BRIAN FLYNN
GLITTERING PRIZES

BRIAN FLYNN was born in 1885 in Leyton, Essex. He won a scholarship to the City Of London School, and from there went into the civil service. In World War I he served as Special Constable on the Home Front, also teaching "Accountancy, Languages, Maths and Elocution to men, women, boys and girls" in the evenings, and acting in his spare time.

It was a seaside family holiday that inspired Brian Flynn to turn his hand to writing in the mid-twenties. Finding most mystery novels of the time "mediocre in the extreme", he decided to compose his own. Edith, the author's wife, encouraged its completion, and after a protracted period finding a publisher, it was eventually released in 1927 by John Hamilton in the UK and Macrae Smith in the U.S. as *The Billiard-Room Mystery*.

The author died in 1958. In all, he wrote and published 57 mysteries, the vast majority featuring the super-sleuth Antony Bathurst.

BRIAN FLYNN

GLITTERING PRIZES

With an introduction by
Steve Barge

DEAN STREET PRESS

INTRODUCTION

"I believe that the primary function of the mystery story is to entertain; to stimulate the imagination and even, at times, to supply humour. But it pleases the connoisseur most when it presents – and reveals – genuine mystery. To reach its full height, it has to offer an intellectual problem for the reader to consider, measure and solve."

Brian Flynn, *Crime Book* magazine, 1948

BRIAN Flynn began his writing career with *The Billiard Room Mystery* in 1927, primarily at the prompting of his wife Edith who had grown tired of hearing him say how he could write a better mystery novel than the ones he had been reading. Four more books followed under his original publisher, John Hamilton, before he moved to John Long, who would go on to publish the remaining forty-eight of his Anthony Bathurst mysteries, along with his three Sebastian Stole titles, released under the pseudonym Charles Wogan. Some of the early books were released in the US, and there were also a small number of translations of his mysteries into Swedish and German. In the article from which the above quote is taken from, Brian also claims that there were also French and Danish translations but to date, I have not found a single piece of evidence for their existence. The only translations that I have been able to find evidence of are *War Es Der Zahnarzt?* and *Bathurst Greift Ein* in German – *The Mystery of the Peacock's Eye*, retitled to the less dramatic "Was It The Dentist?", and *The Horn* becoming "Bathurst Takes Action" – and, in Swedish, *De 22 Svarta*, a more direct translation of *The Case of the Black Twenty-Two*. There may well be more work to be done finding these, but tracking down all of his books written in the original English has been challenging enough!

Reprints of Brian's books were rare. Four titles were released as paperbacks as part of John Long's Four Square Thriller range in the late 1930s, four more re-appeared during the war from Cherry Tree Books and Mellifont Press, albeit abridged by at least a third, and two others that I am aware of, *Such Bright Disguises* (1941) and *Reverse the Charges* (1943), received a paperback release as part of John Long's Pocket Edition range in the early 1950s – these were also possibly abridged, but only by about 10%. They were the exceptions, rather than the rule, however, and it was not until 2019, when Dean Street Press released his first ten titles, that his work was generally available again.

The question still persists as to why his work disappeared from the awareness of all but the most ardent collectors. As you may expect, when a title was only released once, back in the early 1930s, finding copies of the original text is not a straightforward matter – not even Brian's estate has a copy of every title. We are particularly grateful to one particular collector for providing *The Edge of Terror*, Brian's first serial killer tale, and another for *The Ebony Stag* and *The Grim Maiden*. With these, the reader can breathe a sigh of relief as a copy of every one of Brian's books has now been located – it only took about five years . . .

One of Brian's strengths was the variety of stories that he was willing to tell. Despite, under his own name at least, never straying from involving Anthony Bathurst in his novels – technically he doesn't appear in the non-series *Tragedy at Trinket*, although he gets a name-check from the sleuth of that tale who happens to be his nephew – it is fair to say that it was rare that two consecutive books ever followed the same structure. Some stories are narrated by a Watson-esque character, although never the same person twice, and others are written by Bathurst's "chronicler". The books sometimes focus on just Bathurst and his investigation but sometimes we get to see the events occurring to the whole cast of characters. On occasion, Bathurst himself will "write" the final chapter, just to make sure his chronicler has got the details correct. The murderer may be an opportunist or they may have a convoluted (and, on occasion, a somewhat over-the-top) plan. They may be working for personal gain or as part of a criminal enterprise or society. Compare for example, *The League of Matthias* and *The Horn* – consecutive releases but were it not for Bathurst's involvement, and a similar sense of humour underlying Brian's writing, you could easily believe that they were from the pen of different writers.

Brian seems to have been determined to keep stretching himself with his writing as he continued Bathurst's adventures, and the ten books starting with *Cold Evil* show him still trying new things. Two of the books are inverted mysteries – where we know who the killer is, and we follow their attempts to commit the crime and/or escape justice and also, in some cases, the detective's attempt to bring them to justice. That description doesn't do justice to either *Black Edged* or *Such Bright Disguises*, as there is more revealed in the finale than the reader might expect . . . There is one particular innovation in *The Grim Maiden*, namely the introduction of a female officer at Scotland Yard.

Helen Repton, an officer from "the woman's side of the Yard" is recruited in that book, as Bathurst's plan require an undercover officer in a cinema. This is her first appearance, despite the text implying that Bathurst has met her before, but it is notable as the narrative spends a little time apart from Bathurst. It follows Helen Repton's investigations based on superb initiative, which generates some leads in the case. At this point in crime fiction, there have been few, if any, serious depictions of a female police detective – the primary example would be Mrs Pym from the pen of Nigel Morland, but she (not just the only female detective at the Yard, but the Assistant Deputy Commissioner no less) would seem to be something of a caricature. Helen would go on to become a semi-regular character in the series, and there are certainly hints of a romantic connection between her and Bathurst.

It is often interesting to see how crime writers tackled the Second World War in their writing. Some brought the ongoing conflict into their writing – John Rhode (and his pseudonym Miles Burton) wrote several titles set in England during the conflict, as did others such as E.C.R. Lorac, Christopher Bush, Gladys Mitchell and many others. Other writers chose not to include the War in their tales – Agatha Christie had ten books published in the war years, yet only *N or M?* uses it as a subject.

Brian only uses the war as a backdrop in one title, *Glittering Prizes*, the story of a possible plan to undermine the Empire. It illustrates the problem of writing when the outcome of the conflict was unknown – it was written presumably in 1941 – where there seems little sign of life in England of the war going on, one character states that he has fought in the conflict, but messages are sent from Nazi conspirators, ending *"Heil Hitler!"*. Brian had good reason for not wanting to write about the conflict in detail, though, as he had immediate family involved in the fighting and it is quite understandable to see writing as a distraction from that.

While Brian had until recently been all but forgotten, there are some mentions for Brian's work in some studies of the genre – Sutherland Scott in *Blood in their Ink* praises *The Mystery of the Peacock's Eye* as containing "one of the ablest pieces of misdirection" before promptly spoiling that misdirection a few pages later, and John Dickson Carr similarly spoils the ending of *The Billiard Room Mystery* in his famous essay "The Grandest Game In The World". One should also include in this list Barzun and Taylor's entry in their *Catalog of Crime* where they attempted to cover Brian by looking at a single title – the somewhat odd *Conspiracy at Angel* (1947) – and summarising it as "Straight tripe and savorless. It is doubtful, on the evidence, if any of his others would be different." Judging an author based on a single title seems desperately unfair – how many people have given up on Agatha Christie after only reading *Postern Of Fate*, for example – but at least that misjudgement is being rectified now.

Contemporary reviews of Brian's work were much more favourable, although as John Long were publishing his work for a library market, not all of his titles garnered attention. At this point in his writing career – 1938 to 1944 – a number of his books won reviews in the national press, most of which were positive. Maurice Richardson in the *Observer* commented that "Brian Flynn balances his ingredients with considerable skill" when reviewing *The Ebony Stag* and praised *Such Bright Disguises* as a "suburban horror melodrama" with an "ingenious final solution". "Suspense is well maintained until the end" in *The Case of the Faithful Heart*, and the protagonist's narration in *Black Edged* in "impressively nightmarish".

It is quite possible that Brian's harshest critic, though, was himself. In the *Crime Book* magazine, he wrote about how, when reading the current output of detective fiction "I delight in the dazzling erudition that has come to grace and decorate the craft of the *'roman policier'*." He then goes on to say "At the same time, however, I feel my own comparative unworthiness for the fire and burden of the competition." Such a feeling may well be the reason why he never made significant inroads into the social side of crime-writing, such as the Detection Club or the Crime Writers Association. Thankfully, he uses this sense of unworthiness as inspiration, concluding "The stars, though, have always been the most desired of all goals, so I allow exultation and determination to take the place of that but temporary dismay."

In Anthony Bathurst, Flynn created a sleuth that shared a number of traits with Holmes but was hardly a carbon-copy. Bathurst is a polymath and gentleman sleuth, a man of contradictions whose background is never made clear to the reader. He clearly has money, as he has his own rooms in London with a pair of servants on call and went to public school (Uppingham) and university (Oxford). He is a follower of all things that fall under the banner of sport, in particular horse racing and cricket, the latter being a sport that he could, allegedly, have represented England at. He is also a bit of a show-off, littering his speech (at times) with classical quotes, the obscurer the better, provided by the copies of the *Oxford Dictionary of Quotations* and *Brewer's Dictionary of Phrase & Fable* that Flynn kept by his writing desk, although Bathurst generally restrains himself to only doing this with people who would appreciate it or to annoy the local constabulary. He is fond of amateur dramatics (as was Flynn, a well-regarded amateur thespian who appeared in at least one self-penned play, *Blue Murder*), having been a member of OUDS, the Oxford University Dramatic Society. General information about his background is light on the ground. His parents were Irish, but he doesn't have an accent – see *The Spiked Lion* (1933) – and his eyes are grey. Despite the fact that he is an incredibly charming and handsome individual, we learn in *The Orange Axe* that he doesn't pursue romantic relationships due to a bad experience in his first romance. We find out more about that relationship and the woman involved in *The Edge of Terror*, and soon thereafter he falls head over heels in love in *Fear and Trembling*, although we never hear of that young lady again. After that, there are eventual hints of an attraction between Helen Repton, but nothing more. That doesn't stop women falling head over heels for Bathurst – as he departs her company in *The Padded Door*, one character muses "What other man could she ever love . . . after this secret idolatry?"

As we reach the halfway point in Anthony's career, his companions have somewhat stablised, with Chief Inspector Andrew MacMorran now his near-constant junior partner in investigation. The friendship with MacMorran is a highlight (despite MacMorran always calling him "Mr. Bathurst") with the sparring between them always a delight to read. MacMorran's junior officers, notably Superintendent Hemingway and Sergeant Chatterton, are frequently recurring characters. The notion of the local constabulary calling in help from Scotland Yard enables cases to be set around the country while still maintaining the same central cast (along with a local bobby or two).

Cold Evil (1938), the twenty-first Bathurst mystery, finally pins down Bathurst's age, and we find that in *The Billiard Room Mystery* (1927), his first outing, he was a fresh-faced Bright Young Thing of twenty-two. How he can survive with his own rooms, at least two servants, and no noticeable source of income remains a mystery. One can also ask at what point in his life he travelled the world, as he has, at least, been to Bangkok at some point. It is, perhaps, best not to analyse Bathurst's past too carefully . . .

"Judging from the correspondence my books have excited it seems I have managed to achieve some measure of success, for my faithful readers comprise a circle in which high dignitaries of the Church rub shoulders with their brothers and sisters of the common touch."

For someone who wrote to entertain, such correspondence would have delighted Brian, and I wish he were around to see how many people have enjoyed the reprints of his work so far. *The Mystery of the Peacock's Eye* (1928) won Cross Examining Crime's Reprint Of The Year award for 2019, with *Tread Softly* garnering second place the following year. His family are delighted with the reactions that people have passed on, and I hope that this set of books will delight just as much.

Steve Barge

PART ONE
THE INVITATION

I

THE first intimation that Mrs. Warren Clinton had arrived in England from America came from no less famous a person than Anne Assheton. This fact is worth recording because it was so unlike Anne to call attention to the presence of another member of her sex. Everybody had been aware that Miss Assheton was on her way home from Hollywood, and when the *Myrobella* berthed there was the inevitable phalanx of reporters to meet and interview the star. As it happened, Anne had run a throat on the voyage over and had been much less in evidence, in consequence, than usually on such trips. When the reporters swarmed round her she had smiled and posed and let them photograph her and then, to the surprise of all of them, she had dropped her bomb.

"Gosh, boys," said Miss Assheton, smiling her sweetest smile and looking her loveliest. "I wonder you aren't sick of hanging around me. Every time I go backwards and forwards you make a fuss and put it in your papers. It's all the wrong way round." She smiled as only Anne Assheton could.

The bunch of reporters grinned at her as one man. Jerry Redfern of the *Morning Message*, who was standing nearer to Anne than any of the others, permitted his grin to develop into a laugh.

"What are your plans, Miss Assheton? Can you tell us that?"

To the surprise of all of them, Anne shook her head at the question. "No, boys. You've got me all wrong. I mean every word of what I said. Why don't you go in for what really counts in life? *Uplift!* The triumph of mind over 'mutter.'"

The bunch of Pressmen roared at the crack. Anne persisted. "Now, listen. I'll be a pal to you. A real pal. I've been thinking about this for hours on end and I'll put you wise. Mrs. Warren Clinton crossed with me on the *Myrobella*. There's an earful for you."

There were murmurs of incredulity. Jerry Redfern voiced the doubt that was in the minds of all of them. "And who the heck's Mrs. Warren Clinton?"

Anne poured scornful contempt over him. Redfern took a basinful.

"Be your age. Hide that shameful ignorance. It'll wreck a promising career if you aren't careful. Haven't you ever heard of Warren Clinton, the richest guy in Nebraska?"

It seemed that there were mumblings of assent. Anne Assheton went on: "Well, this is Warren Clinton's widow. He passed out last fall and this is one of the richest women in the world. And say—does she love this little country. I'd have you boys know that five mornings out of six on the voyage home I heard her singing 'There'll always be an England' in her bath. And you stick around me with your moon faces when you could get the lowdown from her. Call yourselves reporters! You make me sick. You wouldn't know there was an earthquake till they started to collect for the families of the victims."

Jerry Redfern took the full battery of Anne's world-famous smile. "Miss Assheton," he said, "you're swell as a publicity agent. I'm taking your tip. Where do I find this Warner Clifford dame?"

"I said Warren Clinton, and Warren Clinton it is. She'll be staying at 'Davidge's.' For a time at least. I know that because she told me herself."

"Thank you, Miss Assheton," chorused the reporters. "Now how about those plans of yours? What's the name of your new picture and who's starring with you?"

"I haven't any, and it hasn't one. But I'll let you in on this. You can tell your readers—both of them—that I'm going to spend the next month or so with my husband."

"Thank you, Miss Assheton. Now you're being reasonable and we'll say he's lucky."

They fired more questions at her. Anne Assheton rattled back the answers without the slightest hesitation. She knew them all. And they knew that she knew them. At last Jerry Redfern flung this one at her: "How's Hope Hatteras?"

Hope Hatteras had been the reigning star of Hollywood. Anne Assheton loved her not. There were rumours concerning Hope's waist-line.

"Hope?" repeated Anne Assheton. "Oh, how can I put it? Well—let me say she's just sweet—'sweet and plenty'."

Anne Assheton skipped away and, turning, waved her hand to the Press.

II

Paragraphs of this kind appeared in the following morning's papers. They were headed (or most of them): 'Mrs. Warren Clinton comes to England.' Jerry Redfern in the *Morning Message* went somewhat farther than this and said: 'The famous American philanthropist and social worker, Mrs. Warren Clinton, arrived in this country yesterday. As all our readers know, Mrs. Warren Clinton is the widow of the late Warren Clinton of Nebraska, U.S.A., and besides being that worthy gentleman's widow she is his sole heiress. When we consider that the late W.C. died worth x million dollars, it is easy to see why Mrs. Clinton is reckoned by all those who think they know as the fourth richest woman in the world. More than that—she is as gracious and charming as she is wealthy, and in an interview which she was pleased to give our representative yesterday, soon after she had set foot on British soil, Mrs. Clinton gave us this message for our readers: "I have come to England on no mere pleasure cruise. I was born in this country. I have come here with a definite purpose. I believe in definite purposes. I always have done so. I am here to work for the benefit of, and in the cause of, England herself and of the great British Commonwealth of Nations. I am a rich woman. Too rich. Richer than any woman has a right to be. My husband has left me an immense fortune. That money I intend to dedicate to that purpose of which I spoke just now. It will be my job to find out the best way to do what I want to do. I have plenty of ideas floating about at the back of my mind, but my plans are very far from being perfected. I love England, English people and all that England stands for. I am one of those people who believe that it is only England and her colonies that can save the world. And now to conclude on a somewhat lighter note. I have already met one of your national favourites. I allude to Anne Assheton. The one and only incomparable Anne Assheton. She had the next cabin to me on the *Myrobella*. I couldn't wish to meet anybody more utterly delightful . . . we speedily became great friends . . . Miss Assheton was kindness itself to me despite the fact that she hadn't been too well during the voyage. . . . I am dining with her and her husband, Wilfred Denver, the famous Shakespearean actor, one evening next week . . . and then, as soon as I can, I shall hope to commence my real work.'"

Jerry Redfern, enterprising as ever, managed to secure a photograph of Mrs. Warren Clinton and the readers of the *Morning Message* saw the picture of a charming middle-aged lady, beautifully dressed and wearing an eminently gracious smile. A week afterwards most of them had forgotten her, but little less than a fortnight later they were destined to remember her with a forcefulness that bordered on the frightful.

III

A week or so after Jerry Redfern's interview with Mrs. Warren Clinton at Davidge's Hotel there was hustle and bustle at the Royal Sceptre Hotel, Remington. The manager spoke earnestly to the *maître d'hôtel*. The *maître d'hôtel* harangued the several waiters. The several waiters conferred with the chambermaids. The chambermaids sought the advice and the instructions of the receptionist. The receptionist contacted the manageress and the manageress expostulated angrily with the manager, who happened, rather unfortunately from his point of view, to be her husband. It will be seen, therefore, that there was, to say the least of it, an unusual activity within the classic confines of the 'Royal Sceptre,' Remington. The reason for such activity? Nothing less than the impending visit there of Mrs. Warren Clinton herself.

She had booked that particular suite of rooms at the hotel which the habitual patrons of the 'Royal Sceptre' knew as the 'Nonpareil' and which was far beyond the financial resources of most. The fact was commented on in the *Remington Gazette*, made much of in the *Remington and District Herald* and positively flaunted in the columns of the *Weekly Guide to the Entertainments and Amusements of Remington*. It was acknowledged by everybody in the town to be one of the most outstanding events in Remington's already glorious and distinguished history. Benjamin Disraeli had spoken in Remington. Jenny Lind had sung there. Pavlova had danced there. Ransford, the triple poisoner, had been hanged there—and now Mrs. Warren Clinton of Nebraska, *the* Mrs. Warren Clinton, was due to stay there for a few days at least—perhaps even for as long as a week.

The chef at the 'Royal Sceptre' spent three afternoons on what may be described as a mental refresher course and the wine waiter checked assiduously, more than once, and with the gravest concern, the contents of the 'Royal Sceptre's' cellars. Besides these purely local reactions, the intention of Mrs. Warren Clinton to visit Remington was duly chronicled in the London Press and at least one Society journal made the visit its most noteworthy feature. Directly the news became generally known concerning Mrs. Warren Clinton's visit, other ordinary bookings at the hotel jumped considerably numerically. To tell the truth, the 'Royal Sceptre' had recently passed through a decidedly lean time and the change thus brought about was very welcome to the management.

The affair also produced a municipal entanglement. The Town Clerk of Remington, Mr. Stewart Vernon, scenting a remunerative social contact, mentioned it to the Mayor. That worthy gentleman, it must be. admitted, thought chiefly in terms of the late Warren Clinton's x million dollars. After all, there were several municipal enterprises which had been launched in Remington and which had signally failed to receive anything like adequate support. For one—there was the Organ Fund. If Mrs. Warren Clinton could be interested in even one of these . . . The Town Clerk, however, shrugged his shoulders. He deprecated the Mayor's attitude. As Town Clerk he was vastly more important than any wretched Organ Fund.

Mrs. Clinton arrived at the Royal Sceptre Hotel, Remington, 'twixt sun and shower on a Saturday afternoon in April.

IV

Just about the time that the preparations to which reference has been made were in full swing at Remington, John Maxwell Ramage, K.C., was seated at dinner with his wife. 'J.M.,' as he was known to almost everybody, had wrapped the folds of shimmering success round himself from his first days at Brasenose to the present time. Determined from his earliest days to make his way at any cost, he had been President of the Union, entered the legal profession, been called to the Bar and had now established for himself not only an absolutely outstanding reputation as a barrister, but also an annual income the proportions of which made most people gasp when the figures were mentioned to them.

Ramage had just returned from New York, to which city he had recently been invited for the purpose of giving evidence at the Divorce Commission.

"Life, my dear Angela," Ramage was saying to his wife, "is full of surprises and most amusing from the standpoint of 'value adjustments.'"

Angela Ramage smiled at her husband. "Go on, John. I'm perfectly certain that you have a lot more to say in the matter than that. Come off the mere fringe of things."

John Ramage toyed with the stem of his wine-glass. "Perhaps I have. So I'll obey your instructions, my dear. But when I was speaking just now my mind was going back to my voyage from New York. On the *Myrobella*."

"What about it, John?"

"Well—for me, it was a course of salutary treatment. I suppose that nine moderately intelligent people out of every ten would agree that my recent mission to New York was not undistinguished and certainly not unimportant." He paused—a quiet smile playing round the corners of his lips. "Is that enunciation a reasonable one?"

"U'm—the point is conceded. But please don't exact penalties from me for the concession." Angela deftly peeled an apple.

"Good. That's established then. Now for the real point underlying my remarks. When the *Myrobella* got in, my arrival was entirely unheralded and unsung. So different from my reception in New York when I went out there."

"Don't be babyish—John. I'm surprised at you—worrying over a trifle like that. You get worse—instead of better." There was mischief in Angela Ramage's eyes as she spoke.

Ramage still smiled. "No. You misjudge me. I have no anxiety in the matter. Far from it in fact. On the contrary, I found and am still finding much cause for amusement."

"How do you mean?"

"I will try to explain to you. Whereas my return, as I said, passed entirely unnoticed, and as far as I know has failed to evoke a single line in any of the daily papers, there were two ladies who had also sailed on the *Myrobella* who, when they landed, positively 'hit the high-spots.' In the language of the profession, they were 'wows.' Whereas I was no more than the most sickening of 'flops.' Hence—my amusement."

Angela Ramage wrinkled her brows. "I don't know that I understand. Who were those two ladies? Is that your real point?"

"Naturally, my dear Angela. Their names were Anne Assheton, the film star, and a certain Mrs. Warren Clinton of Nebraska, U.S.A. I had heard of the former, I admit, but of the latter I confess most unashamedly I had never heard."

Angela nodded. "Tell me more. What actually happened?"

"When we were prepared to disembark, do you mean?"

"M'm. Tell me the details."

John Ramage paused for a moment before replying. "Well, the usual crowd of reporters and journalists surged forward and made a complete bee-line for the incomparable Miss Assheton."

"Neglecting you?"

"Oh—utterly."

"I can understand it, I think. It's simply the translation of the popular appeal. That is to say, with the emphasis on the adjective. You, my dear John, distinguished as you may be in your own particular circle, make no appeal whatever to the *hoi polloi*—and that's all there is to it."

Angela purred. She was pleased with herself. The occasions when she was able to score over her husband were by no means so numerous that she failed to exult when an opportunity of the kind did present itself. But John Ramage was unperturbed.

"I accept the rebuke," he said quietly. "Time is a great healer. Although I'm rather afraid that when I saw and realized what was happening when Anne Assheton was surrounded, I was inclined to look down my nose and mutter such ungallant phrases as 'wretched film-star.'"

A peal of laughter came from Angela. "I can well believe it. But you haven't told me yet about the other woman. The Clinton woman.

What happened to her? Did she attract a similar horde round her?" Ramage shook his head. Angela couldn't help thinking, as she looked at him, what a handsome man he was.

"Not at first," he replied in answer to her question. "That was the peculiar part about it. I believe I'm right when I say that Anne Assheton actually put the reporters on to her. She and Mrs. Clinton had been close companions on the voyage. Often together in various places. Just fancy, my dear Angela, a popular film star indulging in an excess of altruism. And a female one at that."

"If it happened, and you say it did, it's just another indication of the superiority of the so-called weaker sex. I'm glad you told me about it. I shall be able to use it against you in argument in the future." John looked at her across the table. "Judging by the newspaper reports which followed, the various Press representatives who were cluttering up the place took the Assheton tip and ran Mrs. Warren Clinton to earth in the London hotel to which she had gone after disembarkation. So there you are—you have the entire picture as it presented itself to me when we sat down to dinner. Assheton 1, Clinton 2, Ramage also ran. In full perspective subsequently it has caused me, as I said, a certain amount of amusement."

"It *is* rather quaint, with the world in its present ghastly state, when you come to think it over properly." Angela crinkled her nose as she spoke. She could see now that her husband was not in his best mood for teasing. She pushed her glass over to him. "Pour me out another glass of port, John, will you, please?"

Ramage did so. "As it happens," he said, "while I have but an ephemeral interest in Miss Assheton and the profession which she presumably adorns, I find myself most unusually interested in Mrs. Warren Clinton. But *why* exactly—frankly, my dear Angela, I don't know." Angela sipped her glass of port. "And that's unlike you, John, isn't it?"

V

On the 4.10 p.m. train out of Paddington *en route* for Remington, John Maxwell Ramage, K.C., read and re-read the following letter:

'Davidge's Hotel,
London, W.C.2.
April 17.

My dear Mr. Ramage,

You will doubtless be surprised to receive this letter. I am almost unknown to you, although I am aware of the fact that we travelled together from New York on the Myrobella. But as one who firmly believes that the British Commonwealth of Nations urgently needs, during these perilous days, the services of all her brilliant sons, I am asking you to be my guest next week-end at the Royal Sceptre Hotel, Remington. Please accept this invitation and treat it as in the strictest confidence, because I hope to make you a most important offer as a result of your visit.

Believe me to be,
Your sincere admirer,
Miriam Clinton.'

John Ramage fingered his chin reflectively. He felt certain that there was a great deal more behind this letter than appeared on the surface. It was up to him, therefore, to read between the lines. He carefully folded the letter, replaced it within its envelope, put the envelope back in the breast-pocket of his light overcoat and turned in his seat to gaze out of the window of his first class compartment.

VI

Doctor Angela Ramage, M.P. for West Markham, slowed down her coupé in a narrow street of the village of Brooch, parked it in an appropriate place and then entered a small tea shop for an attractive interval of coffee and buns. She found a suitable table and seated herself. After she had given her innocent order to the waitress who attended her, Angela Ramage took a letter from her handbag and proceeded to read it with the utmost care. As she read it, her distinctly good-looking and engaging face wrinkled in the lines of perplexity. It may be remarked that this was the fourth time that morning that she had read this letter. Its contents ran as follows:

'My dear Mrs. Ramage,

You will doubtless be surprised to receive this letter from me, as I am, I fear, entirely unknown to you. But I am one of those people whose opinion it is that the British Commonwealth of Nations stands today in imminent peril. This peril is all the greater because of the great struggle which must surely come between the forces of Freedom and those of Slavery. Because of this feeling of mine, linked as it is with the conviction that Britain needs the services of all her brilliant children, I am asking you to be my guest next weekend at the Royal Sceptre Hotel, Remington. Please accept this invitation and treat it as in the strictest confidence, because I hope to make you a most important offer as a result of your visit to me.

Believe me to be,

Your sincere admirer,

Miriam Clinton.'

Angela Ramage sipped her coffee, munched another tempting-looking bun, and tucked the letter in her bag again. When she had finished the coffee she lit a cigarette and cupped her chin in her left hand. Angela finished her cigarette, pushed the stub in a convenient ash-tray, paid her bill and then made her way slowly from the little shop to the waiting car. Deep in thought, she pressed the self-starter and continued on her way to Remington. Funny that she had received the invitation! She wondered if it were because her husband had been invited.

VII

The 4.10 p.m. train out of Paddington which carried John Ramage to Remington stopped at Reading. This was its first scheduled stop. One of the passengers who joined it at Reading was Wilfred Denver. Actually, he entered the next compartment but one to that which was occupied by Ramage. He took an Egyptian cigarette from a gold cigarette-case, settled himself in a corner seat, lit the cigarette and took a letter from an envelope. This letter he unfolded, preparatory to reading.

'My dear Mr. Denver,

You will doubtless be surprised to receive this letter. Although by now I am positive that you will have heard of me. Because I haven't the slightest doubt that your charming wife will have told you of my love for and my fears for this Empire of ours. As one of the leading figures in the noble profession which you adorn and have adorned for so long a time now, I am writing to ask you to be my guest over the next weekend at the Royal Sceptre Hotel, Remington. Please accept this invitation and treat it as in the strictest confidence, because I hope to make you a most important and remunerative offer as a result of your visit to me.

Believe me to be, therefore,

Your sincere admirer,

Miriam Clinton.'

With a smile playing round the corners of his mouth, Denver replaced the letter in his pocket and thrust his hands deep into the large pockets of his heavy overcoat. His smile gradually broadened as he thought matters over. It must be understood that he was the husband of no less a person than Anne Assheton. Anne Assheton, who had been the close companion of Mrs. Warren Clinton on the voyage of the *Myrobella* from New York to England, and whom he had left a couple of hours previously.

VIII

Capt. Ronald Playfair, V.C., entrained for Remington from Exeter. He was fortunate enough to live in a charming house in the valley of the Sid. He was of middle height, spare, dark and dapper. His eyes were quick-moving and intelligent. When he took his seat in the train he rubbed the ridge of his jaw reflectively, for the main reason that, for once during his varied career, he was feeling far from sure of himself. The letter which he had received some days previously and whose summons he was now obeying, was worded as follows:

'Dear Captain Playfair,

Although my name may be unknown to you, yours is extremely well known to me. Your exploits during the War of 1914-1918 which culminated in your winning the Victoria Cross, the services you have rendered to your country since then, the repeated and persistent efforts you have made to urge England to become more aware of the gravity of her position amongst the nations and of the dangers which surround her—all these have impressed me immeasurably. I am writing to you, therefore, asking you to be my guest next weekend at the Royal Sceptre Hotel, Remington. Please accept this invitation and treat it as in the strictest confidence, because I hope to make you a most important and remunerative offer as a result of this visit.

Believe me to be,

Your sincere admirer,

Miriam Clinton.'

The words of the letter were by now too familiar to Capt. Playfair for it to be necessary for him to re-read it. They had impressed him so much that they were almost burned into his brain. Nonchalant and debonair and looking as fit as the proverbial fiddle, he leant back in his seat and hunched his shoulders against the upholstery of the compartment. It certainly seemed to him, as he thought matters over, that one power which Mrs. Warren Clinton undoubtedly possessed was that of money. Capt. Playfair knew full well the value of this power. From this interview which lay just in front of him there might come a great opportunity for him. Capt. Playfair's clean-cut features relaxed into a smile. The train from Exeter entered a tunnel. Capt. Playfair lit a cigarette. When the train emerged from the tunnel he was still smiling.

IX

Sir Edward Angus, Conservative Member of Parliament for the Rigby Division of Holme, and in the minds of most good judges 'the coming man in British politics,' glanced with a certain amount of irritation in the direction of his chauffeur. He then voiced this irritation in words.

"In my opinion, Kingsford, you have come at least fifteen miles out of your way." His voice was tinged with asperity.

"I don't think so, Sir Edward. At least—not in the long run. On this road, sir, I shall be able to by-pass Lanham and make Remington from the north. You need have no fear, Sir Edward."

"H'm—you seem pretty sure of yourself. Only hope you won't be disappointed—that's all."

Sir Edward, having delivered himself of these two sentiments, slumped back in his seat again. The words of the letter which had so recently reached him repeatedly flooded his brain and stirred his thoughts. The various phrases persisted . . . 'your fighting speeches in the House in which you have called attention to the urgent peril of your country . . . my sincere conviction that England needs you in a position of extreme authority where your outstanding abilities might be exerted to the utmost . . . my guest . . . next weekend . . . Royal Sceptre Hotel, Remington . . . invitation in strict confidence . . . important and remunerative offer . . . sincere admirer . . . Miriam Clinton.'

Sir Edward Angus smiled a smile of supreme self-satisfaction and carefully polished his horn-rimmed spectacles. If Kingsford were right in his contention concerning the by-pass, they would be in Remington in a little less than an hour. From his own point of view Sir Edward regarded this as so much the better.

X

Yet another car was on its way to Remington. The occupant of this car was the Very Reverend Dean Langton of St. Sepulchre's Cathedral, Mannington. Modern critics were unanimous in ranking him with the greatest preachers of all time—in the same class as Spurgeon, Parker, Scott-Holland and Campbell. In addition to the possession of his silver tongue, he was a man of magnificent presence. With aquiline features, a height of over six feet, a crown of silver hair, Theodore Langton was fully equipped physically for the reigning position in the pulpits of the land. He had physique, presence, power and personality. His chauffeur had been in his employment for a period of between eleven and twelve years. The strength and accuracy of Theodore Langton's memory were household words wherever he went. His more intimate friends claimed on his behalf that his memory was equal to the reputed memory of the great Macaulay.

As he sat in his car he pondered over the terms of a most unusual communication with which he had been favoured by a lady who signed herself as 'Miriam Clinton.' As in the instance of Sir Edward Angus, the sentences which the lady had used were continuously active in Dean Langton's brain. 'You . . . whom I am bound to regard as the greatest religious force and influence of our time . . . one of those who must put his hand to the plough in the leadership of the great British Empire . . . the greatest spiritual adviser of modern times . . . my guest for the coming weekend at the Royal Sceptre Hotel, Remington . . . an alluring and attractive offer . . .'

The dark eyes of Dean Langton gazed fearlessly and steadfastly in front of him. It was intensely gratifying to think that there were powerful financial interests extant in the world which were not entirely oblivious to the spiritual needs of mankind. The opportunities for doing good which would come to a woman possessing the wealth that Mrs. Warren Clinton possessed were immeasurable. It was a pity that there were not more people in the countries of the earth of her public spirit and noble disinterestedness. If Mrs. Warren Clinton would be content to let him influence and advise her . . . Dean Langton clenched his fists . . . he was already visualizing himself as the Supreme Champion of Good, challenging imperiously, and with glittering success, the Powers of Darkness and the Squadrons of Evil.

XI

Lord Esmond Curte flew to Remington. For years he had made it his practice and habit to fly to most of his appointments and engagements in his own 'plane. From his home in Nottinghamshire, close to the banks of the Trent, and from his own park, within which he had established his own private aerodrome, his 'plane made many speedy and successful flights. He saw no reason to depart from his customary procedure on the occasion of his visit to Mrs. Warren Clinton.

Curte was a man in the early fifties. He was tall, thin and spare. Most of the hair he had possessed had departed this life. He had fierce features, a slightly curved—almost predatory—nose and eyes of that particular shade of blue which almost invariably accompanies the quality of cool courage. Opponents of his opinions were quick to call him a reactionary. Self-styled democrats were even quicker to describe him as 'a Ruddy Fascist.' Even if neither of these two opinions was strictly veracious, it is certain that Lord Esmond held more belief in the ancestral homes of England than he held in the artisans' dwellings to be found in certain parts of it. Curte was that *rara avis* amongst Englishmen—an orator. But, of course, with an entirely different style and quality from those which characterized Theodore Langton. Curte was, at the age of fifty-five, still a bachelor. In this connection it had often been said of him by his closest friends that women occupied no place whatever in his existence. Curte was, as far as the ordinary emotions of life are concerned, an isolated, aloof figure. But there was a certain splendour in that isolation and an austere grandeur in that aloofness.

As his pilot, Capt. Maitland, D.F.C., brought the Curte 'plane nearer and nearer to the town of Remington, Lord Curte, like so many other distinguished people were doing at the same time, turned over in his mind the terms of the letter which had been recently forwarded to him by Mrs. Warren Clinton. 'One of the most notable figures in English public life today . . . one of the few people in whose hands lies the salvation of the British Empire . . . a man with the reputation of being trusted by all the classes . . . an invitation to be my guest for the coming weekend at the Royal Sceptre Hotel, Remington . . . material gain . . . Miriam Clinton.'

Esmond Curte looked down through the window of his aeroplane and saw the fair countryside of his native England spread beneath him. The undulating valleys, the dotted fields, the alternate lines of green and yellow, the luscious fields of the counties of the West, so full of sap and sunny . . . all these but served to accentuate Curte's deep love of his native country. He turned and spoke to Maitland.

"How long?" he enquired tersely.

Maitland glanced at his wrist-watch. "A quarter of an hour, sir," he answered, "no more than that. It's been a good trip all the way. Conditions couldn't have been better."

Curte nodded in agreement. He fell to wondering what Mrs. Warren Clinton would be like. Women, in his opinion, were such strange, inconstant, unstable creatures. He had kept away from them all through his life. He had no intention of ever abandoning that condition, and yet, here he was now, on his way to be interviewed by a woman whom he had never seen and whom he didn't in any way know. He searched his soul for reasons. Why was he going there? Because this woman had flattered him? Perhaps. Or rather more than perhaps—certainly. Curte was nothing if not introspective.

XII

Rosamund Kingsley drove her own car towards Remington. As she had driven it over the greater part of the continent of Africa and as she hoped to drive it in the comparatively near future over the greater part of other continents. She was in every way a remarkable woman. Allied with undeniable charm, she possessed that rather rarer quality in a woman—icy courage. And in the early thirties she still retained both allurement and glamorous attractiveness. Her father had been a Major in the Royal Artillery, and right from her cradle days Rosamund had been determined to be the famous explorer she had eventually become.

She was fair, her eyes blue and her hair corn-coloured. Men liked her, almost without exception, immediately and instinctively. Her recent adventures with a pygmy tribe in one of the most unexplored tracts of Africa had attracted worldwide notice and publicity, and she had been back in England but a little more than a month when she had received a letter from Mrs. Warren Clinton. Like certain other letters with which the reader is familiar, this had been couched in highly flattering terms.

'In many respects I have come to regard you as the foremost woman of our times . . . your fearlessness and fortitude are acknowledged the world over . . . the intrepid spirit which has sustained you throughout your almost unparalleled achievements is the admiration of all nations . . . the accepted leader of our militant sex . . . there are certain selected people whom England needs today at this, perhaps, the most critical moment in her history, and you are one of them . . . there can be no reasonable argument about this .

. . an invitation to be my guest at a gathering which I am holding over the coming weekend at the Royal Sceptre Hotel, Remington. . . . I hope to make you a most remunerative offer . . . yours, in the most sincere admiration—Miriam Clinton.'

Miss Kingsley stopped her car at a convenient spot by the roadside and indulged in the luxury of an Algerian cigarette. She smoked no other kind. She liked Algerian cigarettes. The harsh, almost acrid tang of the tobacco suited her palate. She frowned at nothing in particular and then smiled. After that she smiled again and then frowned. To tell the entire truth she was not attracted by Mrs. Warren Clinton's invitation to her. But at the same time she had to confess to herself that she was something more than merely interested. She was indeed on the way towards being intrigued. Far more than she would have believed, previously, that she could have been. She found a certain satisfaction in what had happened to her. She turned over the possibilities it presented in her mind. No doubt this American woman was absurdly rich. She remembered reading about her somewhere in one of the newspapers. Her husband had left her an immense fortune. She might well be a woman who was ready and content to pour riches into a crucible of Good instead of squandering them selfishly on personal pleasures as so many rich people did. In short—a rare creature. Rosamund Kingsley took a final draw at the cigarette she was smoking and tossed away the stub. She glanced at her wrist-watch. What she saw pleased her. She pressed the self-starter. Barring accidents she would be in Remington in less than an hour.

XIII

As Rosamund Kingsley took the wheel of her car to resume her journey to Remington, another car flashed by her, rather unpleasantly closely, and was out of her sight in an inconceivably short space of time. It was a 'Bentley,' and had Rosamund known who was the driver, and the nature of his errand she would have been even more intrigued with her present position than she actually was. For the reason that in that 'Bentley' sat no less a person than Cedric Garnett. Now Garnett was a superb physical specimen. At Oxford he had been a Triple Blue. At Rugger, Rowing and Cricket.

The unusual combination should be noted. He had managed to obtain the first and second of these distinctions by playing Rugger and Rowing in alternate years. He had hooked for the pack in the XV, rowed Four in the boat and captained the Varsity XI at Lord's against Cambridge. Since he had come down he had not looked back. He had been capped against Ireland at Twickenham, against Wales at Cardiff Arms Park, against Scotland at Murrayfield (his side winning the Calcutta Cup), been in the Leander crew that had won the 'Grand' at Henley, and in addition he had captained five Test elevens at Trent Bridge, Lord's, Leeds, Old Trafford and the Oval against Australia. He stood six feet two inches in his stockinged feet and weighed thirteen and a half stone. Nevertheless it must be conceded that the letter he had received a day or so previously had rather bewildered him.

Certain phrases in it still hammered against his brain. 'When I was in Germany a short time ago and saw so many thousands of robust young men, marching with the vigour and precision of well-trained soldiers . . . stripped to the waist . . . their splendid brown bodies gleaming in the hot sun . . . singing as they marched with unflagging energy and boundless enthusiasm . . . I was not only exhilarated . . . I will confess that I was enthralled! Their unquestioning devotion to their country . . . it came as a severe shock to me that I saw more magnificent, well-built young men in Germany *in one morning* than I have seen *all the time* I have been in this country . . . no discipline . . . no training . . . C 3 bodies . . . lounging about at street corners waiting for the results of horse-races that they have made bets on . . . watching dog-racing and football matches . . . sprawling ill-shaped in cinemas. You are the one man in the country who can help in this particular direction. It is because of that fact that I am appealing to you now. England must awake before it is too late. The time for this awakening is unhappily all too short. You are one of the few men living who can awaken her . . . sending you an invitation herewith to be my guest for the coming weekend at the Royal Sceptre Hotel, Remington . . . I earnestly ask you *not* to refuse, in fact I beg of you . . . for the sake of your country and also because I hope to be able to make you what I think you will regard as an attractive and most remunerative offer . . . believe me to be, in the most sincere admiration . . . Miriam Clinton.'

Cedric Garnett took one hand from the wheel and fingered the point of his jaw. The car slackened speed. 'Afraid,' he muttered to himself, 'must be phoney. Woman screwy. Bats in the belfry or something. At the same time, must look into it. Owe it to myself. Not so well-lined that I can afford to neglect such an offer. For the good reason, my dear Cedric, that you never know, and there's just the chance that the old girl may be quite pukka and A1 at Lloyd's.'

In his driving-mirror he could see a small two-seater on his tail. He had noticed that it had been there for some little time. The thought then struck him that this looked very like the car he had passed about half an hour previously. There had been a distinctly attractive woman in it. Distinctly easy on the eye. He chuckled to himself. She'd be surprised if she knew where he was bound for. Probably thought he was joy-riding, the same as she herself was. She'd open her eyes pretty wide if she realised that he was answering a call. Yes . . . that was right . . . the description was apt . . . it was a call . . . a summons . . . and more than an ordinary summons . . . more like a tocsin! To *him*. The car she was in was nearer to him now. He didn't mind that a bit. He could see the driver better. She looked more attractive still at closer quarters. Usually, Garnett was inclined to be contemptuous of women drivers . . . but there was something about this girl and the way she handled the car she drove that made him assess her differently.

XIV

It will have been observed by the meticulous that Mrs. Warren Clinton, of Nebraska, U.S.A., had summoned nine people to her side. They shall be detailed by name—the occasion is opportune for that purpose and the time is appropriate. John Maxwell Ramage, Angela Ramage, his wife, Wilfred Denver, Capt. Ronald Playfair, Sir Edward Angus, Dean Theodore Langton, Lord Esmond Curte, Rosamund Kingsley and Cedric Garnett. Altogether—a most distinguished gathering. They had been deliberately chosen by the lady concerned by reason of their outstanding qualities and their potent personalities. Every one of them had responded to the invitation with a certain degree of willingness. The invitation had flattered them, but one and all they had studiously ignored the flattery and were unanimously prepared to regard it as a genuine compliment to their capabilities and a tribute to their sterling worth.

As may be imagined, they arrived at the Royal Sceptre Hotel, Remington, at different times. It should be recorded that Curte came last. The field where he landed his 'plane, or rather where Maitland landed it for him, was a greater distance from Remington than he had calculated. Kingsford, Sir Edward Angus's chauffeur, had barely had time, however, to garage Sir Edward's car before Curte arrived, and actually passed Capt. Maitland on his earnest way to the saloon bar of the hotel. The various guests, as they arrived, were informed by the receptionist of the numbers of the bedrooms that had been allotted to them. Mrs. Warren Clinton herself received her guests in the largest apartment of those that comprised the 'Nonpareil' suite. The leading toast-master of the day, Carte Knighton, announced the various names as they entered, in that sonorous voice of his which originally had set his feet on the rungs of the ladder which had led him to the pinnacle of his profession.

It has already been stated that Curte came in at the tail of the field. What the emotions and the impressions of the various distinguished people were, when they first found themselves gathered together as the guests of Mrs. Warren Clinton, will never be accurately known. Certain it was that she received each one of them warmly, shook hands with each with the utmost cordiality, thanked each one almost effusively for having accepted her invitation and come to Remington, and then informed them that they would shortly be entertained by her to dinner. Dinner, she told them with more detail, would be served within an hour.

"In the meantime, ladies and gentlemen," continued Mrs. Warren Clinton, "if you care to go into the room on the immediate left of this, you will find what I hope is an excellent buffet, where you can all get to know each other, those of you who haven't met one another before, and find general entertainment before dinner is served. So please go in, make yourselves thoroughly at home and enjoy yourselves." Mrs. Warren Clinton spoke in a rather thin, high-pitched voice, which had, as might have been expected, seeing the number of years she had spent in the States, a strong American accent.

The guests, having been received by her, drifted, some already in pairs, some one by one, into the room where the buffet had been installed. It may be interesting and possibly instructive to observe how they eventually paired. When they partook of their first liquid refreshment in Remington, Mrs. Clinton, the hostess of this most unusual gathering, went in with John Ramage. Playfair, after a sharp glance round the room, joined Curte. Sir Edward Angus felt himself attracted by Dean Langton. Wilfred Denver, seeing Angela Ramage unattended, went to her side, and Cedric Garnett, with an acute reminiscence of his journey down, gravitated towards Rosamund Kingsley. Mrs. Clinton and Ramage talked law and order. Playfair and Curte talked military strategy, Langton and Sir Edward Angus discussed Christian Socialism, Denver and Angela Ramage argued about contemporary Drama, and Garnett and Rosamund Kingsley jointly enthused over the activities of the open air.

Gradually, but with steady insistence, any constraint that might possibly have existed when the guests first came together was dissipated and the hum of spontaneous conversation notably increased in volume. The time passed quickly. Other contacts were speedily made, the groups changed according to their personnel and Mrs. Warren Clinton passed from one to another of her guests with the charm and the aplomb of the perfect hostess. She had been serious with Ramage, she spoke gravely with Curte and Playfair, she joked with Rosamund Kingsley and Cedric Garnett, she almost subdued herself when in the company of Sir Edward Angus and Dean Langton and she rather playfully insinuated herself between Denver and Angela Ramage. Half an hour passed, three-quarters, and then the clock in the Apartment chimed the hour. The doors of the dining-room were flung open by the waiters, who were clad in the most punctilious evening-dress. Behind them stood the figure of Carte Knighton, the world-famous toast-master.

"Ladies and gentlemen," he announced, "dinner is served."

The guests made their way to the seats at the table, which had been assigned to them. At a sign from Mrs. Warren Clinton, sitting at the head of the table, Dean Langton rose to say Grace. Needless to remark, the Dean accepted the opportunity with both hands and filled several unforgiving minutes.

XV

The dinner which Mrs. Warren Clinton placed before her guests, with the professional assistance of the 'Royal Sceptre' chef, was excellent in every respect. This fact was conceded without a note of dissension. The wines had been chosen with a sureness of selection which was satisfactory to even such a connoisseur as Lord Esmond Curte. When the last course had been finished, the waiters attended to their duties and withdrew. The doors were closed and almost immediately an atmosphere settled upon the room. Perhaps it was John Ramage who was the first to sense it. He was seated between his wife and Denver. But whether it was Ramage or another who first reacted sensibly to this new atmosphere which had descended upon the room, it is certain that all the occupants were aware of it before many seconds had passed. They all turned, more or less instinctively, towards that end of the table where sat their hostess. It was plainly evident that they were expecting something from her. They were not to be disappointed. In a silence, during which a pin could have been heard to drop, Mrs. Warren Clinton rose from her chair. Ramage, from his seat, took stock of her. Better stock then he had so far been able to take. He could see her better and appraise her more fully at a distance than he had been able to do at the moment of their first introduction. Although Mrs. Clinton had travelled on the *Myrobella* with him, he had seen but little of her on the boat and had seldom been in her company.

She was a woman who still had pretensions to good looks. When she was young, thought Ramage, she must have been exceedingly pretty. Her speaking voice was not quite as high-pitched as her purely conversational voice had been, but if anything the American accent was even more marked.

"Ladies and gentlemen," said Mrs. Warren Clinton, "I hope that you have thoroughly enjoyed your dinner. It would be a disappointment to me to think that any one of you hadn't. Because it is my intention now to come to the real purpose of our gathering here this evening. You may have already noticed that there are ten of us present. Nine guests and I, your hostess. You—I say, without hesitation—belong to the 'Upper Ten.' That is to say, the 'Upper Ten' of Intelligence. The aristocrats of Intellect. You have been chosen by me with the greatest possible care. For some time now I have been following your respective careers with the utmost interest. Both yours and others. Because you were not my only studies. And yours have stood the acid test of my consideration better than all the others. That is the reason why you are with me this evening." Mrs. Clinton paused and sipped from a glass of water. "It has been evident to me for some time," she continued, "that this country, the Empire and all that you and I hold dear, our sense of freedom, our way of living, our faith, our religion, our private lives, are in deadly peril. You are British, I am an American who had the honour to be born in England and to fight that menace to which I have just referred, we must be not only willing, but also prepared to stand together. That is the second reason why you are here this evening. Having progressed so far, I am now going to ask you for your acquiescence in what I have said, remembering that I am placing my entire fortune at the disposal of the British Empire. Will all those who feel that they are ready and willing to hear what I have to say further in the matter, signify in the usual manner by raising their right hands? I assure you that you will not commit yourselves to any action from which you may feel inclined subsequently to recoil or withdraw. Your hands—please—that is, of course, if you find yourselves in agreement."

The response was unanimous. But John Ramage noticed that there were two people present who, judging from their manners, were feeling a trifle diffident. The reference is to Wilfred Denver and Dean Langton. The latter, Ramage thought, looked just a little scared. With Denver, the look was not one of fear, but rather one of doubtfulness. Having looked round the table in order to gauge the measure of response which her previous statements had evoked, Mrs. Warren Clinton continued:

"Before, however, I take any further steps in the project which I shall eventually place before you, I am going—with your permission, naturally—to put you to two additional tests."

Langton shifted uneasily in his chair. Mrs. Warren Clinton leant forward a little over the dinner table, towards the two rows of her guests. Langton wondered what was coming next. Mrs. Warren Clinton started to speak again.

"The first test which I feel it is incumbent upon me to give you will be a test of your intelligence, initiative and quick-thinking. Please take your menus, you will have already observed that you have each been supplied with one. Here are pencils for you." Mrs. Clinton bent down, found small pencils and passed them round the table. Each guest, a little bewildered, a little amused perhaps, took one. "And put down this list of words. There will in all be nine of them. 'Orpheus.' She paused between the utterance of each word. 'Edyrn.' She spelt this to them carefully. 'Ulema,' 'Roup,' 'Iphicles,' 'Reldresal,' 'Eagle (two headed),' 'Mazikeen' and 'Premonstratensian.' I will repeat the words, so that you may check up on them. As I said, there are nine of them."

Mrs. Clinton smiled. "One for each of you. Because there are nine of you. Each one of those words has a certain counterpart or association. The test will be for you to find those counterpart words. It will not be an easy task. I am going to ask you to remain in this room so that there will be no opportunity for any one of you to have recourse to any outside aid. The test will finish at ten o'clock and you will all agree that under the conditions I have outlined your chances of success are absolutely equal. I can answer no questions about the test. But I will say this. Although each of the words I have dictated to you may have more than one association of meaning, you will know, when you reach the conclusion of your task, whether or no you have discovered the correct one. And there is in each instance only *one* correct counterpart. Please note that carefully. Now, ladies and gentlemen, I will leave you—to be with you again punctually at ten o'clock. The test will commence when the clock strikes the hour, and I should like a condition of complete silence to be maintained throughout. Thank you, ladies and gentlemen. Till ten o'clock, then."

Mrs. Warren Clinton bowed to the company, walked across the room and made a dignified exit.

XVI

Sir Edward Angus said: "Very remarkable. I think I made a great mistake when I came."

Dean Langton smiled rather unhappily and said: "Really . . . I don't know . . . this is rather . . ."

Angela Ramage bit her lip and said nothing. This, it may be said, was most unusual. Her husband, John Ramage, seated next to her, furrowed his brows into a whimsical expression and muttered something under his breath which his wife didn't catch and requested him to repeat.

"Bit of a teaser," he replied.

She nodded but said no more, relapsing somewhat sullenly into her previous condition of silence. Cedric Garnett leaned back in his chair and blew cigarette smoke through his nostrils. There was a certain ostentation in the way he did this.

"Don't know about any of you chaps," he said rather aggressively and unnecessarily loudly, "but not my line of country at all. Haven't an earthly. Sheer waste of time coming."

Wilfred Denver stared insistently at the line of words he had scribbled on the back of his menu. An acute observer would have noticed that his stare held a quality which was very like to a keen interest. His eyes ran backwards and forwards along the row of words and altogether he gave the impression that the words really did mean something to him. Every now and then he rubbed the ridge of his jaw with the tips of his fingers as though he had already embarked on the effort of solving the problems which his hostess had just presented to him. Esmond Curte, on the other hand, frowned prodigiously. His features took on their more predatory appearance and all their fierceness shone through them. His fingers worked incessantly with the top right-hand corner of his menu and he glared at the various members of the assembled company who were seated around him with his blue eyes and in such a manner that the Dean and Angela Ramage had qualms of definite anxiety.

Rosamund Kingsley looked half-amused and half-annoyed. She was seated opposite Garnett and she had, therefore, heard all that he had said. To admit the truth, she felt very much the same way about things as he did. If it weren't Cedric Garnett's line of country, it was equally certainly not hers. She contented herself by thinking about the second test which Mrs. Clinton had stated she would impose upon them and wondering what particular form this would take. She imagined, as she thought over things, that in all probability it would be entirely different from the one which faced her now. The remaining member of the guest party, Capt. Ronald Playfair, sat still in his chair, dark and debonair. A whimsical smile played round the corners of his mobile sensitive mouth. It was often said of Ronald Playfair that when he got out of bed in the morning he looked more spruce and more debonair than most men did after they had completed the most meticulous of toilets. He thrust his two hands into his pockets, tilted back his chair, and elevated his glance to the ceiling. As he shifted his body in the chair, the clock struck the hour. Its chimes quivered through the atmosphere of the room. Nobody spoke a word. The silence was complete. Mrs. Warren Clinton's first test had begun.

XVII

Denver started to write first of all of them. For some reason which he couldn't have satisfactorily explained had he been asked to, he listed as an opening move the capital letters of the nine words which had been dictated by Mrs. Clinton. 'O.E.U.R.I.R.E.M.P.' The three last letters caught and held his eyes. He thought of what his hostess had said. That the task, as it were, would eventually 'prove itself.' That he would *know* if his answers were correct. In a flash he had rearranged the nine letters. To read 'OUR EMPIRE.' He smoothed back his hair in satisfaction. It occurred to him that he had at least accomplished something. He then began to study the words with extreme care. His task was to find a word of close association with each. He came to the conclusion, after a few minutes' thought, that the nine 'answer' words would, in themselves, form an anagram made up of their respective capital letters, just as the nine original words had. He had to discover, therefore, an appropriate 'association word' of nine letters, with the two words 'Our Empire.' He glanced again somewhat ruefully at the original words. He could do something with 'Orpheus,' 'Iphicles' and 'Eagle' (even though the last-named might be of the two-headed variety), but the remaining six conveyed little or nothing to him. Still—he could and would attack the more simple words first of all—after the manner which he had always employed for the answering of examination papers when he was a boy at school.

Wilfred Denver scratched his cheek and bent to his task. Garnett contented himself, during these early moments, by looking round at the various guests and their different occupations. Those who had started to write at once were Ramage, Denver, Dean Langton, Sir Edward Angus and Lord Esmond Curte. The two ladies and Capt. Playfair, up to the moment, had not made a start. Garnett grinned mischievously in the direction of Rosamund Kingsley and endeavoured to convey to her in the effort that he sympathized most thoroughly with her in the totally unnecessary predicament in which she now found herself.

After about a spell of ten minutes, Ronald Playfair pulled his menu towards him and began to write. Garnett fell to wondering what he was actually putting down on the card. Playfair by now was writing steadily. Words appeared to be coming to him with unusual fluency. Cedric Garnett grinned again. So far as he himself was concerned, his interest was now centred upon the second test to which Mrs. Clinton was submitting him. He took a cigarette and lit it, tossing the match on to an ash-tray which was on the table some distance away from him with commendably sure and accurate aim. Thus the time dragged by. Garnett helped himself to a drink from a bottle of wine which was standing close to his left elbow. The clock chimed the successive quarters with steady insistence. Its hands crept to ten o'clock, the limit of time which Mrs. Warren Clinton had named as the end of the test. When but five minutes remained to go, Denver flung down his pencil and pushed his card away from him. The gesture seemed to hint at impatience. But two of the figures round the table were still writing—these were John Ramage and Dean Theodore Langton. The first chime of the clock striking ten sounded. Ramage and the Dean stopped and there entered Mrs. Warren Clinton. She smiled at them encouragingly.

"Thank you, ladies and gentlemen," she said, "will you be good enough to hand me your cards."

Then, without waiting for any other spoken answer, she moved along the table collecting the cards one by one. When she had them all in her hands, she turned and made another announcement.

"You may amuse yourselves for the next half-hour in any way you please while I look at your answers. At half-past ten I shall be with you again."

At that Mrs. Warren Clinton disappeared with the test papers.

XVIII

Punctually at half-past ten Mrs. Clinton kept her promise. She appeared in the doorway. "I am now going in to my little room. I use it chiefly for any reading and writing that I do. I want each one of you to come in to me in the alphabetical order of your surnames. So please begin to sort yourselves out in readiness. Sir Edward Angus, will you come along with me to start, as it were, the ball rolling? Thank you. Sir Edward."

Sir Edward Angus bowed to his hostess and accompanied her to the little reading-room. The door closed behind them. At quick intervals the other guests, in turn, took Sir Edward's place. Curte, Denver, Garnett, Rosamund Kingsley, Dean Langton, Playfair, Angela Ramage and then, finally, John Ramage. By forty-eight minutes past ten the various personal interviews were over. It was plain to see, as each person concluded his or her interview with Mrs. Clinton, that every one of them was tremendously puzzled by what had been submitted to them. For some little time Mrs. Clinton remained in her private apartment. As the clock chimed the hour of eleven she came back to her guests.

"Ladies and gentlemen," she said in a clear voice, entirely free from emotion, "as a result of my two tests I am able to announce that I have made my selection. You, to whom I have unburdened this evening my secret hopes, my fears and my own plans to combat the latter, will understand that I have not made my choices carelessly or without the most assiduous consideration of the claims of everybody The successful names are those of Mr. Wilfred Denver and Mrs. Angela Ramage. My congratulations to both of them. I will now wish you good night. Till breakfast-time tomorrow morning, then. Good night everybody—and thank you all ever so much for your invaluable help and assistance."

Mrs. Warren Clinton waved her hand and departed. The guests with one accord turned to Denver and Angela Ramage and showered questions and congratulations upon them. Ramage noticed that Denver looked pleased, whereas his wife looked surprised and startled. John Ramage walked over to her.

"So you're bearing your blushing honours thick upon you—eh? Well—let me add my congratulations to the rest. But I'll tell you candidly, my dear, that you wouldn't have carried my money. So—with the congratulations—apologies."

His wife started to reply but thought better of it and shook her head. The idea that she was worried persisted in his brain. She turned her head—half away from him. He put his hand on her arm, but Denver came up and what John Ramage had intended to say to his wife was diverted from his mind.

Playfair, Curte and Garnett formed themselves into a group.

"If you ask me," said the first-named, "it's all damned unreal. Feel as though I've been assisting in a sort of modern Arabian Nights' entertainment. Don't know how you fellows feel about things."

Curte laughed, but the laugh held uneasiness. "Much the same as you, I think, if I take the trouble carefully to analyse my innermost feelings. Got an idea at the back of my mind somewhere that it isn't going to end just here."

"I'm inclined to agree with you," supplemented Playfair; "for some reason that I'm totally incapable of explaining, I've been on thorns all the evening. Ever since the grub stakes packed up and our lady friend read us the words of the chorus." He turned to Cedric Garnett. "What do you think about things, Garnett? Have you found any degree of satisfaction in any part of the performance? Because I'm damned if I have."

Garnett laughed. The laugh bordered on the boisterous. "If you ask me, our hostess is a bit 'nuts.' You know what I mean." He tapped his forehead with significant emphasis. "A trifle 'bats in the belfry.' Call the whole business a mutual 'leg-pull' and you won't be far out."

Curte shook his head. "I'm not altogether sure that we can dismiss matters quite so cavalierly as that. If I thought it was only that—"

He broke off abruptly. Garnett cut in at the opportunity.

"Don't forget I called it a 'mutual' leg-pull. To me that part of it's as plain as a pike-staff. Mrs. Clinton flattered us by the invitations. Tickled all of us where we itched and we in turn flattered her by responding so thoroughly and so readily to her bait. Because that's all it was—'bait.' And we all opened our blinking mouths and swallowed it—hook, line and sinker."

Garnett took out his cigarette-case and handed it to the two others. "Well—don't you agree? When you look the problem straight in the face? When you cut out all the 'boloney'?"

Playfair looked at Lord Esmond Curte. Curte returned the compliment. They each shrugged their shoulders. Curte looked across the room. Another group was in close conversation. It consisted of Dean Langton, Sir Edward Angus and Angela Ramage. Angela herself appeared to be saying but little. Sir Edward was holding the floor. He was talking with a strong measure of agitation. Every now and then Dean Langton shook his head as though he were in disagreement with much of what Sir Edward Angus was saying. John Ramage looked at his watch. He was tired. The day's proceedings had wearied him. He decided that it would not be long before he went to bed. He and Angela had separate bedrooms, he had noticed from the slip the receptionist had handed to him, which possessed a communicating door. He went across to speak to his wife. She detached herself adroitly from the Dean and Sir Edward Angus. Ramage told her of his immediate intentions. She nodded to him in assent.

"I'm tired, too, John. Feel gloriously sleepy. If you're going up, I'm coming with you. Let's have one more drink at the buffet." He shook his head, but she caught him by the arm and piloted him over to the bar. Ten minutes later they went upstairs to bed. Soon after that, John Ramage called 'good night' to her from his room.

She returned the greeting. "Good night, my dear. I shall be asleep as soon as my head touches the pillow."

XIX

When Ramage awoke on the following morning he walked through the communicating door of the apartment into his wife's bedroom. To find the room empty. Of Angela Ramage there wasn't a sign. Ramage looked round curiously and advanced towards the bed. It would be wrong to say that there was evidence that the bed had not been slept in. It looked as though Angela had lain in it for a short time and had then got out. Ramage looked puzzled at the turn of events and then—suddenly—desperately anxious. His wife's night attire was on one of the pillows. He turned and retraced his steps. He wasn't sure what he should do for the best. Hang it all— the situation, to say the least of it, was damned awkward. There was a bathroom attached to the two bedrooms and it was obvious that Angela wasn't in there because Ramage, from where he was, could see into it.

He returned to his own room so that he might think things over for a moment or so. He looked in the glass and fingered his chin reflectively. Most awkward and so entirely unlike Angela. After a few minutes' intensive concentration he decided to proceed with his morning's toilet and await developments. But before doing so he went back to Angela's apartment and opened the door of the wardrobe. As far as he could tell from memory, the frocks she had brought with her on the journey to Remington were all there. Although this fact strongly suggested that she had not gone out, Ramage shook his head in bewilderment. Where on earth was she? He shook his head again, went back to the bathroom, turned on the water for his bath and busied himself with his shaving tackle. He stropped the razor almost mechanically. All the time he listened—to find out whether any sounds came from the room that had been Angela's. But all was silent. The only sound came from the stropping of the razor. In this manner John Ramage bathed, shaved and dressed on this particular morning.

At half-past eight he went downstairs to the breakfast-room. Only two of Mrs. Warren Clinton's party had so far put in an appearance. These two were Garnett and Playfair. Ramage wished them good morning and answered their attempts at conversation in curt monosyllables. By now the anxiety that he had felt when he first missed Angela was momentarily increasing. Rosamund Kingsley came in looking the picture of health. Ramage went straight up to her and greeted her.

"Seen my missus in any of your travels this morning, Miss Kingsley?"

Rosamund replied with a shake of her head. "Not so much as a glimpse of her, Mr. Ramage. I wish I had. I've been round the town before breakfast and I should have much preferred to have had a companion. Why do you ask—is she lost or merely mislaid?"

"I'm hoping neither. But if she doesn't turn up in the next ten minutes or so I shall begin to think that something's happened to her."

Miss Kingsley smiled. "She'll be in in a moment or so—don't you fear! If nothing else calls her, there's always the aroma to assail one's nostrils of coffee and bacon. It never fails to work with me, Mr. Ramage. Sends me scuttling along to breakfast no matter where I am when I first smell it." She screwed up her face attractively and smiled at him.

Ramage kept turning his head towards the door. But no sight of the missing Angela rewarded his gaze. Breakfast was scheduled for nine o'clock and gradually, one by one, various members of Miriam Clinton's guest-party came down to the coffee-room. Ramage sized them up as they appeared in turn, all of them apparently in the best of spirits. After a time he noticed that besides his wife, Angela, there was another member of the party missing—Wilfred Denver. Ramage looked at his watch. It had now turned nine o'clock and he knew, only too Well, that it was not one of Angela's habits to be late for breakfast. No matter where she might be. Ramage took a quick decision. He walked quickly into the hall of the hotel and made for the office of the receptionist. That young lady was engaged in the time-honoured practice of making out bills.

"You will pardon me," said John Ramage with a quiet insistence, "but will you kindly tell me where I can find the manager?"

"I'll get him to come along at once," was the bright reply.

The girl turned to a table at her side and used the 'phone. Ramage watched her with a curious concern. She quickly got the response she needed.

"The manager will be along in a few minutes, sir."

Ramage waited near the office for the manager's arrival. The girl was as good as her word. The manager put in an appearance in less than five minutes. He went straight up to where Ramage was standing.

"I believe that you wanted to see me, sir?"

He seemed both cordial and amiable. Ramage drew him to one side.

"It's like this," he said nervously. "My wife seems to have disappeared. It sounds absurd, I know, but she wasn't in her room when I woke up this morning and there's no sign of her anywhere. I wouldn't have worried you—but I'm desperately anxious about her. I mean I can't understand it—and it's all frightfully disturbing. I felt that I must have a word with you about it." Ramage broke off. The manager looked anxious.

"Very strange, sir. It's Mr. Ramage, isn't it?"

"Yes. My wife was here with me. Although we travelled down separately."

"Yes, sir. So I understood from Mrs. Clinton. But to get back to our pressing problem. Isn't it possible that Mrs. Ramage may have popped out for something? What do you think yourself, sir?"

Ramage scouted the suggestion. "I can scarcely believe that my wife would have gone out without her clothes. For I can assure you that all her clothes are still upstairs in her wardrobe."

This reply made a deep impression on the manager of the 'Royal Sceptre.' "Is that so, sir? Well, of course, I didn't know that—I was only making what I thought was a likely suggestion. I'll tell you what—I wonder if Mrs. Clinton herself can throw any light on the matter—"

He walked back to the reception office and dialled on the telephone. Ramage followed him and stood outside the office watching him. Suddenly the manager put the telephone down and came out to Ramage.

"Funny business—all of it," he said. "I can't get an answer from Mrs. Clinton's bedroom. Frankly, I can't make it out."

"She may have come down to breakfast. It's a possibility."

The manager shook his head. "Not she, sir. Not Mrs. Warren Clinton. Ten o'clock's more like her time. At least, judging by her habits since she's been here. Still—I'll take a glance at the breakfast tables in case. Wait here, Mr. Ramage, will you, please?"

The manager darted off. Ramage still waited. He hadn't to wait long. The manager was breathing heavily.

"Not in there, sir. Think I'd better have a tour round. Come with me if you don't mind, sir."

With a bunch of keys in his hand he made his way up the main staircase, followed by John Ramage. "Mrs. Clinton's is the first on the left. Just over there past the writing-room."

They came to the room he had indicated. The manager tapped on the door. There was no answer. He tapped again. With a similar result.

"H'm," he muttered. "Funny. May be just an ordinary case of oversleeping."

He rubbed his chin reflectively. "Don't quite know what to do. Bit of a problem."

"Is the door open?" enquired Ramage.

"Shouldn't think so. Hardly likely. All the doors can be closed from the inside and lock themselves when anybody comes out of the room. That's why you all have keys handed to you when you come."

While he was speaking he tried the handle of the door. "No. It's fastened as I expected. I think I'll knock again before I do anything drastic."

The manager lifted his hand again and rapped loudly on the panel of the door. Again his effort went unrewarded. He turned and looked at Ramage. He looked at him searchingly. "Shall I chance it? What do you think?"

Ramage thought. "On the whole I think I should. Considering all the facts."

"Perhaps I should. But it's on the cards I may want you to stand by me. Anyhow—here goes."

The manager used a key and turned the handle of the bedroom-door. Ramage was at his elbow. But the man's body prevented him from seeing clearly into the conditions of the room. The convulsive start which the manager gave came as a shock to the other man just behind him.

"Shut the door—quickly." The manager's voice was hard and unsteady. Ramage obeyed the order mechanically. He turned, shut the door and pushed the catch into its place. Then he turned again because he knew that he must—that he could do nothing else. He took two steps forward. The hotel manager was standing by the side of the bed—the bed which should have been Mrs. Warren Clinton's bed. The bed-clothes were partly turned back. Two bodies lay in it.

A glance showed that they were dead bodies. If the manager couldn't identify them with certainty, Ramage could. For the bodies at which he looked were those of Angela, his wife, and of the man whom he knew as Wilfred Denver. There was no sign of Mrs. Warren Clinton.

XX

Mrs. Clinton's bedroom was uncomfortably crowded. In addition to the bodies of Wilfred Denver and Angela damage there were Suddards, the manager of the Royal Sceptre Hotel, Dr. Morton, the Remington Police-Surgeon, and Inspector Legge. When discovered, each body had been nude. Dr. Morton covered them reverently with sheets and draped the dignity of death. Denver and Mrs. Ramage had each been shot through the left eye.

"Death instantaneous," announced Dr. Morton. "There are no other marks on the body. Judging by the discoloration round the eyes, the pistol or revolver which was used was held very close to the face."

Inspector Legge looked at Denver's face. "Strange," he said, "there's scarcely any disfigurement. Scarcely any blood effusion."

"That's quite likely," agreed Dr. Morton. Inspector Legge walked round the room.

"Funny, nobody heard the shots. Puzzles me."

"The walls are thick," replied Suddards. "And the room is one of a suite. There was nobody in the next three rooms, for example. So it's quite likely."

Legge rubbed his top lip. "And you tell me that there's another lady disappeared. Besides these two people?"

"Yes, Mrs. Clinton. Our principal guest. Come in here, Inspector."

Inspector Legge followed Suddards into the room that had been used for the buffet on the previous evening. Here there were signs of indescribable confusion. The furniture everywhere was overturned and there was a patch on the carpet which looked suspiciously like the stain of blood.

"Looks worse," muttered Inspector Legge. "Who was attacked in here? Those in there," he jerked his head in the direction of the bedroom, "or somebody else?"

He mentioned no name, but despite his reticence Suddards knew that he was referring to Mrs. Warren Clinton. The Inspector went through the remaining rooms which comprised the suite which that lady had requisitioned. In all these rooms everything appeared to be in normal order. There was no disturbance of any kind. There was no confusion. Also, there was still no sign of Mrs. Warren Clinton. Inspector Legge turned towards Suddards, the hotel manager, and spoke abruptly.

"I shall have to interview all those people who you tell me came here as Mrs. Clinton's guests. As far as I can see into things at the moment, there's something 'fishy' about the whole thing. Two people dead in . . . er . . . extremely indelicate circumstances . . . er . . . to say the least of it . . . and another person missing. You'd better make arrangements for me to see all those people I mentioned. In that further room there. See that nobody leaves and let me have a list of their names at once, will you?"

Suddards nodded agreement. He knew only too well that he had no alternative.

"I'll bring you the list, Inspector. Then you can go in the room you've suggested you'll use, and send for the people in the order you want them."

"Very good. While you're doing that, I'll have another word with Dr. Morton. I'll be ready for the others in ten minutes. Not a moment later."

Suddards went thoughtfully down the main staircase. When he returned the Chief Constable had arrived and given Legge certain instructions.

PART TWO
THE CRISIS

I

CHIEF-Inspector Andrew MacMorran, of New Scotland Yard, listened attentively to the story which the Commissioner of Police was unfolding to him. Anthony Lotherington Bathurst sat at his side. Sir Austin Kemble was reciting the events which had gone to make up what the Press had already labelled as 'the Remington sensation.'

"Colonel Henderson is the Chief Constable down there and he happens to be a very old friend of mine. We were in the Service together. Directly he realized what the case meant, he called in the 'Yard.' Got through to me here at once. I only wish other people in similar circumstances to Henderson would do the same. Would save us no end of trouble."

"Ay, sir," replied MacMorran. "I'm in direct agreement with that."

Mr. Bathurst intervened. "And you say that Mrs. Warren Clinton has disappeared?"

"That's so, Mr. Bathurst. Vanished into thin air. Nobody has set eyes on her since she said 'good night' to her guests that evening in the Royal Sceptre Hotel, Remington."

"Of course—that's as far as you know."

"Of course. As far as is known."

"It's conceivable," said MacMorran, "as I see things, that this Mrs. Clinton may well be the guilty party. After all, according to the story which we're asked to believe, she invited these people down to Remington in the first place. Who is the woman and what is really known about her?"

The Commissioner told MacMorran.

"Nebraska—eh?" returned the Inspector.

"I know her by name," supplemented Anthony, "her reputation for riches has been well exploited in the Press for some years now. She's been described by many of the American journalists in that singularly illuminating phrase, 'a definite character.'"

Sir Austin Kemble nodded. "Quite so, Bathurst. I've read such accounts of her myself."

"It's all rather fantastic, Sir Austin. Don't you think so?"

"Perhaps it is. At the moment. But we don't know all, do we? In fact, on the contrary, we know very little. When we begin to dig into things a bit we may well find a very different complexion put on the matter."

Sir Austin pursed his lips after he had delivered himself of this judgment. MacMorran coughed discreetly. Anthony Bathurst rubbed his hands.

"It's an attractive case, I admit. I think the Inspector and I should pass a hearty vote of thanks to your friend Colonel Blimp for having tossed it into our laps. At any rate, that's how I'm feeling about it."

"His name's not Blimp—it's Henderson—Colonel Henderson—I imagined that I made that clear."

"I'm sorry," murmured Bathurst. "I meant to say Henderson."

Sir Austin glared at him suspiciously. Then he seemed to remember the terms of what had been his original intention. "I want you and MacMorran to go down there, Bathurst. Down to Remington. Today, some time, if it's at all convenient. There's a fast train from Paddington somewhere about midday." Sir Austin consulted a slip of paper. "12.14 actually. Colonel Henderson told me. Can you do it?"

"Yes. I've nothing on that can't be put off."

"Good. That's settled then. There's one thing—you won't find the scent stone-cold. Henderson says that his men have the matter well in hand. That is, of course, up to a point."

"Right," replied Anthony, picking up his hat. "I'll meet you at Paddington, Andrew, as the clock is striking twelve."

II

In the train with MacMorran, on the journey down to Remington, Anthony read many newspapers. Their accounts of the double tragedy at the Royal Sceptre Hotel were extremely varied. Past Reading, Anthony tossed the papers over to the Inspector.

"On the whole, Andrew, not very illuminating. I shall steadfastly refuse to come to any conclusion whatever."

"I entirely agree, Mr. Bathurst."

"Who's the man in charge of the case at Remington? Any idea?"

"An Inspector Legge. I've never met him that I can remember. To all accounts, he's an excellent man. This affair, though, is probably too big for him. Taken him out of his depth a bit. That's why they asked the 'Yard' to take a hand."

Anthony nodded. "I suppose so. But tell me, Andrew—I'm interested to know—how does the affair strike you?"

"In what way—exactly?" McMorran was nothing if not cautious. "Well—do you see anything behind it—beyond the mere fact of murder? *And*—shall we say, the somewhat sordid infraction of the seventh commandment?"

MacMorran puffed solemnly at his pipe. At last he ventured an opinion. "Well—to tell the truth—I do—and that's a fact."

"What do you see, Andrew?"

"Don't know—quite. But something big. That's the only way in which I can describe it. I feel that there must be big interests at stake. The feeling's in my bones."

Anthony nodded almost as though he were in complete agreement. "Go on, Andrew. Expound. Tell me more—you've started something in my mind."

MacMorran pressed down the burning tobacco in his pipe. "Well—in the first place, what's behind this American woman? Why did she decide to come over here,? A very rich woman at that. What's the real truth behind her visit? She must have been up to something. Take these so-called party invitations to start with."

The Inspector paused. Anthony took things up from where MacMorran had left them. "Yes. I could bear to know a great deal more concerning them. So far I have but the haziest of notions as to what they were all about. I've read the notes that you gave me on the case and I'll frankly confess that they left me completely puzzled. By the way—what is Mrs. Warren Clinton's age? I don't remember that I've run across it anywhere in your notes."

MacMorran thought. "In the early sixties, I believe—sixty-two."

"Thanks. Her husband, I fancy, died in the October of last year. Am I right?"

"You are, Mr. Bathurst. In Nebraska, U.S.A."

"Well—I'm keeping an open mind. In many respects I'm inclined to regard it as the strangest case that has ever come our way. If I'm asleep, wake me up, Andrew, when we run into Remington."

III

Anthony Lotherington Bathurst sat with Inspector Legge of the Remington police and Chief-Inspector MacMorran of New Scotland Yard. Legge had recounted the details of the murders in the 'Nonpareil' suite of the 'Royal Sceptre.' They sat in the manager's office on the ground floor of the hotel. Legge was talking when Anthony intervened with a question.

"You say that there is a patch of blood on the carpet in this buffet room?"

"Yes. Doctor Morton, the Divisional Surgeon who was called in directly the bodies were discovered has tested it and is satisfied that the stain on the carpet is human blood."

"I should like to visit the rooms," said Anthony, turning to MacMorran.

Legge led the way to the 'Nonpareil' suite. He explained how the bodies of Denver and Angela Ramage had been found.

"What clothes were they wearing?" asked Anthony.

"None," replied Legge curtly. "Each body was nude."

Anthony nodded. "I see. Was Mrs. Ramage an attractive woman, can you tell me? I've seen her photographs, especially since she entered Parliament, but I always think that photographs give you very little real idea of what a person is like—particularly with regard to a woman."

"I asked the same question," said Legge. "I am informed that Mrs. Ramage was a distinctly attractive woman."

"Thank you, Inspector. Mrs. Ramage's husband was also a member of Mrs. Clinton's party, I understand?"

"That is so, Mr. Bathurst."

"Now tell me this, Inspector. What success have you had in tracing Mrs. Clinton?"

"None at all. All the enquiries we have made so far have yielded nothing."

"I see. So that we start by being properly up against it."

Legge smiled ruefully. "I'm afraid that is so, Mr. Bathurst."

"Ah—well—we won't be discouraged on that account."

"I should suggest," ventured MacMorran, "that our first step should be to interview, one by one, the various members of Mrs. Warren Clinton's guest party."

"I entirely agree, Andrew. Eminently sound idea! Have you considered the order in which we should interview them?"

MacMorran looked puzzled. "No. I hadn't considered that point at all. Quite frankly, Mr. Bathurst, I don't know that I get you."

Anthony smiled. "I don't know that I get myself. But it struck me that we should interview Ramage last of all. He was with Suddards when the bodies were discovered and he also happens to be the husband of one of the victims. I feel that we should have the opportunity of hearing the accounts of the various other people before we hear his story. Do you agree, Inspector?"

MacMorran accepted the position. "Yes. I accept that. Have you any preconceived ideas as to the order in which the others should be interviewed?"

Anthony shook his head. "No, none at all. In your hands, Inspector."

"Good. Then we may as well have them in here. And to show there's no favouritism, I'll see them in strictly alphabetical order. Let me glance at the list."

MacMorran ran his eye down the list of names before speaking to Inspector Legge. "Ask Sir Edward Angus to come in, will you, Inspector Legge?"

Sir Edward was quick to obey the summons. His face was familiar to Anthony, and when he took the seat that Legge offered to him he polished his horn-rimmed spectacles with a silk handkerchief and nodded genially to the three men he saw confronting him. Before he questioned him, MacMorran made him aware of the rules with regard to the submission of any statement he cared to make. Sir Edward Angus smiled affably at the Scotland Yard inspector.

"I understand thoroughly," he declared. "Please ask me any questions you feel you would like to."

"Thank you, Sir Edward. You are, of course, a Member of Parliament?"

"Conservative member for Holme. Rigby Division. Have held the seat for more years than I care to remember." Sir Edward's brown, bird-like eyes twinkled with good humour as he made the statement.

"Tell us the circumstances which brought you here as Mrs. Warren Clinton's guest—will you, Sir Edward?"

Angus related the receipt of the invitation from the missing lady.

"May I see this letter?" asked MacMorran.

"I regret that I didn't keep it," answered Angus. "As a matter of fact I did retain it until yesterday. When, however, I got here and was introduced to the lady who had sent it, I destroyed the letter. I didn't see, to be perfectly candid, what useful purpose would be served by my continuing to keep it. But I think that I can repeat its terms, almost word for word. This is what Mrs. Clinton's letter contained."

Sir Edward Angus repeated aloud the terms of the letter as he claimed to remember them.

"Just a moment, sir," said Anthony—"but when did you receive this letter?"

Sir Edward thought over the question. "About ten days ago. Certainly not more."

"Thank you, Sir Edward." Anthony nodded to MacMorran and the latter carried on from the point where he had been stopped.

"You accepted Mrs. Clinton's invitation?"

"Naturally—seeing that I'm here now." Again the Member of Parliament smiled.

"What was the intention behind the invitations? Can you tell us that, Sir Edward?"

Sir Edward Angus shook his head. "No. I don't know that I can. I'm afraid that the only person who can satisfactorily do that is Mrs. Warren Clinton herself."

Anthony smiled to himself at the neatness of the reply. But Mac-Morran was by no means perturbed. He went straight to his point.

"What happened during the time you spent at this hotel, up to the moment of the crimes being discovered?"

"We were received by our hostess, given light refreshments and then asked to sit down to dinner. After dinner a curious thing happened." Sir Edward proceeded to recount the test which Mrs.

Clinton had outlined to them. Anthony evinced keen interest when he heard Sir Edward describe this. Angus went on. He recited the conditions of Mrs. Clinton's first examination of them all.

"And what were these 'test' words, Sir Edward? Can you remember them?" The question came from Anthony.

"Oh, yes. They were certainly unusual: I can say that without fear of contradiction. Let me see now. The words were: 'Orpheus, Mazikeen, Premonstratensian, Iphicles, Roup, Edyrn, Ulema, Reldresal and . . . er . . . dear me, what was the last one . . . oh, I remember—Eagle (Two-headed)'."

Anthony looked puzzled. "Were they given to you in that order, Sir Edward?"

"Oh—no. I've mixed them up . . . I named them as they occurred to me."

Anthony wrote the words down. "From the point of view, Sir Edward, of Mrs. Clinton's marking, how many correct answers did you give?"

"I haven't the slightest idea. Not the foggiest. That's one of the most remarkable features of it all. Mrs. Clinton collected my answers as I had written them, immediately after ten o'clock, and quite frankly—that's the last I either heard or saw of them."

Anthony shook his head wonderingly. "Extraordinary—all of it, I agree. But you referred, Sir Edward, to a second test which the lady imposed on you. What form did that take?"

"A barrage of questions. Put to me privately, of course. In this very apartment. Concerning my individual attainments and powers."

"Give me an example, please, Sir Edward."

"Certainly. With pleasure. Was I a good shot? An accomplished swimmer? Able to ride a horse? Did I understand the mechanical parts of a motor-car and a tank? There were several others, but those are representative."

Anthony smiled. "How were you able to answer? In the main."

"My answers were mixed, naturally, but I can swim and I can ride. I suppose, on the whole, I put up a 'fifty-fifty' performance." Sir Edward Angus chuckled as he made the statement.

"What happened after that?" asked Anthony.

"I was dismissed after being thanked very charmingly for having taken part in the proceedings. By the way, I was the first guest to be questioned. I rather fancy she saw us in alphabetical order." Sir Edward paused, to go on again almost immediately. "At eleven o'clock, Mrs. Clinton came back to us and announced that she had made her selection. She had chosen Denver, the actor chap, and Mrs. Ramage, the lady M.P. for West Markham."

Anthony started. Sir Edward noticed the movement.

"I can see that you're thinking what I'm thinking. Coincidence, isn't it?"

"More than that, I'm afraid, Sir Edward." Anthony shook his head gravely. "The whole business may be fantastic—but I'm afraid that these are deep waters. But tell me—what happened after Mrs. Clinton had made the announcement of her selection."

Sir Edward moved easily in his chair. "Well—we more or less accepted the position, wondered whether we were the victims of something in the nature of a practical joke, talked together for half an hour or so, and then gradually drifted off to bed. It was about all we could do."

"I see."

MacMorran put a question. "What was the number of your bedroom, Sir Edward?"

"Number 54."

The Inspector referred to his list. "Thank you."

"May I glance at that, Inspector?" said Anthony.

MacMorran handed the document to him. Anthony thanked him. MacMorran had more questions.

"Did you hear anything in the night, Sir Edward?"

"Not a thing. As you will have seen, the bedroom I occupied was some considerable distance from Mrs. Clinton's suite."

"And you saw nothing, I suppose, during your stay with your fellow-guests that aroused any suspicion on your part?"

"Nothing at all. As a matter of fact I thought it was a distinctly distinguished gathering. There was no discord of any kind. I think that we more or less regarded ourselves as fellows in the same boat."

"One question from me, Sir Edward." The speaker was Anthony Bathurst.

"Yes. I shall be delighted to answer it. That is, if I can, of course."

"Who was responsible for the allocation of the various bedrooms? Can you tell me that, Sir Edward?"

Sir Edward thought carefully. "No. I can't tell you that. The number of my bedroom was given to me by the receptionist. But I don't know by whom the arrangements were actually made."

Anthony nodded. "I understand the position. Once again, thank you, Sir Edward."

MacMorran rose. "I don't think I shall need you any more, sir." Sir Edward bowed and made his departure. Anthony looked at Inspector MacMorran. "Notice the coincidences, Andrew? Nine guests invited. Nine words included in the test. Two successful people nominated by Mrs. Clinton. The same two found murdered. In the wrong bed. Distinctly interesting, Andrew, to say the least of it. Who's next on the list?"

"Lord Esmond Curte," replied MacMorran.

IV

Lord Esmond Curte entered almost on the heels of Sir Edward Angus. His attitude was both cynical and supercilious.

"Sit down, my lord," said Inspector MacMorran.

Curte obeyed without saying a word. At a nod from MacMorran, Legge took charge of the preliminaries. This accomplished, he told Curte what lay behind the interview. Curte moved his head, giving the indication that he understood everything perfectly. MacMorran questioned him with regard to his original invitation. Curte gave a terse explanation. It coincided with Sir Edward Angus's statement. Other questions followed to which Esmond Curte gave similar replies to those Angus had given. Anthony listened rather lazily until MacMorran brought Curte to the point of the 'test' examination.

"Mrs. Warren Clinton called out a list of nine words. Some of 'em I'd never heard of before. Most of 'em in fact. Don't mind confessing as much."

"Can you remember any of the words?" asked Anthony.

Curte looked annoyed. "I might be able to. If I tried hard enough. 'Eagle (Two-headed), Orpheus, Iphicles, Roup, Ulema' . . ." Curte came to a somewhat abrupt conclusion. "How many's that?" he asked.

"Five. You want to think of four more."

"I don't. You're quite wrong, believe me. Five only—eh? Let me see if I can improve on five." Curte wrinkled his brows "Edyrn . . . Mazikeen . . . no, I'm afraid that finishes me. My mind's a complete blank as regards the rest. Sorry—but what the hell's it matter—after all? There's no need to make the business any more ridiculous than Mrs. Clinton made it." Curte made a quick gesture of annoyance. Anthony smiled at him.

"What were you supposed to do with these words?"

Curte explained as Angus had before him.

"And how many correct answers did you give, my lord?"

"Good Lord, I don't know. Haven't an earthly. The old girl never let on. Didn't breathe a word."

"How do you think yourself you got on?"

For the first time the faint flicker of a smile flitted across Curte's face. "I don't think that I set the Trent on fire. Far from it. Let's leave it at that."

MacMorran glanced at his notes. "After that, my lord, I understand that you had a private interview with your hostess. Is that correct?"

"Entirely. We all did. She sent for us one after the other and 'chin-wagged' at us rather relentlessly."

"What happened during this interview?"

"Oh—she asked a number of damn fool questions. Candidly—I wish to God I'd never accepted the invitation. Serves me right, I suppose."

"Can you give us any idea of the nature of these questions?"

"Naturally I can, since I was asked them. Could I row a boat? Had I any knowledge of jiu-jitsu? Was I a fluent speaker of German? I remember that to that particular question I answered that I wasn't. Anyhow—I didn't satisfy the good lady's demands, so why the hell should we worry? Denver seemed to fit the particular bill that she wanted fitted—and then, evidently, paid the penalty."

Anthony seemed interested by this last remark. "Tell me, sir, do you connect the two events? Do you think that Denver was murdered *because* he was chosen?"

Curte regarded him almost contemptuously. "Why, man, wasn't Mrs. Ramage killed as well? Can there be any reasonable argument about it? The two people chosen by Mrs. Clinton and then a few hours afterwards found murdered in their beds!"

"Bed," said Anthony simply. Curte seemed a trifle taken aback.

"Er—yes," he corrected himself . . . "bed. I was forgetting for the moment." His face looked ugly.

"Some people would argue, you know, that it's a distinction with a big difference."

"I suppose so. From my point of view, though, it doesn't affect the point. I'm simply dealing with the fact that the two people were murdered—not with the reason that took them to the same bed."

"Exactly," said Anthony drily.

MacMorran sailed in with his normal questions. Lord Esmond Curte replied to them all with a direct candour.

"The number of my room was 61. I heard nothing whatever in the night that aroused the slightest suspicion and I'm afraid that beyond what I've already told you I cannot be of any assistance to you in your investigations."

MacMorran thanked him for his attendance.

"Do you want any more of me?" asked his lordship.

"For the time being, sir," replied the Inspector, "I don't think so."

Curte stood up before lounging out. "See you again, then," he remarked with a nod.

When he had closed the door behind him the Inspector looked at Anthony with a question. "What did he mean by that exactly?"

"I fancy, Andrew," said Anthony, "that he was simply repaying you in your own coin. In a way, you know, you asked for it."

MacMorran frowned. "I don't see why. I only gave a plain answer to a plain question."

His frown deepened. Turning to Legge, who had continued to hold a watching brief, he said: "Get Garnett in, will you, do you mind—Mr. Cedric Garnett."

V

Anthony Bathurst was perhaps more interested in Garnett than in any of the other members of Mrs. Clinton's guests, That is to say, more *personally* interested. Not so much from the standpoint of the crimes and who had committed them, but because of Garnett's many-sided distinctions in the world of sport.

When he came into the room, piloted by Inspector Legge, Anthony saw at once that physically Garnett was a magnificent specimen. Well over six feet in height, finely-proportioned, his straw-coloured hair a trifle unruly, these features helped to suggest that here indeed was one who might have been a Viking of old. A few feet from the doorway Garnett stopped and surveyed the two men who awaited him.

"Come in, Mr. Garnett," invited the Inspector, "come in and sit down."

Garnett took a step or so forward, thrust out a leg, crooked it round a chair, pulled the chair towards him and sat in it. A debonair giant who had looked on life and found it good. MacMorran put the usual questions to him with regard to the genesis of the gathering at Remington. Garnett, in a soft and pleasing voice for so big a man, gave the same answers as those of the guests who had preceded him. Anthony watched him with increasing interest, He knew Garnett's outstanding record in the realm of sport and secretly held him in the highest admiration. MacMorran proceeded by a series of steps to the first Clinton 'examination.' Garnett tossed his fair head back and laughed happily.

"Examination! I'll say! I have a job to spell 'believe' and 'receive,' so you can guess how brilliantly I fared. To tell the truth, I wasn't able to answer a single one of the questions. Most of the ruddy words I'd never even heard of. Don't mind admitting it. Erudition has never been my long suit."

Anthony smiled at Garnett's frank admission. "So there's no need for me to ask how many marks Mrs. Clinton awarded you?"

Again Garnett laughed with boisterous good humour. "None at all, I should say. A complete and utter 'blongey.' I can assure you that the hour which Mrs. Clinton allowed for that ridiculous business was completely wasted as far as I was concerned. God's good time at that! Time, alas, that will never come to me again."

Garnett smiled, showing his white even teeth. MacMorran decided to go ahead on the normal lines.

"Then, I take it," he said quietly, "you were sent for to undergo a second inquisition?"

"That's right. Had to sit for my viva voce. What a scream! The old cow kidded us all right when she enticed us down here. Well—they say there's a mug born every minute. I'll say it's true—and none better."

"Mrs. Clinton questioned you?"

Garnett nodded. "She did—and all. My hat—the questions that dame put. Could I pilot a plane? Could I play a musical instrument? Had I any knowledge of curling and ski-ing? Did I know anything about the combinations of safes? These—and several others."

"Can you do any of the things mentioned?"

Garnett shrugged his shoulders. "I can pilot a plane, with moderate skill. That was about the one question to which I could truthfully answer 'yes.'"

Anthony cut in. "What was your opinion, Mr. Garnett, when this interview with Mrs. Clinton was over?"

"Opinion?"

Garnett looked at Anthony blankly. "As to what?"

"With regard to the inner meaning of the whole business. A business which I feel bound to point out has ended in a peculiarly horrible double murder."

"Oh—I get you! Why—that the whole thing was 'nuts'! 'Haywire'! The old girl was 'dotty' all right—not a doubt of it."

"You are aware, of course, that Mrs. Clinton herself has disappeared?"

"I've heard as much," replied Garnett with an almost elaborate carelessness.

MacMorran came back. "You don't feel, I suppose, Mr. Garnett, that you can assist the police in any way?"

"Can't offer a thing, Inspector. Sorry and all that." Garnett swung one leg over the other.

Suddenly and somewhat surprisingly, Legge, who had been unnaturally silent, put a question to him. "Had you ever met Mrs. Clinton before, Mr. Garnett?"

"Never. Here—take a squint at this. Here's the original letter the old girl sent me."

Garnett fished in his pocket and eventually produced a letter. He hesitated evidently as to whether he should hand it to Legge who had put the question to him, or to MacMorran who was obviously conducting the inquiry. The latter solved the difficulty. He held out his hand for the letter. After the slightest of pauses, Garnett gave it to him. As MacMorran took it, Anthony leant over towards him and whispered something. MacMorran wasn't sure of what Mr. Bathurst had said to him. He would have raised the question had not Anthony moved away from him and towards Inspector Legge. Instead, therefore, MacMorran contented himself with reading the letter which Garnett produced as having been written to him by Mrs. Warren Clinton. The Inspector read it carefully and then passed it over to Legge with the remark, "Let Mr. Bathurst have it after you."

Legge nodded his agreement. When Legge gave the letter to him, Anthony felt a strange thrill of interest. Here in his hands was one of the beginnings of an affair which had culminated in the deaths of two people. People to whom life had not been unkind and who were entitled to think and believe that in their futures it might prove to be even kinder still. Anthony felt that Garnett was watching him closely as he read the letter. More closely perhaps than he had watched either MacMorran or Inspector Legge when he had read it. Garnett turned his head and carefully regarded his finger-nails.

Anthony noted the insistence of the physical in the terms of Mrs. Clinton's letter. Also the somewhat extravagant phrases—particularly towards the conclusion of it. 'You are the one man who can save the country.' Anthony folded the letter, replaced it in its envelope and returned it to Cedric Garnett.

"I'll tell you what strikes me as strange," he remarked.

"Yes," replied Garnett. "I shall be pleased to hear."

"Why—this. In the letter which Mrs. Clinton writes to you, in which she *introduces* herself to you as it were—she pays you the highest tribute and applies the most flattering descriptions. With which condition I, of course, can find no quarrel."

Anthony smiled as he spoke. Garnett bowed—with the suspicion of a smirk on his lips. Anthony went on.

"Yet—despite this complete nomination and acceptance of you as the potential saviour of the British Empire—when you arrive in response to her own invitation you are subjected with the others to what may be fairly described as a searching test of your general abilities. From my point of view, the two conditions, to be perfectly candid, don't fit." Anthony looked Garnett straight in the eyes. But all Garnett did was to move his head in agreement.

"I'm entirely with you. As a matter of fact, that's just what I thought myself. And for two pins I'd have told her so. I felt that she'd won the toss and put me in on a real 'sticky dog'—if you know what I mean."

Anthony intimated that he did. "What was the number of your bedroom, Mr. Garnett?"

"Fifty-eight, Inspector. And a very comfortable spot at that. I've no complaints on that score." Garnett smiled and his eyes twinkled at the savour of reminiscence.

"I take it you heard nothing unusual in the night?"

"The only sounds I heard in the night came from that big clock which stands at the foot of the main staircase. It has a particularly arresting chime which attends to the quarters, the halves and the three-quarters. To say nothing of the forwards. I mean the hours." Garnett grinned at his little joke.

MacMorran had one further question for him. "And you feel that you are unable to help us in any way, Mr. Garnett?" MacMorran waited, pencil poised over note-book for Garnett's reply. But Garnett found no inspiration.

"Sorry, Inspector, but there's nothing I can do about it. Only too delighted—if I could."

"Thank you. That will be all, then, for the time being, Mr. Garnett."

Garnett rose from his chair. Anthony leant over and spoke to MacMorran in a low tone.

"Yes," replied the latter. "I'll get Legge to attend to it. Legge! Ask Lord Curte to come back, will you? There's something we forgot to ask him when he was in here."

Inspector Legge followed Garnett out of the room to return within a few minutes with Lord Esmond Curte.

"Sorry to trouble you again, my lord," opened MacMorran, "but there's something else I'd like to ask you. Have you in your possession the letter which Mrs. Clinton sent you in the first instance?"

Curte looked surprised but nodded and answered 'yes' without the slightest hesitation. Thrusting his hand into his pocket, he produced the letter in question.

"Here you are, Inspector—you can look at it."

Curte gave MacMorran the letter. After the latter and the local inspector had read it, it came to Anthony. He soon saw that it was couched in similar terms to that which had been sent to Garnett. Curte smiled as he watched Anthony reading it. His blue eyes sparkled with mirth and the almost hawk-like fierceness of his face softened temporarily under the influence of the smile.

"Chucks bouquets at me, doesn't she? Quite embarrassin'."

"And yet you were not the selected candidate."

"No, that's perfectly true. But Denver may have appealed to the old girl more. There's always that possibility, you know."

Anthony handed back the letter. "Thank you."

MacMorran added his thanks to Anthony Bathurst's. Curte made his second departure. MacMorran turned to Legge again.

"Ask Miss Kingsley to come in," he said quietly.

VI

When Rosamund Kingsley came in, Anthony felt that here was a really outstanding woman. Beyond her physical attractiveness there was an indefinable quality about her to which it would have been excessively difficult to put the right name. No fault could be found with Mrs. Clinton's judgment as far as the selection of Rosamund Kingsley was concerned. With her corn-coloured hair and her blue eyes she suggested to Anthony the sagas of the Northland.

"Sit down, Miss Kingsley," said Inspector MacMorran, "and tell us all about this unpleasant business. Go back to the start of it all."

In a rather cold but beautifully modulated voice, Rosamund Kingsley related how she came to receive the letter of invitation from Mrs. Warren Clinton.

"Do you happen to have that letter with you, Miss Kingsley? If so, we'd like to have a glance at it."

"I had anticipated that request. Here it is, Inspector."

The three men read the letter in turn, Anthony last of the three. "Very similar to the others," he remarked as he returned it to the girl.

"Go on, Miss Kingsley," said MacMorran, "tell us what happened to you after you arrived in Remington."

Miss Kingsley obliged. Her story was on all-fours with those of the others. When she came to the account of the examination, Anthony listened carefully. He wanted to see the details, if any, of differences between her account and the accounts of the men. He was remembering that this was the first woman they had interviewed. Indeed it would be the only one, for of the other two who had come to Remington, one was dead and the other missing. But as far as he was able to see, as he listened, Rosamund Kingsley's story of the Clinton examination was subsequently identical with all the others. He questioned her.

"How did you get on with those words that were submitted to you, Miss Kingsley? I'm interested."

Rosamund laughed happily. "I was pretty hopeless, I'm afraid. If you ask me, I should probably have filled the bottom place. Many of the words were entirely unknown to me. Who's ever heard of such etymological monstrosities as 'roup' and 'ulema'? All I know is that I haven't." She laughed again and her eyes remained merry.

"What was the number of your bedroom, Miss Kingsley?" asked MacMorran.

"Seventy-two. That's on the floor above the room where the murders were."

"You heard nothing during the night?"

"Nothing at all. Not a sound. But don't attach the slightest importance to that. I invariably sleep like a top. Many of my best friends say that I can sleep standing up. You probably know that I've slept in the oddest places and among the quaintest people."

Anthony nodded and smiled at her. "You've no contribution of your own to make, I presume, that will help us in any way? You noticed no incident or episode that seemed to you suspicious or abnormal?"

Miss Kingsley considered the question. "Certainly not suspicious and perhaps not abnormal, but . . . strange. And that was this.

It occurred when Mrs. Clinton announced the results of her tests and the names of the two people she had selected. Mrs. Ramage and Wilfred Denver. Denver looked complacent. I mean by that, as though he had *expected* to be selected, whereas Mrs. Ramage looked to me as though she were absolutely astounded at Mrs. Clinton's choice. I mean—choice of herself."

Anthony saw her point. It was useful. Perhaps the most valuable contribution which had so far come to them.

"Thank you, Miss Kingsley. Information of that kind can't be over-valued. Up to the moment we have been almost startlingly unsuccessful. Yours is the first ray of light to pierce the darkness."

"I am glad," she replied. "Will you be wanting me any more?"

MacMorran looked at the two others. Anthony and Legge shook their heads in response to the unspoken question.

"No, thank you, Miss Kingsley. If I require you again we'll let you know."

Rosamund Kingsley made her exit.

"Ask Dean Langton to come in, Inspector."

Legge went to the door and Anthony prepared himself for another of the more interesting interviews.

VII

Anthony knew Langton from his Press photographs. Directly the Dean entered Anthony felt that he was primarily an incongruity—that he should never have been *dans cette galère*. The Yard Inspector, almost unconsciously, or so it seemed, became ultra-deferential. MacMorran evidently had the true Scotsman's deep regard for the Manse and the cloth. Langton's account of the affair was like all those which had preceded it. As before, MacMorran asked to see the letter from Mrs. Clinton which had brought the Dean to the gathering at Remington.

"I'm sorry," replied, Langton, "I haven't it with me. Had I known that you would have . . ."

Anthony cut in: "Tell us what it said, sir. Doubtless your memory will be equal to the occasion."

"Oh—quite." The Dean furrowed his brows. "The terms of the letter were these. The lady was good enough to emphasize the spiritual influence which I have been privileged to exert for some little time now ... and er ... called attention to what she described as my ... er ... undoubted powers of leadership. Because of these things, she invited me to Remington for this weekend. I accepted the invitation. I accepted it ... er ... from the highest possible motives. I think I am justified in making that much clear. The fact that Mrs. Clinton offered me what she called an 'alluring and attractive' proposition did not weigh at all. Not an iota."

The Dean of Mannington caressed his cheek, with his long, sensitive, tapering fingers. Before MacMorran could speak Dean Langton went on.

"And I'm going to say here and now, in order that you may understand clearly how I think and feel about things, that I bitterly regret ever having come here. I feel that in some obscure way which I am unable to explain I have been tricked."

The Dean looked supremely indignant as he gave expression to his protest. Anthony attempted to temper the wind to the troubled Dean.

"We've heard a good deal, sir," he said quietly, "about a curious test which Mrs. Clinton imposed on you who were her guests. Will you be good enough to give us some account of it? I should value your version of this incident very highly."

Dean Langton nodded gravely. "I shall be pleased to do as you wish. Mrs. Clinton announced to us a number of words. The whole affair to my mind bordered on the fantastic. I was familiar, as you may guess, with the whole of the words. But whether I was able to fulfil the conditions of the 'association' words, putting in a nutshell Mrs. Clinton's conditions as she explained them to us, I cannot say." Anthony moved his head as an indication that he understood. He had already heard of this particular point and had given some attention to it.

"At my second interview," went on the Dean, "she asked me if I had ever played hockey. I hadn't."

MacMorran continued with his customary questions. "What was the number of your bedroom, sir?"

"No. 62. I was allotted the bedroom next to the one occupied by Lord Esmond Curte."

"You were not disturbed at all during the night, I suppose?"

Dean Langton showed surprise. "Disturbed? Dear me—no. Why should I . . . oh—you were referring to the murders. Why, no. I can safely say I didn't hear a sound. I was tired, I was in a highly critical state of mind and I was extremely annoyed. I went to bed with those emotions in conflict in my mind and I slept. I can say no more than that, gentlemen."

The Dean looked gravely resolute and as though the Hound of Heaven were trotting sedately along at his side. MacMorran's eyes met Anthony's. What he saw satisfied him.

"Thank you, sir," he said to the Dean of Mannington. "You will not be required any more."

VIII

"Capt. Playfair," said MacMorran, "please sit down."

Playfair accepted the invitation easily and comfortably. 'Oh—yes,' though Anthony as he looked towards him, 'there is certainly something about you. And, what is more, you know it.' Playfair's eyes were taking a quick and comprehensive survey of the room and its occupants. All that emanated from him suggested to Anthony high-tempered courage.

MacMorran commenced to question him. The questions were by now all too familiar. As were the answers. Playfair ran true to form.

His account of the Clinton adventure contained nothing different from the many accounts which had preceded it. He described the initial letter which Mrs. Clinton had sent him, and the flattering expressions which had accompanied it. He produced the letter. He spoke of the introduction to Mrs. Clinton upon the arrival of the guests. Eventually he came to the moment when Mrs. Clinton announced that the examination would take place.

"Of course," he declared, by way of explanation, "most of the stuff she put over to us was definitely very far from being down my street. Directly I realized what was coming I knew it didn't interest 'yours truly.' So I just folded up."

He shrugged his neat compact shoulders with an eloquence that couldn't be ignored. "I just sat there and accepted the inevitable." Anthony determined to put a question to him immediately. "What, in your opinion, Capt. Playfair, was behind it all?"

It seemed to Anthony, as he asked the question, that Playfair hesitated. For perhaps something like a split second.

"In my opinion," he replied, "for what it's worth, Mrs. Clinton was a fervent patriot. There *are* some, you know. Not enough of them really. With her, the salvation of the British Empire had become an obsession. Better than that, let me say—more like a crusade. A cause to which she had solemnly dedicated herself. When her husband died and she found herself controlling a huge sum of money, she resolved to take certain steps in support of this overwhelming allegiance of hers. What actually those steps were to be I am unaware." Playfair paused. Before he could go on Anthony intervened.

"Having those ideas, then, Capt. Playfair, you have something definite to suggest to us with regard to the murders."

"Oh—yes, undoubtedly. Look at it logically. Admitted that Mrs. Clinton thought as I have just described and that she chose from the ranks she had assembled at her side the two people whom she regarded as the pick of the basket. She had examined us according to her lights, remember. Well—isn't it likely that the people against whom her effort was directed took a hand in the game for self-protection, very likely, and wiped out the two people she had chosen? It certainly seems so to me."

Playfair leant back and took a deep breath. He had spoken quietly and almost as though he were labouring under the stress of a deep emotion. MacMorran wrote in his note-book. Anthony saw clearly the lines on which Playfair was thinking. He resolved to ask Playfair another question.

"When you were called in, Capt. Playfair, for your second interview with Mrs. Clinton, what particularly did she ask you?"

"She asked me three questions. I was unsatisfactory at each of them. One—had I any experience as a 'parachute-jumper,' two—had I ever bred canaries, and three, had I ever studied the causes of sleeping-sickness? I was no good for any one of them, so I was turned down. I wasn't disappointed. I expected it. As things turned out, I may have been luckier than I thought."

Playfair grinned ruefully. Anthony smiled back at him. By a coincidence, Playfair, coming almost last, had contributed more than any of his predecessors.

"What was the number of your bedroom?" asked MacMorran.

"My bedroom? No. 55. Next to the room where Sir Edward Angus was. I remember that I said 'good night' to him as I went in to bed. He was standing just outside his bedroom door."

MacMorran carefully noted the answer. "No suspicious noises in the night?"

Playfair grinned again. "Sorry, Inspector. None at all. If I could produce one for you—believe me, I'd be delighted."

Anthony looked at him quizzically. "Nothing more to help us? Such stuff, for example, as dreams are made on?"

Playfair shook his head. "Beyond what I've handed you *re* motive, I'm as puzzled as you are. Honest Injun."

The Inspector decided to dismiss him. "Well, many thanks, sir. These inquiries may be tedious but they're very necessary. If I want to have another word with you, I'll let you know."

Capt. Playfair bowed and made his way out. MacMorran spoke to Legge. "That leaves Mr. Ramage, Inspector. Husband of the murdered woman. Ask him to step this way, will you?"

Inspector Legge departed on his errand.

IX

Ramage came in and sat down. His scholarly face showed signs of the tragic ordeal through which he was still passing. MacMorran expressed official sympathy in a few words.

"Thank you, Inspector," returned John Ramage.

Ramage, under the Inspector's direction, told the usual story of Mrs. Clinton and her invitations. He produced the letter which she had forwarded to him. The two police inspectors and Anthony read it.

"And your wife had a separate letter, I understand?" said Mac-Morran.

"That is so. I was away at the time and rather surprised when she told me, but my wife was, of course, a Member of Parliament and highly successful in her own sphere—medicine—so I gave the matter a little reflection and decided that perhaps things weren't quite so surprising after all."

"Now proceed, Mr. Ramage, and tell us what happened after you arrived at Remington."

Ramage described in detail what had occurred. MacMorran picked up a point.

"Am I to understand that you and Mrs. Clinton had met before, Mr. Ramage?"

"Yes. We had been fellow-passengers from America on the *Myrobella*. But I had spoken to her on but few occasions. She struck me as being a woman of undoubted personality and certainly one who knew her own mind."

"I see. Go on, please, Mr. Ramage."

Ramage continued. His voice was low and inclined to be toneless, but he spoke without a tremor. He came to a description of Mrs. Clinton's examination.

"How did you fare yourself?" asked Anthony.

Ramage shook his head with a hint of sadness. "Well—that's rather difficult for me to answer. I knew most of the words Mrs. Clinton gave us, naturally, but I'm by no means sure that I discovered the 'companion' words in accordance with the terms that the lady laid down to us and which I tried to explain to you just now." Ramage proceeded to describe what followed.

"What questions did Mrs. Clinton ask you at the interview?"

"Well, to tell the truth, rather extraordinary ones. I was extremely surprised. There were three in all. Firstly, had I ever grown chives; secondly, was I interested in numismatics, and, thirdly, was I at all acquainted with the Black Forest?"

"How did you answer, Mr. Ramage?"

"'No,' to the first two questions, and 'yes' to the third."

Anthony noted the terms of his reply.

"Well," continued Ramage, "as you know now, Denver and my poor wife were the successful people. Mrs. Clinton chose them and announced the choice to the rest of us."

Anthony thrust a question at him. "Mr. Ramage—forgive me asking you this. You knew Mrs. Ramage's capabilities better than anyone else. Were you surprised at Mrs. Clinton's choice?"

Ramage thought a moment before he answered. "Well, I'll endeavour to tell you exactly how I felt about that particular point. At first, when I heard Mrs. Clinton's announcement, I was, frankly, definitely surprised. But when I came to think it over more carefully

I was inclined to revise my original opinion. My wife," his voice faltered for a second, "was an exceedingly capable and well-informed woman. Quite likely she distinguished herself with her answers to the 'word list'."

Anthony was in again immediately. "Did Mrs. Ramage give you any idea as to how she had got on?"

"No. We scarcely had time to discuss details of that kind very closely. That discussion, no doubt, would have come later. Now, alas, it will never come." Ramage stopped but quickly recovered himself. "I can tell you, however, what my wife did tell me. The details of her interview with Mrs. Clinton. As with me, Mrs. Clinton asked her three questions. My wife informed me what they were. The first was: 'Could she speak German well enough to pass muster as a German.' The second was: 'Had she a sound knowledge of economics.' The third was: 'Had she any training or experience in "Map-reading".' As it happened, she was able to answer 'yes' to all three of them." Anthony nodded. "So you see, therefore, that when I came to think things over with closer consideration, my wife's selection as one of the two successful candidates was by no means so surprising as it had seemed to me at first."

John Ramage passed his hand across his forehead. It was the gesture of a tired, almost broken man. MacMorran made certain notes before putting a further question.

"Had your wife ever met Mr. Denver?"

"You mean—before coming to Remington?"

"Yes—that was my meaning. I'm sorry if I wasn't clear."

"I believe she had. It was one of the first questions I asked myself when I first heard of the tragedy. I suppose it was natural that I should ask it. But a stray chord of memory tells me that she and Denver had met once before. It was in London last summer at the Theatrical Garden Party. My wife attended it every year. I think I can just remember her telling me on the last occasion she went that she had been introduced to Wilfred Denver."

MacMorran wrote again—quickly and energetically. Anthony waited for him to finish. At the appropriate moment he questioned Ramage again.

"When did you last see your wife, Mr. Ramage?"

"I think it would be as well if I told you all that happened. When Mrs. Clinton announced to us all that Angela and Denver had been chosen by her, I formed the opinion that Denver looked pleased at the decision, whereas she did not To my mind she looked a trifle shocked. Yes, I think 'shocked' is a word which fits the condition quite satisfactorily. Anyhow, I went over to her and congratulated her. But before she could reply to me and assist me in my diagnosis, Denver came sailing up and she went off with him somewhere. But not for long. For my wife came back. She had evidently left Denver and was talking to Sir Edward Angus and Dean Langton when she spotted me and joined me. We agreed that we were both tired and decided to go to bed. So we had a final drink and a few minutes later went upstairs to bed."

"Just a minute, sir," said the Inspector, who for a few seconds had been in whispered conference with Legge, "but what was the number of your bedroom?"

"My wife and I had been allotted separate bedrooms, with a communicating door. Neither she nor I, I may say, had any voice in that arrangement. It had been made for us. The numbers were 45 and 46. Well, there isn't very much more for me to tell you. As I said just now, Angela and I were both very tired. We went to our respective beds and I went to sleep, I should imagine, almost immediately. At least, I have no memory of lying awake. When I woke up in the morning I went to my wife's apartment. She was not there. And she wasn't in the bathroom either. Her bed indicated to my eye that she couldn't have slept in it for very long. After a time, and due consideration of almost every probability and even possibility—and you must bear in mind that by this time I was desperately worried—I came to the conclusion that I must report to the manager the stubborn fact that my wife was missing. You more or less know the rest."

Ramage paused, his face working with emotion, MacMorran coughed. It was his cough of official discretion. "You will forgive me, Mr. Ramage, if I put a painful question to you. Had you before last night's tragedy any suspicions as to your wife's relations with Wilfred Denver?"

Ramage's voice, when he answered, came like the crack of a whip. "None, Inspector. None at all. And what's more, I have none now. I desire you to make a special note with regard to that."

The veins in John Ramage's forehead and temples quivered and throbbed. Anthony felt strangely attracted to him. Ramage attempted to fortify his previous statement.

"I know full well of the unhappy circumstances in which my wife's body was found. I know even better of the construction which will be placed upon those circumstances by the majority of damned good-natured people." His voice was tinged with scorn and he paused for the merest fraction of a second. "But I am certain that, when the time comes for the truth to be told with regard to this appalling tragedy, no stigma will be left attached to my wife's name and reputation. There will be both a convincing and an adequate explanation." Anthony looked at him and put yet another question. "Can you tell me what clothes of Mrs. Ramage's are missing?"

"As far as I can say, Mr. Bathurst, some underclothes and a silk-wrap. You know what I mean, I expect, an affair of the dressing-gown type."

Anthony noted Ramage's answer. "I don't think we need detain Mr. Ramage any longer," announced Inspector MacMorran, "unless, of course . . ." he looked enquiringly at Legge and Anthony. The former shook his head.

The latter said: "No, Inspector, I have nothing more to ask Mr. Ramage for the time being."

X

Anne Assheton was *en route* for Hollywood when the news of her husband's death came to her over the radio. Other details of the Remington murders followed. There had been a time when she had been genuinely fond of Wilfred Denver, and the news of this murder, conveyed to her as it was down a channel which she invariably associated with dance-music, shocked her. She was dabbing her eyes with her lace square of handkerchief when Captain Lovell of the *Myrobella* came to assure her of his sincere regret and overwhelming sympathy. The gallant skipper had an eye for a pretty girl, and when Beauty was in the trappings of Distress he always felt that it made an even greater call upon his gallantry.

"I shall have to go back to England, Capt. Lovell," sobbed Anne. "I simply must. I've no option. Though I don't know what Benny will say about my contract. He worked so hard to get me signed up with him. Had to fight Scrawner Brothers tooth and nail to pull it off."

Anne's sobs developed dangerously. Capt. Lovell murmured more appropriate sympathy. He went so far as to pat the incomparable Miss Assheton's hand. After a time Anne's tears subsided. Capt. Lovell had been at his own superb best. She repaired her ravaged complexion, and whilst this operation was in progress she began to wonder what she had best wear for dinner—In the circumstances, with a haste perhaps that bordered on the indecent, she decided that black would be most becoming. Besides, she always looked her best in black. It must be recorded that Anne at dinner that evening put up an extremely able performance. All her gestures and all the movements of her eyes and head were just right. As she got into bed that night she didn't know which part she wanted to play the more, 'St. Joan' or the 'Second Mrs. Tanqueray.'

XI

The days that followed brought Anthony and the Inspector nothing that might have been reasonably regarded as a relative of success.

Enquiry succeeded enquiry, questions were asked of nearly every Remington inhabitant—but all these efforts were of no avail. At the end of the week MacMorran returned to the 'Yard.' Anthony, however, made up his mind to stay in Remington (for the time being at least). Legge was also on the spot, ready to give Anthony any assistance should he need it. Anthony decided to lie low, to watch points and generally keep himself in the background of the case as far as possible. He therefore booked rooms at one of the smaller hotels—the 'Raven' to be precise—and prepared himself to settle down there with Remington and district as his diocese for the next week or so.

He made it his business to watch the various steps and actions taken by that miscellany of Mrs. Clinton's guests and knew at the same time that this duty was not his alone, but was being looked after also, at the various other ends, by certain men under the command and orders of Chief-Inspector Andrew MacMorran. This knowledge gave him an added confidence, with the result that his time at the 'Raven' passed much more pleasantly than it otherwise might have done.

The first item of importance occurred on the third day after MacMorran had returned to London. Anthony had a visitor. The visitor was announced as Capt. Ronald Playfair. Anthony received him with a warm cordiality. Playfair sat down. He seemed uneasy, Anthony thought, as he looked at him. It was unlike Playfair to be off his stroke. Anthony let him take first knock.

"I say, Mr. Bathurst," he said, "I'm a bit scared about worrying you like this and I wouldn't have done so if that Policeman Johnny had stopped on here instead of skedaddling back to the 'Yard.' But since he did, and you're here alone, I'm afraid you'll have to have it coming to you."

Anthony smiled at him. "Go ahead."

Playfair leant forward towards him. "I think I've discovered something. I'm 'on to something,' I think, as you chaps usually put it." His eyes were eager—almost enthusiastic. Anthony saw and recognized the signs.

"Good man," he declared encouragingly, "let's have the whole story."

Ronald Playfair lowered his voice. "I'm taking an extra slice of care," he remarked, "as part of a deliberate policy. I believe in looking ahead and I believe in keeping your eyes skinned. Don't you agree?"

"I most certainly do," returned Anthony.

At that precise moment the telephone rang in Anthony's room at the 'Raven.' "You'll pardon me," he murmured to Playfair as he reached forward and lifted the receiver.

"Certainly."

"What's that?" Playfair heard him say. "Where?" he said, and then immediately followed up that second question with "When?" Playfair waited. "That puts a different complexion on matters," said Anthony. "I'll await more news—in the meantime, many thanks, Andrew, for 'phoning me. And ring me if you want to, by all means. . . . I'll make it my business to be in."

Anthony replaced the receiver. Then he turned to Playfair. "It may interest you to learn. Captain Playfair," he said, "that the body of Mrs. Warren Clinton was discovered this morning in a trunk at Waterloo Station. And there is every evidence, I am given to understand, that the body had been in the trunk for some days."

It was abundantly clear that Playfair was taken aback by the news that Anthony gave him.

"Another murder, I suppose?"

"It would appear so."

"How was she killed?"

"She has been shot. I understand there's a bullet-hole in the temple. An entrance wound only. The police hope to find the bullet."

Playfair sat and stared at Anthony. For once his habitual sang-froid had temporarily deserted him.

PART THREE
THE WARNINGS

I

ANTHONY spoke. "You were about to remark, when that interruption came—"

Playfair came back with the semblance of a start. "By Jove—yes, your news of Mrs. Clinton's death absolutely side-tracked me. Put me out of my stride completely. Let me collect my scattered thoughts for a second."

Anthony waited for him. He hadn't to wait long. Playfair picked up the threads of his story. "I suppose you don't know a lot about Remington?"

"Not a frightful lot. Why do you ask?"

"Well—I'll try to help you. You know the railway station?"

"Yes."

"Well—if you turn to the left when you leave the station and come straight down the road that leads to Winton you run into a block of rather charming flats. Can you recall where I mean by any chance?" Playfair looked hard at Anthony as he put the question.

Anthony nodded. "As it happens I know those flats very well. But go on."

"I'm concerned with one of the basement flats. The farthest one from you as you travel away from the station. As you walk by it, the front window is almost on eye level. As a matter of fact, I went by it on the actual afternoon of Mrs. Clinton's gathering. As I passed by I noticed something that struck me as bordering on the peculiar. As I tell the story to you now it may sound appallingly trivial. But at the time I noticed it it didn't. In the window was a big red china dachshund."

Anthony looked up. He was interested.

"As it stood and faced the window, its nose pointed to the right-hand corner. It was so, so un-English, that it caught my eye, I suppose, more than the china figure of a cat or a horse, say, might have done. Well, when I got into the 'Royal Sceptre' I discovered that I'd run short of my own particular brand of tobacco. I was annoyed. I'm always annoyed when that happens. But as I had bags of time before Mrs. Warren Clinton was due to perform, I made up my mind to retrace my steps and buy some. I had spotted a decent-looking tobacconist's in the High Street as I had come along. So I went back. On my way I had to pass the flat with the dachshund in the window. As I went by something made me turn my head and look in. Can't tell you why—but I did. To my utter astonishment the red dog had gone. In the space of less than half an hour. But there was a blue one in its place—its nose pointing in the same direction as its predecessor."

Capt. Playfair paused for a moment. He glanced at Anthony. The latter was carefully filling his pipe.

"H'm—interesting, I agree. But I've an idea that you haven't told me all the story. Am I right?"

"You are. Listen to this. Since the murders I have been by that window on six or seven occasions. Scarcely ever have the dogs or the positions been the same on two successive occasions. I'll swear to that. First the red one way—then the blue another—and so on. What do you make of it, Bathurst?"

Anthony shook his head. "Mustn't rush me. But I'll grant that it's interesting and, if you like, peculiar."

"Nothing else strikes you about it, I suppose?" Playfair leant forward eagerly.

"You mean that the crimes are 'international' in origin?"

Playfair nodded. "In a way. But that's only *part* of what I mean. I suppose in order to convince you of certain things, I had better make a clean breast of it. It's like this. I used to be in the Intelligence Service." He waited to see the effect this statement had on Anthony. Then he went on. "I was X22. After the war finished I spent several years in Germany. I was in Berlin in the February of 1933 when the Reichstag went up in flames. I shan't forget that night in a hurry, I can assure you. To avoid the crowds in the Königsgrätzer Strasse I ran down the Wilhelmstrasse and turned from there into the Dorotheenstrasse. Past the President's house, I realized what had happened. Talk about heat: I could literally feel it on my face."

Anthony became aware that as Playfair spoke he was watching him intently.

"As the floors fell in and the fire-engines came crashing down the Dorotheenstrasse and took their places at the Reichstag entrance, I saw hundreds of people with the sign of the red dachshund in their lapels. I was present, too, when Van der Lubbe came to trial. He was just a fat, overgrown moron. I wouldn't have trusted him to set fire to a Chinese cracker. Now you know why I'm more than interested in the window of that flat." Playfair stopped and wiped his forehead with his handkerchief.

"Tell me what you really suspect, Capt. Playfair?"

"With pleasure. That Mrs. Clinton, in some way unknown to us, had got wise to something. Probably a plot against the British Empire. Think of the letters that she sent to those of us whom she invited to Remington, and the terms in which they were written. And when you think of those things and remember that not only is Mrs. Clinton herself dead, but that the two people she selected for the cause are also dead, and murdered at that, well—the idea comes to me that those dachshunds may have meant something after all."

"I don't quite see how—although, of course, I admit the possibility. For instance—wasn't the secret of Mrs. Clinton's selection known only to the people whom she had invited to Remington as her guests?"

"I suppose it was."

"Well, then, if that be accepted, the murderer must be one of those guests. That's so, isn't it?"

Playfair proceeded to defend his position. "All right. I'll concede that. And there still may have been some collusion between that guest and somebody who lives in the flat where the dachshunds are. They may have even been signals of some kind to the murderer. Surely you can see that?"

Anthony nodded in agreement. "Yes—as I said, I admit the possibility. I'll promise you, Capt. Playfair, that the clue will be followed up and I thank you for having brought it to my notice. Why did you leave the Intelligence Service?"

Playfair laughed and shrugged his shoulders. "I grew tired of the work after the war and wanted a change. I'm afraid I should never be the man to stop in any job after I had grown tired of it."

"When did you leave Germany?"

"In the autumn of 1935. I didn't like the way things were going. In fact I thought the second war would come some years even before it did. I didn't want to be anywhere but in England when it did break out. So I asked the powers-that-be to accept my resignation. To my pleasure and perhaps a little to my surprise, they raised no objection—and I came home." Playfair laughed again. "I never thought I should come to take part in anything like this 'Royal Sceptre' business."

"These things are beyond our own shaping," returned Anthony.

"Yes. I suppose they are. Ah, well, Mr. Bathurst, I shall go on keeping my eyes open, and I've no doubt you will do the same."

"You may rely on me," replied Anthony.

II

Anthony stood with Chief-Inspector MacMorran in the latter's room at New Scotland Yard.

"You're on to something, Andrew, I feel certain. Otherwise you wouldn't have sent for me to come up. What is it?"

MacMorran pushed over several sheets of closely-typed paper. "There's Sugden's report on his autopsy on the body of this woman, Mrs. Warren Clinton. Read it carefully."

Anthony found a comfortable seat and read Sugden's report. "Body well-nourished. Age—probably somewhere in the early sixties. Killed by a bullet wound through the temple. I probed for the bullet and found it embedded in the brain."

At this moment MacMorran ventured an interruption. "Dr. Sugden has shown me the bullet. It's slightly battered about the nose and carries two or three scratches. Sugden says that the scratches were caused by his instrument when he was looking for it. There are other marks, too, made by the rifling of the barrel. There's no doubt that the weapon used was a small light revolver." MacMorran leant forward eagerly. "And the rifling marks are similar to the marks on the bullets which killed Denver and Mrs. Ramage. I've examined 'em all three and you can take my word for it"

Anthony nodded. "I think I know the type of revolver you're referring to. It's American made and has become an almost common property in this country. Many people buy 'em for self-defence against Bill Sikes. They're useful toys at a pinch and can be carried comfortably in a hip-pocket."

"Yes, that's true. Now don't forget something, Mr. Bathurst. With regard to the deaths of Denver and Mrs. Ramage. Each was shot through the left eye. In each case the eye was destroyed. And in each case the brain was shattered at the base. But there was no sign in either instance of the weapon having been placed against the eye or even close to it. Funny place to shoot anybody, don't you think?"

"The fact should help us, Andrew. Doesn't it prove that the murderer had sufficient time or was so conveniently placed that he was enabled to take deliberate aim?"

"Yes. I'll accept that. It's all very feasible."

Anthony turned his attention again to Dr. Sugden's report. "Now how long does our friend Sugden consider that Mrs. Clinton had been dead when the body was discovered? Because that's one of the most important factors in the case—as I see it."

"I understand—at least a month."

"And how long is it since the deaths at Remington?"

"A month last Saturday."

"H'm. Near thing—eh? Can't Sugden cut it any finer than he has?"

"Not with any absolute certainty."

"Pity. What do the cloakroom people say about the leaving of the trunk? Does their information help us at all?"

"The trunk was left at the cloakroom at Waterloo on the day following the Remington murders. Here's the ticket that was handed over for it."

The Inspector passed to Anthony a small, jagged slip of paper. The paper was cheap and of inferior quality. Anthony saw the pencil scrawl that ran across it.

"What time in the day was this issued—have they told you?"

"They can't be sure. I've been to Waterloo myself on that inquiry. But judging from the total number of tickets that were issued on that particular day, the balance of probability is that this ticket was issued early in the morning. Certainly prior to midday."

"Is any information forthcoming as to the person who deposited the trunk?"

"Yes. But not a lot." MacMorran chose his words carefully. "The trunk was received by a Southern Railway cloakroom attendant by the name of Webster. He seems a very decent sort of fellow and I think he may be regarded as reasonably reliable. He's been in the railway service for twenty years. As far as he can remember, and I've interviewed him twice on the matter, the trunk was handed in to him by a middle-aged woman of the poorer class. But beyond that he won't budge."

"Looks to me, Andrew," said Anthony, "that we're up against more than one person on this job. Quite likely against a combination."

"You mean a gang."

"All right. Have it your own way." Anthony smiled. "What about the trunk itself, Andrew? Does that tell us anything?"

"I thought you'd be asking that and I've been waiting for the question. I reckon I'm going to give you a bit of a surprise. The trunk is Mrs. Warren Clinton's own property." MacMorran spoke the words with relish.

Anthony looked up. "Is that a fact?"

"I only deal in sober facts. I love 'em, Mr. Bathurst. They get you somewhere. Fantastic theories don't."

Anthony grinned. "All right. All right. I can take it. Tell me, though, how do you know the trunk belonged to Mrs. Clinton?"

"Her name's inside the lid. And the trunk's of American manufacture. I think those two facts are good enough to base my conclusion on."

Anthony became grave. "It's important, Andrew, if what you say's true. Looks as though she were murdered at the hotel and the body brought away. In other words, that the trunk was *handy*, that is to say near to her when the murder took place. But why take the trouble to move the body? That's what's puzzling me, Andrew. Don't get it. By the way, have you been able to check up those cars yet?"

"Do you mean at the hotel at Remington?"

"Yes. As I asked you to—before you came away."

MacMorran nodded. "I remember. I made exhaustive inquiries. Had I run across anything in any way suspicious I would have told you. But I didn't. Not a single man or woman had left the hotel on the morning the bodies were discovered and not a single car had been taken from the hotel garage. You can rest assured on both those points."

"Is that so? Well, then, will you tell me, Andrew, how the body of Mrs. Warren Clinton came to Waterloo?"

"There are other means of transport besides cars," retorted the Inspector.

"Such as?"

"Trains, aeroplanes . . . and er . . ."

"Roller-skates, I suppose?" Anthony shook his head. "Sorry, Andrew. Nothing doing. Apologies if I disappoint you."

But MacMorran was staring ahead of him—with a curiously fixed look on his face. "Now that's rather remarkable . . ." he started.

"What's rather remarkable?"

"Why—my remark about aeroplanes. I've thought of something."

"What's that?"

"Why—that that 'lord' chap—Lord Esmond Curte—flew to Remington in his own 'plane. From somewhere near Nottingham. Don't you remember? Makes you wonder somewhat, doesn't it?"

"Yes—but Curte was there all right in the hotel on the morning after the night before. He didn't get away with Mrs. Clinton's body. We ourselves interviewed him the day after that."

"Very likely we did," exclaimed MacMorran with something like triumph in his voice, "but what about his professional pilot? The man who flew the 'plane to Remington. Maitland! Maitland was at Remington with him I What about Maitland? Mr. Bathurst, I've been slow. Too slow to catch cold. There's a possibility here that I haven't even considered."

The Inspector turned impetuously to Anthony, who seemed lost in thought. "Did you hear what I said, Mr. Bathurst?"

"No, Andrew. I'm sorry. I was thinking of something else. Something that came via Capt. Playfair yesterday. Listen—and I'll tell you all about it."

MacMorran settled in his chair to listen. But his mind was full of Lord Esmond Curte and his pilot—Maitland.

III

When Sir Edward Angus eventually left Remington after the police had directed their necessary inquiries, he made straight for London and the smoking-room of his club—the 'Lexicon.' He had missed the congenial atmosphere of the club for some weeks now, through no fault of his own, and the fact was causing him a considerable amount of annoyance. Sir Edward liked a smooth routine.

When he arrived at the 'Lexicon' the big smoking-room was comfortably crowded, but there was an isolated corner dotted with empty chairs by the many-paned window against which Sir Edward had sat on innumerable occasions. At the extreme edge of this far corner sat Adrian Anstey. Anstey hailed Sir Edward, when he saw him advancing towards him, with a whoop of delight. For the reason that Sir Edward Angus was one of the very few members of the 'Lexicon' who could bear to listen to him. Adrian Anstey was tall and thin. He had an overhanging fair moustache and an 'Adam's Apple' that always reminded Sir Edward of his own days at Repton when he had drawn maps of Ireland and printed in with impish delight that contour of the coast which demanded in the neatest of letters the singularly attractive title 'Bloody Foreland.' Another remarkable feature of Anstey's appearance was the colour of his eyes. The right eye was light blue. The left eye was dark brown. Many people, as he talked to them, became conscious of these odd eyes, and forgot what he said to them. Which annoyed Adrian Anstey immensely. So much so that his voice would suddenly become harsh and disagreeable and his eyes flash with an active animosity. Almost invariably he wore a high white linen collar and a broad white piqué tie. Both collar and tie were relics of the sartorial traditions of a previous generation.

Sir Edward answered Adrian Anstey's hail with becoming modesty, and after nodding to a chain of other acquaintances walked towards him and shook hands with some degree of cordiality.

"Angus—of all people that on earth do dwell," cried the tall man from the depth of his arm-chair, "and in addition to that, the very man whom I was desirous of seeing above all others." He gripped Sir Edward's hand with unusual warmth and fervour. Sir Edward wondered what the reason was to cause Anstey this paramount desire. He took the armchair next to him and seated himself on the extreme edge of it. Then he gave way to habit, removed his horn-rimmed spectacles and polished their glasses with his silk handkerchief. He expressed wonderment in words.

"And what, my dear Anstey, have I done to deserve such a compliment?"

He held out his cigarette case to his companion. Anstey grinned. He was pleased.

"Thanks. I don't see why I shouldn't smoke a cigarette with you." He took one from Sir Edward's case. "And as for your other question—haven't you been close at hand to the most sensational murder case for many years?"

"I suppose I have—in a way. But I'm not clear as to the reason of your interest in it."

Sir Edward looked hard at Anstey as he spoke. Anstey returned the look with serenity and complacence.

"Didn't I know Angela Ramage? Don't I know poor old John Ramage? Do you know, Sir Edward, that I haven't seen him here since the murder?"

"I'm not surprised at that. Ramage is pretty hard hit. He can't be expected to prance about just as he did when his wife was alive. Have a heart, Anstey."

Anstey shook his head reproachfully. "Don't underrate my intelligence. To do that always annoys me excessively. Coming from you it would be almost intolerable. What I said was a mere statement of fact. Neither more nor less." He leant over an arm of his big chair towards Sir Edward and spoke in a lowered voice. "Who shot Denver and Mrs. Ramage? And why were they shot? They're the questions I've been wanting to ask you."

Sir Edward bore the attack with steady composure. "My dear Anstey—what gives you the idea that I can supply the answers to those two questions?"

Anstey gazed amiably at his companion. "You were there. You know what happened before the murders. You know, too, what happened after the murders took place. You met and talked with the dramatis persons. I should be doing you less than justice, Sir Edward, if I didn't imagine that you had collected the scattered pieces of the jig-saw puzzle and fitted them together. You see—I know you so well."

Anstey leant backwards in his seat and blew a smoke-ring towards the ceiling. Sir Edward Angus waved a hand vaguely.

"And yet I haven't. You must believe me when I say that."

Anstey smiled a smile of indulgent superiority. "I find it, I confess, difficult to believe you. But let me put my question in a different form. Whom do you suspect?"

Sir Edward felt a tinge of annoyance. This ill-judged persistence of Anstey's bordered on rudeness. "Shouldn't I properly refer you to Scotland Yard?"

"Oh come, come, Sir Edward," Anstey held up his hand as if in gentle reproof. "Surely between you and me . . . after all . . . who benefited by the deaths? Ramage himself? Have you thought of that?"

Anstey paused, as though it were his intention to let the full significance of his suggestion percolate to the other's mind. Angus bridled even more unmistakably. "And I suppose, too, that according to you, Ramage benefited by the death of Mrs. Clinton? Sheer nonsense, Anstey, and what's more you should be well aware that it is nonsense."

As he half-turned in his chair Sir Edward saw one of the club waiters approaching him. The man carried a letter in his hand. He came to the side of the chair where Sir Edward was sitting.

"You'll pardon me, sir," he said deferentially, "but this letter has just come for you."

"Thank you, John," replied Sir Edward. He took the envelope. Anstey nodded significantly towards it.

"Somebody's timed your arrival to a nicety. Cue for letter. Couldn't have been done better on the professional stage."

Sir Edward made no reply. His mind was fully occupied. He had opened the envelope and was reading the letter. As he read it he began to frown. The letter bore no address or date. It had been typed and ran as follows:

'Dear Sir Edward,

During the course of the next few weeks you will, doubtless, be asked many questions with regard to the recent murders at Remington. Some may be intelligent—the majority will be inordinately and vulgarly curious. You are hereby commanded to give no information whatever to anybody. This is an imperative order which must be obeyed and it applies with equal force to your chauffeur, Kingsford. You will convey it to him. If you should be foolish enough to disregard it—your blood will be on your own head, and both you and Kingsford can take this statement literally. You will not readily forget, we feel convinced, what happened to Denver and Mrs. Ramage. To say nothing of Mrs. Warren Clinton. To convince you of our powers, we will communicate with you again at 11.30 this evening. Till then, dear Sir Edward, au 'voir. Or better still—auf wiedersehen! Heil Hitler!'

Sir Edward, having read the letter, looked up from the pages. He desired to see Whether Anstey had been able to see what he had been reading. But Anstey appeared to be completely oblivious of the matter. Sir Edward thrust the letter into a pocket, crumpling it in the process, and rose from his chair. His nostrils quivered. He was intensely annoyed. Excusing himself to Anstey, he sought out John, the waiter who had brought the letter to him.

"John," said Sir Edward quietly, "that letter you brought me a few moments ago—when exactly did it come? I'm sorry to trouble you over it, but it's rather important, as it happens."

John, who was something of a personage, let it be said, was immediately upon his dignity.

"It was delivered by post, sir, but a few moments before I brought it to you. It is my invariable habit, if I may say so, sir, to deliver members' letters the *moment* they come into my possession."

"I see. Came by the last post, did it?" Sir Edward took out the envelope and examined it. There was the address: 'Sir Edward Angus, c/o The Lexicon Club, Manners Street, W.1.' The postmark was London.

He went back to the corner where Adrian Anstey was still sitting. "Well, my friend," he said, "I'm afraid I shall have to be getting along. Something's turned up unexpectedly that needs my immediate attention. So I shan't be able to satisfy your curiosity with regard to the Remington crime after all."

He turned on his heel as Anstey growled an unintelligible reply. He was determined now to return to his own flat. Whilst there the time passed irritatingly slowly. The veiled threat contained in the letter was the one and only thing that he could force his mind to consider. Indeed, after a time, it became an obsession. These people, whoever they were, and who had chosen to threaten him, had spoken of their 'powers.' To 'convince' him of these powers they had pledged themselves to communicate with him again at half-past eleven that evening. Sir Edward found himself glancing at the clock on the mantelpiece every few minutes. Ten o'clock came and he felt that his patience would be at an end long before the required hour and a half had passed. The clock that he watched chimed the quarters, but Sir Edward Angus had never in the whole of his life known any period of fifteen minutes take so long in passing as each of these periods took. Many a time the words of Wilde flooded his thoughts. 'And through each brain on hands of pain, another's terror crept.'

At last the laggard clock chimed the half-hour after eleven. Sir Edward gripped the arms of his chair and waited for he knew not what. He was not destined to be disappointed. Almost immediately after the dying away of the chimes his telephone rang. Sir Edward rose mechanically to answer it. A deep-throated, distinctly melodious voice came from the other end.

"Sir Edward Angus! Although you don't know my name, or whom I have the honour to represent, you are well aware of the connection between us that has occasioned this telephone call. We told you in our letter that we would supply you with convincing evidence of our powers. To do that will be an excessively simple matter. Please put your hand in the right-hand pocket of the coat you were wearing when you were out today."

Sir Edward interrupted the speaking voice. "I am not able to—at the moment. I have changed my clothes since I came in."

"No matter. Go to your coat directly I ring off. Do you ever carry 'Swan Vestas'?"

"No, never. And why waste my time with such an irrelevant and absurd question?"

The voice at the other end remained unruffled and unperturbed. "Never mind. Look in the pocket I indicated and you will find a full box of 'Swan Vestas' in there. And please realise that the hand which placed them there could, with equal facility, have used a knife. There is a certain place between the ribs, you know, Sir Edward . . . but there—I am sure there is no need for me to go any further! Goodnight, Sir Edward . . . and er . . . Heil Hitler."

The deep voice ceased speaking. Sir Edward Angus replaced the receiver and then thoughtfully made his way to his bedroom. Opening his clothes-cabinet, he took from its hanger the jacket he had taken off an hour or so previously. He thrust his hand into the right-hand pocket. His fingers closed on an unfamiliar box. He took the box out. It was a new packet of 'Swan Vestas.' Sir Edward rubbed the point of his chin. As he had previously stated, he never bought such things. He never used them. This box which he was handling as he stood there must have been placed in his pocket at some time between his leaving the company of Adrian Anstey and his reaching the comfort of his flat. He recalled the words of his recent telephone message—'the hand which placed them there could, with equal facility, have used a knife.' Very true! Too true! Sir Edward shivered a little before sitting down to think matters over. Then he deliberately walked to his telephone again and dialled for 'Scotland Yard.' When he was through, he asked for Chief-Inspector MacMorran.

IV

Lord Esmond Curie's letter was delivered to him in his house at Nottingham by his immaculate manservant whose name was Pollard.

"A letter, my lord. From its appearance I feel that it may be of some importance."

Lord Esmond took the letter from the salver upon which it had been presented to him. He opened it and within the space of a few seconds his face had grown hard and ugly. The typed words of the letter ran thus.

'To Lord Esmond Curte.

You flew to Remington a short time ago to be the guest of the late Mrs. Warren Clinton. Foolish on your part, don't you think? Our meaning is—foolish to have travelled by 'plane. The word is emphasised. Because you also returned by 'plane. In other words, why deliberately call attention to yourself and your movements? To act in this way never pays. In this reference, therefore, we feel compelled to give you one instruction at least. An instruction which it is imperative must be obeyed. Your pilot, Capt. Maitland, will be interrogated by certain officers from Scotland Yard. It is certain that this will take place. On no account must he inform them that he saw Frederick Kingsford, chauffeur to Sir Edward Angus, when he was on his way to the bar in the "Royal Sceptre" before Mrs. Clinton had interviewed her guests. Please impress this on Capt. Maitland most particularly. We should hate to think that any harm was likely to befall either you or him. After all, three distinguished people are already dead, making thirty per cent of the invited party. It would be a tremendous pity if, for any reason, we were compelled to increase that percentage. You agree with these admirable sentiments, don't you? To convince you that our threats are no idle boasting, we will communicate with you again somewhere near midnight tonight. Till then, Lord Esmond Curte, auf wiedersehen! Heil Hitler!'

Curte examined the envelope in which the letter had been sent. The postmark was St. Albans. Then he glanced up. Pollard had silently disappeared. Curte's fancy took strange paths. Sitting there in his study alone and unseen, he felt that the advent of this letter had already made him a watcher and a listener. He was already watching and listening for something which might strike at him out of the darkness as it were, and he felt a tinge of annoyance with himself that his imagination had already launched a campaign against him, which had for its objective a persuasion that he was facing a very live menace and confronting a very real fear. He tried to smile at what he endeavoured to call his stupidity. He looked at the letter again. In order to be fitted into the envelope, it had been rather carelessly folded in two. The crease was ragged—by no means sharp or well-defined. Curte wondered why this was. His thoughts went to the night of the murders at Remington. There had been one particular moment which his memory recalled most vividly. The moment when Mrs. Clinton had requested him to come into her room for what she had described as his 'second test.' He remembered with infinite detail the various expressions on her face as she had sat there and interrogated him. Now it grew darker as he in his turn sat there in his study. Until complete darkness came. And he was alone. She hadn't been. For a time his eyes were handicapped by the darkness. Then, gradually, he became like a man who has been blind but has afterwards recovered some shadow of his vision.

He sat in a black corner of the room. He could see the open door at the end of the room. The door through which Pollard had passed but a few minutes ago. For all he knew, as he sat there enemies might be outside his house at that very moment. Outside the door of this room even. His eyes kept on turning towards the door. As he looked a cold fear came and clutched at his heart. Something dark filled the doorway with an almost menacing suddenness. Lord Esmond Curte half rose in his chair, with the instinct dominant in his mind that he must defend himself at all costs. Then the room was flooded with light. Pollard had entered the room and switched on the electric light. He advanced slowly towards his employer.

"You will pardon me, sir, if I remind you, but you are due at 9.30 this evening at Lady Shacklock's Charity Ball. In the Trent Hall. It struck me that the engagement might possibly have slipped your Lordship's memory."

"Thank you, Pollard," returned Lord Esmond Curte. "You will see that my things are in readiness."

He rose. Pollard bowed. He had noticed that Lord Esmond's voice was unsteady.

V

Lord Esmond Curte's car, its low headlights flooding the darkness with a clear diamond-like beam, swung along the road from his house to the city. Then, throbbing slowly and almost deliberately, it came to a stop outside Trent Hall. Curte alighted and went to the front of the car to seek his chauffeur.

"You know where to go, Dixon, don't you? Pick me up again here at half-past eleven. Don't be a minute late on any account. I must be back home again before midnight."

"Very good, my lord," replied Dixon. "I shall be here punctually with the car at half-past eleven."

Up went his hand to his cap. Curte moved quickly up the flight of stone steps which led to the main entrance to Trent Hall. The big doors were open. The guards at the entrance, knowing him well, saluted and passed him in. Curte went from the vestibule to the cloakroom and from the cloakroom to the large hall itself. Lady Shacklock floated over effusively to welcome him. After giving him a plump, warm hand, she fluttered back to an ante-room, guiding him skilfully as he accompanied her. A drink was poured out for him. A Pol Roger of commendable quality and excellence. His hostess sprinkled him with sprays of clipped conversation. Curte shook himself mentally, many times.

"A splendid evening . . . most distinguished gathering . . . everybody present who was anybody . . . a most abnormal percentage of military . . . most charming of Lord Curte to have spared the time." Thus his hostess.

Lady Shacklock was bejewelled and buxom. Curte himself murmured commonplaces in reply to her splashes of colourful chatter. He drank his wine and put the glass down on the long white-clothed table. There were clusters of men and women all along it. His glass was immediately refilled. Curte began to study the various guests. A girl standing but a few paces away from him caught his eye. Somehow her face seemed vaguely familiar to him, but he couldn't place her. The thought came to him that he must have seen her in the Pavilion on the Trent Bridge cricket ground. Her face was familiar to him even in detail. It was a face which would always arrest attention. He was still gazing at the girl when he felt a light touch on his arm. The touch came from his hostess. The Shacklock simper was in full bloom.

"Now . . . now . . . Lord Curte," said her ladyship, "at your age, you know—"

Curte smiled and shook his head. "Who's the lady . . . her face seems familiar, that's all."

"It's a friend of Dulcie Ratherdon's . . . I didn't catch her name as she came in. But I'll find out for you. You just wait here a moment."

Lady Shacklock billowed away and Curte saw her anchor alongside a tall man and tap him almost peremptorily on the arm. He saw her speak and the man reply. Lady Shacklock showed beaming thanks and returned to Curte full of champagne and information.

"I've found out for you," she announced triumphantly. "I asked Marcus Ratherdon himself. It's a girl named Felicity Frayle. She is rather a peach, isn't she? Marcus says her name is a flagrant example of wishful thinking. But, of course, Marcus would say that. The years don't change him an iota."

Lady Shacklock giggled exuberantly. Curte returned thanks for the information she had brought him.

"Have another drink," said Lady Shacklock. Curte nodded and turned towards the buffet. His glass was filled again.

"When you've drunk that," remarked his hostess, "you must come out of here and let me introduce you to people. There are quite a dozen here whom you don't know."

In time Curte suffered himself to be led from the bar. In the main hall an orchestra was playing softly and with alluring rhythm a fox-trot that was the rage of the moment. It was easy to see that the evening was a huge success. The floor was crammed with dancing pairs. Curte let his glances wander everywhere.

"Do you want to dance?" enquired Lady Shacklock.

"I might," grinned Curte, "under certain conditions."

"I get you," said Mona Shacklock. "Leave it to me and I'll see what can be done."

Curte nodded his thanks. Lady Shacklock moved away. For a time he stood in the doorway and watched the swaying fortunes of the dance. The fox-trot finished. But the dancers wanted more of it. From their hands came the traditional sounds of applause. The leader of the orchestra started another fox-trot. He did not always act according to custom. Curte made his way down the ballroom towards the raised stage where the orchestra were. He began to watch them. He was interested. He liked watching men playing musical instruments . . . the drummers, the violinists and the saxophonists. Suddenly he heard Lady Shaddock's voice again.

"I really must introduce you to Lord Esmond Curte . . . this is Miss Frayle."

Curte bowed to the girl standing by Lady Shacklock. He surveyed her with unconcealed approval. She smiled at him.

"Shall we dance?" he said to her without a moment's hesitation.

"Why not?" she replied easily. He put his arm round her and they swung into the rhythm of the number. Her beauty made Curte catch his breath.

"Feel sure we've met before." He looked down at his partner.

"Do you?"

"Yes. Feel positive. But can't think where. Do tell me, Miss Frayle."

She shook her head. "Sorry—but the idea's all on your side. It's not my usual form to mix with lords and ladies." She smiled demurely at him.

"I must be wrong then. I must have been thinking of your sister . . . or else your cousin."

"You can't have been." Her face looked up at him. "For the excellent reason that I don't possess either."

Curte laughed lightly. "I accept the rebuke." He again looked down at his partner with keen appreciation.

"Lady Shacklock tells me," she said lightly, "that you're the lion of the evening. It was only on those grounds that I consented to be introduced to you. I think that you ought to know that."

"Lady Shacklock," he replied, "has a positive genius for exaggeration."

The number was nearing its finish. Curte noticed it and went on, "How about a drink?"

"Sounds a bright idea to me."

"Good. I know a rather decent little corner . . . if you'll do me the honour."

"To drink alone is unattractive," she riposted . . . "lead me to this rather decent little corner."

Curte took her to part of the main corridor of the hall where one corner had a perfect screen of palms. He found Miss Frayle a seat and went off himself in search of two Pol Rogers. Returning with the two filled glasses, he seated himself next to her.

"Happy days," he wished her.

"And nights," returned Felicity Frayle. She disposed of her champagne.

"Are you staying in Nottingham?" he asked her.

"No. I'm at a little place about thirty miles out. It's called Whysall just beyond Attewell. I'm staying with the Ratherdons. I was at . . . er . . . school with Dulcie Ratherdon."

"Where is your home, Miss Frayle?"

Her eyes fluttered at him. "I have no real home. Both my parents are dead. I chase round whenever and wherever I like. You see—I can't settle down anywhere. I've always been like that and I'm very much afraid I shall never change. Until I marry and settle down. Tell me," she placed a beautifully manicured hand on his knee, "do you think I'm attractive enough to get an offer?"

Curte fell heavily. "My dear Miss Frayle . . . offers will be as thick as leaves in . . . er . . ."

She cut in before he could think of the word that was eluding him. "Sherwood Forest?"

"No. Can't think of the place I want. Wretched word begins with a 'V'—that's as far as I can get at the moment."

She smiled at him mischievously. "Never mind—I know what you mean." The smile became ravishing.

For want of anything else to say, Curte said: "I don't think I know the Ratherdons."

"That's very likely. They haven't been at Whysall very long. Now would you like to take me back to the ballroom?"

Curte looked at her. "You wouldn't care for another drink?"

Miss Frayle shook her head. "No, thanks. Really, I'm a natural teetotaller—rather unique for a girl these days, don't you think?"

"I suppose it is. That is to say, it would be if you were."

Felicity Frayle grinned back at him. "Don't be so enigmatic."

A little smile twisted Curie's mouth. "You know very well what I mean, so don't pretend that you don't."

Miss Frayle bit her lip. "You're direct now. *Not* enigmatic."

"Which do you prefer?"

"I don't know that I really prefer either. It's a matter of complete indifference to me."

"In that case, then," returned Lord Esmond, "you had really better go back to the ballroom. Come with me. I'll escort you."

Miss Frayle tossed her pretty head and Curie piloted her back to the ballroom. He left her in the doorway. She pulled down the corners of her pretty mouth. She said: "Thank you very much, Lord Curie," and sailed away down to the other end of the ballroom. Curte watched her cynically. Harsh lines began to show again on his features. Lady Shacklock swept up to him immediately.

"Lord Curte . . . you must do something for me . . . please."

He looked up at her. "This is Mrs. Blaker-Rashleigh, Lord Curte. Mrs. Blaker-Rashleigh wants to dance."

"She does? Well then, I'm her man."

He took the arm of the tall woman who confronted him. He saw that she was wearing a flame-coloured gown. "Shall we?"

Mrs. Blaker-Rashleigh murmured something that might have been anything. Lord Curte swung the lady into the quick-step that held the floor. He commenced a conversation with her, but his eyes scarcely ever left the form of Felicity Frayle, standing by the wall at the other end of the room. Mrs. Blaker-Rashleigh twisted a little as they adroitly avoided another couple who appeared to be bearing down upon them.

"I say," remonstrated Mrs. Blaker-Rashleigh in a hollow sort of voice, "did you see that?"

But her partner's eyes were still fixed on Felicity Frayle.

*

Curte arrived back home a trifle later than he had intended. At ten minutes past midnight his telephone bell rang. Pollard, who had waited up for his employer, moved silently across the carpet to answer it.

"Very good," Curte heard him say, "if you wait for a few seconds I'll inform his lordship."

"Who is it, Pollard?" he asked.

"The gentleman wouldn't give his name, sir," replied Pollard, "but he requested that he might speak to you personally. I understand from him, sir, that it's by way of being an urgent call."

Curte walked across the room and picked up the telephone receiver. A man's voice greeted his first words.

"Thank you. I am delighted to think that his lordship himself is answering me right away. Although you don't know my name, and you are equally unaware as to whom I represent, I might even say whom *I have the honour to represent*. You are doubtless pretty certain by now that I am ringing you in relation to the communication that you received only a few hours ago. To be exact—yesterday. We informed you then that we should speedily convince you that our threats were no idle boasting. To do so has been a comparatively simple matter. If you will feel in the breast pocket of your dress-coat you will find a card there of which you had no knowledge. This card has been inserted in your pocket during the evening. Are you still listening? Of course you are. Take my tip then and keep silent with regard to Kingsford. Good night, Lord Curte . . . or rather let me say good morning."

Directly the voice ceased, Curte was annoyed with himself. He realized that he had listened all the time to this audacious message and had failed to say a single word in reply. He replaced the receiver and there was a queer look on his mouth.

"God!" he said, and then in self-condemnation, "and I was nothing better than a spell-bound rabbit. Just before the snake's about to devour it! I wonder what—"

At that moment he thought of the card that was supposed to be lying in his breast-pocket. For the time being his annoyance at the sheer effrontery of the attack had obliterated everything else in his mind. Now the thought of this 'planted' card came back to him. He removed the white handkerchief from the pocket of the coat and pushed his long fingers down to search for whatever might be there. Yes, the card was there. He took it out. A plain white card similar to the ordinary visiting card. On it had been typed two words: 'Heil Hitler!' The typing seemed similar to that of the letter he had received previously.

Lord Esmond Curte began to pace the room, his hands thrust deep into his trousers-pockets. Then he appeared to make up his mind about something quite suddenly. He threw back his head and walked to his telephone again. He dialled a number quickly—with an almost fierce intention. "Give me 'Trunks'," he said tersely. Some time later he was in conversation with Chief-Inspector MacMorran at New Scotland Yard. And as he listened, MacMorran remembered the case of Sir Edward Angus.

VI

Cedric Garnett was skippering the M.C.C. at Lord's against Yorkshire. It was the first day of the game—the second Wednesday in June. With his usual good fortune Garnett had won the toss, Brian Sellers, the Yorkshire captain, having called wrong to the spinning of the golden half-sovereign which Garnett invariably used for this particular ceremonial. Garnett had put himself fourth in the batting-order, second wicket down. He had hoped that he wouldn't have to go in before lunch, but fate proved otherwise. Hedley Verity had taken two quick wickets round about half-past twelve, and Cedric Garnett found himself partnering Denis Compton with nearly an hour to go before the luncheon interval. Garnett began carefully. He had made up his mind to have a good look at the famous Yorkshire slow bowler before he took any liberties.

Garnett watched the ball with the eye of a hawk. The result was that few runs came to trouble the scorers. The young Middlesex professional took a trio of boundaries off Smailes in quick succession at the nursery end, but the rate of scoring remained so slow that the crowd, even though they were at Lord's, began the time-honoured occupation of barracking. At exactly a quarter past one the familiar figure of a telegraph boy was observed making his way towards the wicket. The square-leg umpire intercepted him. The boy handed the umpire the familiar-looking buff envelope. The man in the white coat took a hasty glance at the envelope and then unceremoniously stuffed it into his pocket. He knew that there were four balls yet to be bowled before his colleague at the bowler's end would call 'over.' It was some little time before these four balls were delivered. Garnett took a sharply run 'two,' followed by a distinctly cheeky single, and Denis Compton played the third ball of the four right along the carpet to 'cover' (no run) and then punched the last ball of the over hard to the pavilion rails, just to prove that a bad ball is a bad ball no matter whose is the hand that bowls it. The bowler's umpire called 'over.' The other umpire with his eye on 'Mr. Garnett' pulled the buff envelope from his pocket and walked towards the preparing batsman. 'Probably,' he thought, 'something good for the 3.30.' He handed Garnett the envelope. Garnett frowned, pulled off his batting-gloves, slit the envelope with his forefinger and took out the telegram. The field waited while he read the message that had just been sent him.

'To Cedric Garnett, Lord's Cricket Ground, St. John's Wood. This is an order to be obeyed at all costs. Keep your mouth shut as to what you did at Remington before Mrs. Clinton arrived.— Heil Hitler!'

Garnett cursed inwardly, thrust the flimsy piece of paper into his trousers-pocket, put on his batting-gloves again and prepared to face the redoubtable Verity. The first three balls he played carefully, but at the fourth, his mind at conflict with itself, he lashed wildly. The voice of the wicket-keeper and the finger of the umpire told him eloquently what had happened. He made his way, annoyed and angry, to the pavilion. At the gate a second telegraph boy met him and to his utter surprise handed him a second envelope. He grabbed it rudely and made his way up the steps to the accompaniment of mild applause. In the dressing-room he read this second wire before he unbuckled his pads.

'You have just been warned. Obey the warning. The proof of our almost unlimited powers will be forthcoming at midnight.— Heil Hitler!'

Garnett rubbed his cheek. After all, three people had died in the hotel at Remington. Three people with whom he had dined but a few hours previously. Damned disconcerting—all of it, to say the least. He wandered into lunch just as the flannelled figures came in from the middle. The Yorkshire skipper came and sat next to him. Garnett hardly heard what he spoke about. The salmon and cucumber and the cold chicken made no appeal to him. At least three times he had to summon all his mental resources to bring himself back from a state that must have been 'miles away.'

Sir Jeremiah Willoughby, the silver-haired President of the Marylebone Club, remonstrated with him, but Cedric Garnett scarcely heard his voice even.

"What on earth happened to you, Garnett? Just before lunch, too. Never thought you'd have a dip just then. Felt certain you'd play for keeps with the hands of the clock where they were."

Garnett muttered excuses to him in commonplace phrases. Sir Jeremiah smiled indulgently at him and the smile was punctuated with repeated shakes of the head. After a time, Garnett edged away and went into the members' bar. He ordered a couple of light sherries, drank them dismally and then made his way to the top balcony of the pavilion. He found a seat in the front row and prepared to settle down for the afternoon. But the game entirely failed to interest him and several times he descended, to wander aimlessly from one part of the pavilion to another. He wished heartily that the time would speedily come when the M.C.C. side would take the field. This pleasure, however, was denied him. By this time Denis Compton had taken full measure of the White Rose attack, and with Brian Valentine, the Kent amateur, as a partner, the score was rising by leaps and bounds. It soon became obvious to Cedric Garnett that unless a most sensational collapse came along after the tea interval the side he was skippering would bat all day. As events turned out this view was correct, and at half-past six the home side had still three wickets to fall.

Garnett, still moody and depressed, dressed early and went along to Murillo's for dinner. He had booked a table there during the afternoon. Somehow the men with whom he dined seemed completely out of harmony with him, so when the meal was over he excused himself to them and drifted along to the Haymarket to do a 'flick' on his own. When he had had enough he called a taxi, shoved his bag inside and gave his home address. It was his habit to take his bag home. The time was a quarter to twelve when he let himself into his flat at Kensington. He poured himself out a stiff peg of Scotch directly he got in. His mind was, and had been almost all the evening, churning over the matter of those two telegrams which had been delivered to him at Lord's during the earlier part of the day. At five minutes to twelve he looked at his wrist watch. Well—it was just on midnight. He hadn't yet seen any particular exhibition of the powers possessed by the people who had taken it into their heads to worry him. Bluff, evidently. Pure bluff—or else somebody playing a stupid practical joke. There were still plenty of fools in the world who did that sort of thing.

Cedric Garnett decided that he would have one more drink and then hit the hay. He poured himself out a second three fingers of whisky. Just as he was raising the glass to his lips his telephone rang. As he walked across the room, to answer it, something made him look at his watch again. The time was exactly twelve o'clock.

"Hallo," he said. "Cedric Garnett speaking. Who are you?"

He told MacMorran afterwards, in the latter's room at the 'Yard,' that his uppermost impression as he answered the call was one of intense curiosity. Andrew MacMorran made careful note of this. A voice came quickly in reply.

"Good evening, Mr. Garnett. Which should almost be 'good morning.' You will be remembering that you have recently been the recipient of two telegrams. In the latter of those telegrams we informed you that we should give you proof of our powers at midnight. We are about to fulfil this statement. Will you kindly get your cricket-bag, bring it into the room in which you are now speaking and return to the telephone."

"Very well," responded Garnett, "I'll do as you ask although I don't really know why I should."

"You will know very soon," came the grim reply.

Garnett laid the receiver on the table and went into the hall. He had left his bag in the corner of the hall when he came in. He carried the bag into the room and picked up the receiver again.

"Well—I've done what you asked. What about it?"

"Good," came the voice back. "Now will you kindly investigate the contents of your cricket bag. It's most important that you should. Try, first of all, for example, the left-hand corner."

Garnett laid down the telephone receiver again and bent to the examination of the bag's contents. He moved pads, batting-gloves and various other impedimenta so that he might plunge his hand into that part of the bag which the unpleasant voice had indicated. He pulled away an old sweater in the process. As he did so his ear caught an unusual sound. Like the ticking of a clock. He thrust his hand deeper towards the corner of the bag from where this strange whirring noise was coming. He found a squarish brown paper parcel. Beads of sweat glistened on his brow. A bomb! Of course—a bomb. How long before the devilish contrivance went off? A chill sweat came to his brow. Then he pulled himself together. Damn it—he wasn't going to show the white feather to this crowd—whoever they might happen to be.

Leaving the brown paper parcel on the carpet by the side of the ransacked cricket-bag, he returned to the telephone, and spoke.

"Well—what's the rest of the lurid story? I've discovered the article which doubtless I was intended to discover. Where do I go from there?"

His tone was light—almost facetious—but in his heart he was feeling nothing like the way he sounded.

"To hell—if you aren't careful. Now listen here, Mister Garnett. You're a wee bit too fresh at the moment for my liking. Just listen carefully and you'll get an earful. When you open that parcel you've just been handling I guess you'll receive something in the nature of a little surprise. Take off the wrapping—do you mind—I'll hold on here. You are quite safe—for the time being."

Garnett, with an angry glint in his eye, picked up the brown paper parcel from the floor and removed the brown paper wrapping. When he saw what it had contained he *was* surprised, as his unknown messenger had so recently stated. He held in his hands a small alarm-clock, such as could be purchased in hundreds of shops. With a feeling of even greater annoyance he went back to the telephone and picked up the receiver.

"Go ahead," he said angrily, "and tell me the rest of your highly interesting story. Because I may as well tell you at once that I don't get it."

"You will, my friend, if you aren't careful. You'll get it all right! We never warn a person more than once. We regard that procedure as definitely uneconomical. Consider, if you value your life, what has happened. That alarm-clock you have just handled could just as easily have been a bomb. And if it *had* been a bomb—well, we shouldn't have troubled to telephone you. Do you get the idea now, Garnett? Yes? That's better. Don't forget our warning, will you? I am sure that you won't. Good morning. Oh—by the way—I should declare before lunch if I were you."

Garnett cursed softly to himself as he replaced the receiver. He was distinctly worried. He had been in many remote parts of the earth and he knew most corners of the more renowned cities. He had survived several ticklish scraps and had experienced many more 'rough houses' than the average man of his age, but this business had jolted him considerably. After all—as he had thought before in the pavilion at Lord's—three people had been murdered in the hotel at Remington and the murderer obviously was a man who would stick at nothing. Garnett went over to his sideboard and poured himself out yet another stiff peg of 'Scotch.' As he drank the warm spirit he came to a decision—he would go and see Inspector Mac-Morran at Scotland Yard first thing after breakfast in the morning.

VII

Rosamund Kingsley had driven to her Club. As there was no parking place anywhere near the Club, she had left the car in a nearby garage. She lit a cigarette as she dashed up the steps of the establishment. When she entered she saw that it was unusually crowded. She hated it when it was like that. She stopped at the office of the receptionist. The girl handed her several letters. Rosamund ran her eye across the envelopes quickly.

"Has anybody telephoned for me this evening?" she asked.

"No, Miss Kingsley."

"You are quite sure? Have you been on duty for some time?"

"Yes, Miss Kingsley. Since two o'clock this afternoon."

"I see. Thank you. Well—I shall be in the bar if anybody rings for me."

"Very good, Miss Kingsley," came the polite rejoinder.

Rosamund Kingsley made her way into the bar. A throng of women was already there. Women of all ages, from slim young things who spoke in loud, high-pitched voices, to those who had decorated a previous generation, but who now did the same things as their daughters and daughters-in-law did, lest they felt in their hearts that they were being left behind.

Rosamund pushed her way through the chattering company of women towards the bar-counter. She constantly described it to herself as the bar sinister. Mainly because she felt a distinct and active animosity towards nearly all the women who crowded round it. She knew only too well that most of them were deceitful, malicious and vindictive. But she felt that she had to be a member of a Women's Club of some kind for certain privileges that membership brought with it, and she had chosen the 'Femina' for the reason that perhaps it wasn't quite as bad as many others she could name. Rosamund caught the eye of the steward and ordered a 'Clover Club.' Rex, the said steward, knew that she would order a 'Clover Club' directly he saw her advancing towards the counter. She scarcely ever ordered anything else.

"Yes, Miss Kingsley," he remarked. "In a brace of shakes."

This last phrase was by way of being a witticism of Rex's which he seldom failed to produce. Within a few minutes Rex leant forward towards her and pushed over the drink.

"There you are, Miss Kingsley. That'll work wonders." He winked. "Make you think you're back with those cannibal savages of yours." He winked again and jerked his head understandingly towards the clutter of chattering women between whom Rosamund had just pushed her way. Rex liked Rosamund Kingsley and Rosamund liked him, so she grinned at him in some sort of reply.

Rosamund hooked a toe round the bar of a high counter-stool and seated herself. "Toss me over a packet of my specials, Rex. Do you mind?"

Rex handed her a packet of Algerian cigarettes. Then another customer mouthed an order at him and he left Rosamund to her cigarettes and her 'Clover Club.' She took a cigarette from the packet and lit it before sampling the 'Clover Club.' A voice near her caused her to look up in the direction from which it had come. The voice was familiar to her ears. When she saw who the speaker was, Rosamund decided not only that she hadn't seen her but that she wouldn't see her. She detested the woman. Every three months her hair changed colour and her face underwent what was very nearly a complete restoration. Rosamund, therefore, affected to be engrossed in her handful of letters. The person who owned the voice came nearer. Rosamund averted her face. The person of the voice passed by and the shadow of her presence went with her. Rosamund Kingsley felt a wave of relief go over her. At that moment she noticed the envelope of one of the letters which the receptionist had handed to her. The handwriting was unfamiliar and, for a reason which she couldn't have explained, it gave her an emotion of vague uneasiness. Almost mechanically she tore open the envelope, and then, as she read, a frown took possession of her brow. The letter, which had been typed, ran as follows:

'Dear Miss Kingsley,

In the near future you will, we feel certain, be subjected to a continual series of interrogations, some absurd, some possibly extremely pertinent with regard to the recent murders which took place at Remington. You are hereby ordered to give no information whatever to any person who may enquire of you. Particularly are you warned to say nothing of the incident which occurred on your journey down to accept Mrs. Warren Clinton's invitation. If you should be foolhardy enough to disregard the command you are being given in this letter, you will pay the inevitable penalty. Remember the fate of Angela Ramage, Wilfred Denver and Mrs. Clinton. It is not the practice of the' writers to bungle—to achieve our ends, we are determined to stick at nothing. To convince you that this is no empty boast, we will give you an example of our power at midnight tomorrow—that is to say at midnight on the evening of the day of the delivery of this letter. Until then, dear Miss Kingsley, auf wiedersehen! Heil Hitler!'

When she had finished reading this effusion, Miss Kingsley's face showed distinct signs of acute annoyance—an annoyance which was very close to definite anger. She crumpled the letter in her hand and turned impetuously to the bar-counter.

"Rex," she called imperiously, "give me a 'side-car,' will you?"

The steward noticed her discomfiture. "Bit o' bad news, Miss Kingsley?" he inquired solicitously.

"No, Rex. Definitely not bad news. As a matter of fact, I can't quite think of the appropriate adjective to employ."

Rex went on mixing the drink. When it was ready for her, Rosamund tossed it off in a twinkling. Then she gathered up her letters and prepared to make her departure. As she made her way out of the 'Femina,' Rosamund's shoulders came into contact with more than one fellow-member of the Club. This contact, it may be noted, was on no occasion the result of an accident. On the contrary, it was invariably deliberate.

Miss Kingsley's home address was at Chislehurst. A faithful maid who had been in her service for several years looked after her with a quiet, methodical efficiency. As she drove her car towards her house she found herself emphatically wondering if any other car were following hers. It was a most unusual mood for Rosamund Kingsley to be in, and she thoroughly hated it. Eventually she reached the house and ran the car into the garage. She had had dinner in town and looked forward to a good night's rest. Rhoda, her maid, as was her invariable custom, was waiting up for her.

Rosamund passed swiftly along the face of the house and came out into the open space of grass in front of the door. On the edge of this space she stopped for the space of a few seconds. She still had that most uneasy idea that she was being followed. But everything around her seemed normal as far as she was able to tell. No movement was visible near her, although a line of bushes, tolerably close to her, might well give seclusion to an enemy. Rosamund decided to take her courage into her two hands. It was not that she was frightened. Her career had given her a sure shield against fear. She was angry and her anger had made her hostile. She was ready for battle and she intended to give no chances to her opponents whoever they might be. She therefore tripped lightly over the grass space, opened the white gate for which she had been making and speedily came to the door which would yield her entrance to her house. This door was not locked, but it was held by a latch. Rosamund moved the latch and was quickly inside.

She stood in the passage, saw her own staircase in front of her, and beyond the staircase, through an open door, she could see the kitchen with Rhoda sitting in it. Rosamund stood there quietly in the passage and watched the maid at her task with her needle. She felt, again with uneasiness, that if she herself could enter in this way then a stranger could also with equal ease and facility. Rosamund had never troubled with regard to bolts and bars. Too much of her life had been lived in the open spaces of the earth. She called Rhoda to tell her that she had returned.

"Would you like anything, Miss Rosamund, before you go to bed?"

Rosamund Kingsley shook her head. "No, I don't think so, Rhoda, thank you. I had some food in town. Has anybody been?"

"No, Miss Rosamund. Nobody has been and nobody has rung up."

Rosamund walked to the kitchen and glanced at the big old-fashioned clock which hung on the kitchen wall. The time showed two minutes to midnight. She thought of the letter that was lying in her handbag.

"It's time I turned in, Rhoda. Time we turned in." She smiled. Rhoda smiled back at her.

"Very well, Miss Rosamund. I won't say that I'm not ready for bed." Rhoda rose and began to put away her needlework. As she did so a soft, almost furtive footstep sounded outside. The maid looked at her mistress. A light tap sounded on the door through which Rosamund had so recently come.

"Who's that?" murmured Rhoda. She had gone pale, and her voice was a little unsteady. "It's so late—it can't be anybody who—"

Miss Kingsley cut her short. "Stay here, Rhoda. Leave this to me."

With her features set and her blue eyes blazing, Rosamund Kingsley retraced her steps through the passage to the door. On her way there she heard the sound of another tap and this time it was a little louder than the first one had been. Rosamund went to the door and opened it, wondering why the person outside who was tapping didn't lift the latch and enter the house. She could see a man standing there. She could see him well. A smallish, wiry-looking fellow, probably in the early thirties, was standing in the moonlight. He had a clean-shaven, long, lean, narrow face. He looked hungry, she thought. As though a square meal would do him a world of good. His eyes, were brown and darted restlessly beyond her into the passage behind. He was dressed, as far as she could see, in a suit of dark blue with a reefer-jacket. He looked travel-stained, for his clothes, as well as looking old and worn, looked dusty as though he had been long on the road and had at last come to the end of an arduous journey.

"Miss Kingsley?" he inquired as he stood there. His voice was harsh and its general tones grated on her ears.

"I am Miss Kingsley—yes."

Rosamund's own voice was cool and hard. Now that she knew what she was called upon to face she had neither fear nor anxiety. "What is it you want?" she added.

The man coughed and as his body moved in the effort she saw that he carried something under his arm. "They sent me," he said somewhat truculently, "and when they send anybody—well—there's nothing for it but to obey."

He coughed again. Rosamund made a quick decision. She wanted to get to closer quarters with whatever it was she was up against. "Come in," she said curtly. It wasn't a request. It was much more like a command. The man crossed the threshold with evident reluctance. He turned and looked at the girl who confronted him, with no particular favour or regard.

"Whom do you refer to when you say 'they'?" demanded Miss Kingsley.

The man frowned at her. "Those that wield the power. You should know the truth of that as well as I do. What do you want to ask questions like that for?"

Rosamund pointed to a chair placed against the wall of the passage. "Sit down there."

But her visitor shook his head at the invitation. "No thank you, Miss Kingsley. There is no need. I shan't take up much more than a moment of your time. I expect you'd like to go to bed. It won't be me that will stop you. Because I'm ready for a spell of 'shut-eye' myself."

"What's your name?" she demanded.

Again the man shook his head. "We don't have names in the Association. We have to go by numbers. Mine is seventy-seven. That's why I'm often chosen to deliver the special messages that they send out. All I know is that I have to give you this."

The man handed Rosamund a parcel. It was the article he had been carrying under his arm. There wasn't the trace of any emotion either in his voice or on his face. He was the authentic robot. He spoke as a piece of mechanism might speak if it possessed the power. Rosamund took a step nearer to him. Her hands held the parcel which the man had handed to her. As her eyes looked down at what she held, the man sprang forward to the door. Rosamund made a quick movement to detain him. But his movement, so rapid had it been, defeated her object and the next thing she heard was the sound of his running feet across the grass outside. The door, caught by the wind, slammed to and she was left there, still with the parcel in her hands.

With a gesture of annoyance Rosamund took a step towards the door. But she realized that pursuit of the man was hopeless. He had too much start of her. She turned on her heel, her eyes still blazing blue fire, and carried the parcel into the kitchen where Rhoda was standing with one hand resting on the table.

"Who was it, Miss Rosamund?" asked the maid.

"The gentleman didn't leave his name," replied Miss Kingsley in grim accents, "he left this with me instead."

She put the parcel on the table. Rhoda eyed it fearfully before suddenly bending down and putting her ear close to it.

"Why, Miss Rosamund, whatever can it be—it's ticking."

Rosamund, sensing the full implication of the word which Rhoda had used, hastily tore off the paper covering. "Get away from it, Rhoda," she cried, "as far away as you can."

Then Rhoda began to laugh—on a high-pitched note. "Why, Miss Rosamund—it's an alarm-clock. There's nothing to be frightened of—surely."

When the object was fully revealed Rosamund saw that Rhoda was speaking the truth. The parcel had contained nothing more perilous than a cheap alarm-clock. On top of the clock lay a folded square of paper. Rosamund snatched at it anxiously and unfolded it. It was a typewritten note.

'My dear Miss Kingsley,

You will remember our previous message to you. Well—this might equally easily have been a bomb—mightn't it? Then where would you have been? Tragic end to career of well-known explorer. Sad—very! A really promising young life—wasted. No flowers by request and Cannibal island papers please copy! Yours till the next time—and take heed of your instructions—Heil Hitler!'

Rosamund Kingsley looked at her maid standing in the corner by the wall—and swore angrily. It was most unladylike of her—but who shall blame her? She then made straight for the telephone in her bedroom, dialled a number and inquired in a cold, hard, unemotional voice for Chief-Inspector MacMorran.

VIII

Dean Theodore Langton sat in his library. Although the season was summer the weather was unusually cold, and the Dean, whose blood was thin, had had a fire lighted in the grate.

"I'm afraid," he said, turning his head towards the priest who stood at his side, "that my decision in the matter you have been good enough to bring to my notice will disappoint you."

The Dean flushed as he spoke. He knew as well as the man to whom he had spoken knew that there was a trifle of sharpness in his voice. The Rev. Philip Greenaway shrugged his shoulders.

"On the contrary, sir, I am quite prepared to accept your decision." He lowered his voice to a whisper. "Thy way not mine, O Lord." Dean Langton looked up at the Reverend Philip. He had known the priest for many years. He knew him to be zealous and unremitting in his care of souls, but somewhat ruthless and definitely subtle.

"The time comes at least once to every man, when he has to answer to his own conscience. That is the time when he must make the great and grave decisions. There is no middle course open to him. He has to face the decision with integrity and cool courage."

The Reverend Philip Greenaway bowed. Any asperity that he was feeling was concealed behind a smile.

"Very truly spoken, sir," he remarked. His thin, dark face began to work under the stress of a great emotion. He picked up one of two books that were lying open on the table and placed it under one arm. "I will make known your decision, sir, to my churchwardens and the members of my Parish Council. I am sure they will understand the reasons that have prompted and weighed with you."

Dean Theodore moved the burning coal with a poker and seemed to be a trifle uneasy. He was uncertain as to what to say next. A piece of smoking coal fell from the fire on to the open hearth. The watery afternoon sun began belatedly to flood the room with an anaemic radiance. There was silence for an appreciable period of time. The Dean was the first to break this silence. He shifted uncomfortably in his chair.

"I shall see you at the church then, Greenaway, on Sunday evening. That settles it. We shall all meet at the church. I trust that we may reasonably expect an . . . er . . . imposing congregation."

"I think so, sir," Greenaway nodded. "The congregation of St. Saviour's rarely fails to respond to a great occasion."

"Thank you, Greenaway." The Dean showed his pleasure at the compliment the priest had paid him. "My sermon," he added, "will, in all probability, be based upon the Credo of St. Athanasius. I have always felt that it is a subject which receives far too little attention from the Anglican pulpit generally." He glanced at the clock. "Were you wanting me for anything else, Greenaway?"

"No, Dean Langton, I think not." Greenaway started to walk away from the table. He paused and then turned to the man sitting by the fire. "Except to say this, sir. That my congregation is well aware of Dean Langton's world-wide reputation for scholarship."

The Dean inclined his head at the additional compliment. The Reverend Philip Greenaway went out of the room and closed the door quietly behind him.

*

The Dean had preached one of his most eloquent sermons and joined becomingly in certain verses of the offertory hymn. Every now and then, as he glanced towards the singing congregation, he would stroke the silver hair at the back of his head with a sweeping gesture of his hand. The diamond in his ring sparkled brilliantly. The offertory was taken, the sidesmen and churchwardens padded to the steps of the chancel, the congregation shuffled back to their seats and then some of them crumpled on to their knees. The Reverend Philip Greenaway began the post-sermon prayers. When the service was complete, the officials gathered in the vestry with enthusiasm to assess the amount of the collection. The Vicar's Warden, almost choking from the pressure of his high collar, came across a folded square of paper in one of the purses. As he picked it out from the varied assortment of coins which were its companions, he saw, to his surprise, that it was addressed to 'Dean Langton.' The Vicar's Warden, almost disintegrating with indignation, took the note to the Reverend Philip Greenaway. When he handed it to the Vicar he submitted the appropriate explanation as to its origin. The Vicar pursed his lips and made it his immediate business to find the Dean, who was disrobing. The Vicar repeated the explanation he had had from his Warden and surrendered the folded square of paper to the distinguished cleric who had been his guest for that evening.

"Extraordinary occurrence, my dear Greenaway," exclaimed the Dean, "to say nothing of the irreverence involved. I've never heard of such a thing—during the whole of my ecclesiastical career. Dear me—I suppose I'd better read it—there's no knowing what it may contain." The Dean unfolded the square of paper with the Reverend Greenaway watching him with curiosity. The lines on the paper had been typewritten and ran thus.

'Note to Dean Langton,

In a short time the Police and others may interview you again in connection with your recent stay at Remington when Mrs. Ramage and Wilfred Denver were murdered. You will know nothing. You are hereby warned to say nothing. Especially are you ordered to silence with regard to your interpretation of the word "Reldresal."

Your obedience to this order is imperative. Should you choose to disobey, your blood will be upon your own venerable head and you need no reminder as to what happened to Denver and his guilty partner at Remington. In order that you should understand exactly where you stand in this matter, you will receive an overwhelming indication of the power we possess, at midnight tonight. Be warned, therefore, in time. Heil Hitler!'

Dean Langton's initial reaction was one of perplexity. He knew that the Vicar of St. Saviour's was watching him curiously. He decided upon a policy of frankness.

"A case for the police authorities, Greenaway," he said frigidly. "I shall lose no time in putting this sacrilegious communication in their hands."

The lines round Greenaway's thin mouth showed an unmistakable distaste for the entire procedure. "Atrocious," he muttered. "To think of the offertory being used for a scurrilous message of this type—I can't find words for an appropriate description."

The Dean was packing his vestments into a handsome suitcase. The Reverend Philip returned the square of paper to him. The Vicar held it between his fingers as though it were pest-ridden. Dean Langton took it, folded it again carefully and then placed it in a pocket. "I hope supper will not be too late, Greenaway. I have rather more than ordinarily pleasant memories of your cold chicken and your burgundy. Let me see. What was it you regaled me with on the previous occasion I supped with you? A Richebourg—or was it a Musigny? My memory, I fear, is beginning to fail me."

He fell in behind the Vicar as they made their way from the vestry. But even the thoughts of cold chicken and burgundy failed to prevent that strange word 'reldresal' continually coming into his mind. His mind began to wander until seemingly far-off he heard the voice of the Vicar of St. Saviour's saying: "Evelyn . . . Here's the Dean."

Dean Langton jerked himself back to reality. When he said 'Grace' at the Reverend Greenaway's table he had almost completely recovered his customary equanimity. It was a few minutes after eleven when he left the Vicarage attached to St. Saviour's and he was home in his house at Mannington as the Cathedral clock chimed the third quarter of the last hour of the Sabbath day. As he entered the Deanery he thought of the threat concerning the mysterious reminder he was due to receive within the space of the next few minutes. The Dean's eyes flashed with the fire of courage and he drew himself up to the full height of his six feet. His thoughts were far away when his manservant met him in the hall of the house.

"Will you be wanting anything, sir, before you retire? If so, and you let me know now—"

The Dean interrupted him. "No thank you, Hedley. I shan't want anything at all this evening. I shall spend a few minutes in my study and then I shall go to bed. You need not wait up any longer."

"Very good, sir. Good night, sir."

Hedley effaced himself. Dean Langton found some papers and went to his study. As he drew up his chair to the desk his telephone rang. The Dean frowned at the interruption, braced himself for the inevitable encounter and answered the ring.

"Good evening, Dean Langton," came a voice. "I feel sure that there is no need for me to introduce myself. Also I shall take up but very little of your time. On the other hand, I shall come to the point at once. But if you will look in your cigar-case—everybody knows how thoroughly you appreciate a good cigar—you will understand a little the strength of the forces that are warning you and may be also arraigned against you. Don't smoke any of the cigars—throw them in the fire when you get the chance. And ponder on what you *might* have done—if we hadn't condescended to 'phone you. Good night and Heil Hitler!"

Before the Dean could reply, whoever it was had rung off. Dean Langton put his hand into the proper pocket and took out his cigar-case. It contained five cigars. He was compelled to examine them closely before he could completely convince himself that they were of a different brand from his own. That his own had been removed from the case and these others substituted for them. Very thoughtfully he made his way to the kitchen, where a boiler was usually kept alight. Dean Langton opened the top and threw the cigars into the boiler. A strong smell of bitter almonds almost immediately pervaded the room. Dean Langton's face hardened. He would have a word with Chief-Inspector MacMorran in the morning, of New Scotland Yard. He felt that he was being taken out of his depth.

IX

Capt. Ronald Playfair, V.C., walked moodily along the banks of the Sid. He should have been in the best of spirits actually, because he was on his way to play golf. He loved the ancient game and he loved every minute he spent in its devotion. But on this particular occasion he had a letter in his pocket and it had been the receipt of this letter which had contributed so actively to his mood of depression. On his way to the links, Capt. Playfair sat on the stump of a tree and re-read the letter which was causing him so much anxiety. It was worded as follows:

'Dear Capt. Playfair,

In a short time from now the Police Authorities will interview you again with regard to the Remington murders. You are advised to maintain a discreet silence in respect of everything you know and everything you think you know. In case you should feel inclined to disregard this piece of advice, we warn you here and now not to do so. Disobedience will mean drastic punishment and when we speak of punishment we would have you know that you are dealing with men who stick at nothing! Take special care to avoid all reference to the figure that hid behind the big clock in the hotel on the evening of the murders. You don't know who it was. But if the police interrogated you, you might begin to think you did and that is just what must not happen. At midnight tonight we will prove to you how powerful we are. Till then—Heil Hitler!'

Ronald Playfair, after he had read, thought of many things. Chiefly to do with the years that had immediately followed the Armistice in the autumn of 1918. He thought of the burning of the Reichstag and how he had run in order to escape the crowds, past old Hindenburg's house in the Dorotheenstrasse. Of the people who had worn the sign of the red dachshund in the lapels of their coats. Then he thought of the coloured dachshunds he had seen in the window of the flat near the hotel in Remington, and he smiled when he remembered how he had told the story and his fears to

Anthony Bathurst. He rose from the tree-stump on which he had been sitting and continued on his journey. It seemed plain to him that these people who had removed Mrs. Clinton, Mrs. Ramage and Wilfred Denver were making no idle boast when they announced that they would stick at nothing. Playfair shrugged his shoulders. He had been gifted with a clear brain. Not only was it clear, but it invariably worked quickly. This clear brain of his told him unmistakably that the murders with which he had become implicated were the work of no ordinary man . . . or even men. Playfair almost entirely relied on first impressions. He often made statements to that effect. First impressions, he was wont to argue, were founded on the evidence of his own senses and not on the senses or emotions of other people not in such a good position to judge as he was himself. On the whole he was disinclined to trust other people. Their opinions, their judgments, their motives and their intentions. He was supremely content to rely upon himself.

Playfair reached his destination, met his friends, played two excellent rounds of golf, winning each time, had an agreeable lunch, an admirable tea, much delectable liquid refreshment and set out to stroll home in comfort. Playfair much preferred walking in Devon to motoring. He lived on the outskirts of Exeter and after a pipe and a read, with a drop of 'Scotch' at his elbow, he looked at his watch, found the time was half-past eleven and decided to go to bed.

A few minutes later he was in his bathroom cleaning his teeth when his eyes caught sight of what looked like a glow of light in the garden. It was a glorious summer night. Playfair, curious to see what was the matter, pushed up the windows of the bathroom and looked out. He soon saw that his eyes hadn't deceived him. There was a glow of light in the garden and what was more, this glow was getting more intense and larger every second. Muttering an exclamation of dismay, he ran downstairs for all he was worth. By the time he reached the bottom of the staircase the reflection of the glow through the windows gave the frightening appearance that the whole house was alight. Even from where he was he could almost feel the heat himself.

Playfair dashed into the garden and saw from a position of comparative safety that his clump of bamboos was burning. The glow by now of the licking flames was spreading fiercely and Playfair realized in an instant that even the house itself was in dire danger. There was only one sensible action that he could take. Playfair was quick to take it. He ran to the telephone in his hall without a second's delay and asked for the Fire Brigade. The response was rapid, and although the flames were terrific when the brigade arrived they were quickly subdued by an extremely efficient and business-like body of men. Then Playfair began to think things. He remembered the letter he had received and the threat it had contained.

When the members of the Fire Brigade had finished their work and had departed, Playfair walked back to the house from the garden in a contemplative frame of mind. Almost coincidentally with his entry into the house, his telephone bell rang. Playfair's face was set as he picked up the receiver to answer the call. A man's voice came over to him.

"Good morning, Playfair. I rather fancy from the time that another day has dawned. How did you enjoy that little show we put on for your benefit a short time ago? It's amazing how bamboo *does* burn, isn't it? Even in a damp country like ours. And the blaze might so easily have been your house with you asleep inside it. We do feel that you should realize the plain truth of that statement. Good morning, Capt. Playfair—don't trouble to find words to answer . . . and . . . er . . . Heil Hitler!"

There was a nasty look in Playfair's eyes as he replaced the receiver. "Really," he said aloud, "quite an interesting performance! Stick at nothing—eh? It seems that my friends are determined to live up to their reputation. But why pick on me? Why should I have been singled out for their attentions?"

Such were the thoughts of Ronald Playfair when he went to bed about half an hour later. First thing in the morning he decided he would get into touch with Anthony Bathurst.

PART FOUR
THE INVESTIGATION

I

ANTHONY Lotherington Bathurst and Chief-Inspector Andrew MacMorran compared notes. The former had heard from Capt. Playfair again and the latter had been entertained by the various stories as related by Sir Edward Angus, Lord Esmond Curte, Cedric Garnett, Rosamund Kingsley and Dean Theodore Langton. The time was eleven o'clock in the morning. Sir Austin Mostyn Kemble, the Commissioner of Police, sat back in a chair—he had come to the Inspector's room out of the largeness of his heart—and turned his head to listen to MacMorran, who was speaking his mind. Anthony Bathurst sat in another chair beneath the window which looked out upon London's river. When the Inspector had come to the end of his narrative, there was a silence. The Commissioner broke it.

"So that, between the two of you, everybody who attended this crazy gathering of the American woman has had one of these melodramatic and highly-coloured warnings." He looked from one to the other of them. "That's so, isn't it? I'm right?"

MacMorran coughed. Anthony expressed his disagreement. "Not altogether, Sir Austin. There's an exception to that. Ramage. The husband of Mrs. Ramage, one of the murdered women. Unless, of course, he *has* been warned in something of the same way and hasn't passed on the glad tidings. There's always that possibility, I suppose." MacMorran made no comment. Sir Austin leant forward in his chair. "Ramage, himself—eh? Looks distinctly fishy—don't you think so? Him being left out like that? The pointing finger—eh?"

He broke off, looking from one to the other of his listeners. Again Anthony demurred.

"With all due respect, sir, I don't think that I agree with you. If Ramage were the guilty man he'd have been almost bound to have included himself in the warnings. Because to leave himself out— well—such a procedure was bound to produce the reaction which it has already. With yourself. Do you agree with me now, sir?"

"Looks very strange," returned the Commissioner. "I'll certainly concede that." He swung round on to MacMorran. "What do you say about it, MacMorran?"

MacMorran leant forward and folded his arms on the desk. "I'm agreeing with Mr. Bathurst, sir, for two reasons. One—that Ramage, if he were guilty, would almost certainly have been up to the point which Mr. Bathurst had just raised, and, two, that in my opinion there isn't the slightest doubt that these murders were not 'private' murders, if you know what I mean, but have been perpetrated by a gang of thugs who have international interests at stake: Everything as far as I can see points to the latter contingency."

Anthony handed round his case and lit a cigarette. He spoke through the smoke. "I'm glad you agree with me, Andrew, with regard to Ramage. Eases my mind considerably."

He addressed his next remarks to the Commissioner. "I've been looking forward to this chat, sir, as there are still one or two sides of the affair which worry me. Worry me considerably. Let me retrace my steps. Our steps, if you prefer it. May I?"

Sir Austin nodded. "I'm glad to have the opportunity. Go ahead, Bathurst."

"Well, sir, let's start with the lady that we'll call the 'prima donna.' Mrs. Warren Clinton. Comes over from the States full of cash and replete with good intentions (all pro-British). When she lands in this country she's fussed over and then betakes herself to Remington. For the ostensible purpose of selecting (so we've been told) two people from a list she has prepared herself, who will help her make this country once again a land fit for Pierrots to live in."

MacMorran checked an inclination to laugh immoderately. Anthony went on:

"She conducts her test of her selected persons, chooses two of them—only to have them murdered almost immediately and then to be removed herself. Pretty crazy—all of it—don't you think so, gentlemen?"

"Definitely," returned the Commissioner . . . "er . . . very definitely."

The Inspector nodded. Anthony continued again.

"It is all 'oddity.' The chosen people are killed. If their deaths are so desirable to the murderers, why wait for the choice before they murder them? And then, why kill the *dea ex machina* herself *afterwards*? I'm still hopelessly puzzled. Where shall I be able to find the answer or the 'equation-equivalent' to the oddity?"

MacMorran shook his head in denial of his ability to answer the query. "Afraid I can't help you—yet."

Anthony grinned. "You're frank, Andrew, at any rate. I appreciate frankness. But let me amplify the general statements which I have just put forward. Starting with Mrs. Warren Clinton. Who is the heir to the Clinton millions, or should it be thousands?"

He waited for the reply. MacMorran took it upon himself to answer. "Victor Ross Beard, a nephew of old man Clinton. The only son of the old man's only sister. The Clintons themselves had no children. I've had that crumb of information from the State Department of Nebraska. Young Beard's about twenty-two years of age and unmarried. At the moment. That position will probably be adjusted in the very near future." MacMorran's smile was cynical.

Anthony expressed his gratitude. "Thanks for the information, Andrew. I shall be interested to make a note of it. Now let me tell you something else."

The Commissioner and the Inspector waited for him. Anthony lit another cigarette before he began again. "Let us consider this 'test,' or examination, which was held under the auspices of the late Mrs. Warren Clinton. We are told by *all* the candidates whom we have interviewed, that various papers were filled in by them which Mrs. Warren Clinton afterwards collected. Do you agree with that statement?"

The Commissioner and MacMorran assented.

Anthony looked up for their reactions. "Good, you agree! Well— the question that's exercising me is this. What became of those papers that the candidates filled up? We know that Mrs. Clinton went round and collected them. Presumably, therefore, they were in her possession when she was killed. Where are they now? What became of them? Legge and I have signally failed, so far, to discover a trace of them. Not even a charred ember."

MacMorran ventured a suggestion. "She may have destroyed them herself. It seems to me it's quite likely. Once they had fulfilled their purpose, she had no further use for them. That's sound, isn't it?" The Inspector cocked a sapient eye at Anthony.

"It's sound as far as it goes. But if you're right in that theory, she got rid of 'em with an almost unnatural alacrity and, further than that, there was no sign of any paper in any one of the rooms the lady had occupied."

Sir Austin made a somewhat belated contribution. "I see what Bathurst is driving at. I think it's rather strange myself."

"I'll carry on," declared Anthony. "Still sticking to the 'test' which Mrs. Clinton gave to her guests, have you considered the words which formed this test? From what I can gather, the words chosen were most unusual. Consider such specimens as 'roup,' 'ulema' and 'Reldresal.' Am I to understand that Mrs. Clinton was sufficiently erudite to make these selections, or am I forced to the conclusion that the list of words was prepared for her by somebody else? Again, gentlemen, I find myself running up against what I have already described as 'oddity'."

Anthony rose and paced the room, his hands thrust down into his trousers-pockets. There was a silence in the apartment. Anthony went and looked out of the window, over the river. The sky had clouded over and a drenching drizzle was beginning to play upon the pane. For some seconds he stood there saying nothing. Suddenly he turned on his heel and spoke to his two companions.

"I don't think," he said critically, "that we've ever had a pond with so many fish swimming in it. With Mrs. Clinton herself, there were ten of 'em all bunched together at the starting-post." He grinned. "All right, Andrew. I know I'm mixing metaphors. Nine besides the hostess. Angus, Curte, Denver, Garnett, Miss Kingsley, Dean Langton, Capt. Playfair and the two Ramages. Two of the nine are eliminated. Nine minus two equals seven. I suppose I sound as though I were wandering. Seven left out of ten really—counting Mrs. Warren Clinton. And there were also *nine* words. We must remember that fact as well."

"Something else," added the Inspector. "Each one of the nine words was supposed to have what Mrs. Clinton called an 'associate' word. Don't you remember? I think that fact may be important."

Anthony looked at him. "Why not indeed, Andrew? I think about it precisely as you think about it. I feel that I shall be forced to give those nine words an evening's extremely close attention."

He swung himself to a sitting position on MacMorran's table. "But let us proceed. We haven't touched any of the sequels yet. After the murders our seven survivors of the Remington tragedy go back very naturally to their own homes. What happens to them when they get there? With the exception of Ramage, the poor devil who has had his wife murdered, each one of them is *menaced*. Threatened with the power of a sinister organization which ends its soothing messages with the somewhat unoriginal phrase—'Heil Hitler.' Whatever opinions any one of us may hold concerning these much vaunted powers, one thing at any rate *does* emerge from the various contacts that have been made. And that is this. Our friends seem to be in a position to get at the late Mrs. Clinton's guests with a degree of ease which suggests a much more than ordinary knowledge of their personal habits and general whereabouts." Anthony paused to emit a cloud of cigarette smoke. "It is obvious, too," he continued, "that unless we envisage a 'sixfold' conspiracy, which I think is manifestly absurd, a number of these 'threat' stories must be authentic. They may even all be. On the other hand, one of them, or perhaps two of them, are 'hoo-ey'."

He turned to the Inspector. "You and I, Andrew, have a spot of sorting out to do."

"I'll say we have. And the sooner we get down to it properly, the better."

Sir Austin rose. "That's a good place where I can leave you. Cheer-o, Bathurst. Let me know if you want anything."

"You bet I will, sir."

The Commissioner took his departure. "Andrew," said Anthony Bathurst, "I'm convinced that we're missing something. That we keep on missing it. It's there but we haven't got our fingers round it. Something vitally important to the solution of our problem. But when we do hit on it—"

"Ay," interrupted MacMorran, "when we hit on it—I'm glad you said 'when'."

Anthony smiled at him. "Let me finish, you old blighter. *When* we hit on that one thing—well, we shan't have any problem left."

"I'm thrilled that you should think so," growled Inspector Mac-Morran.

II

At Anthony's request, MacMorran himself took over the Playfair strand of the inquiry. Playfair's personal history and record generally impressed the Inspector to an unusual degree. MacMorran told Anthony so. The latter listened and agreed.

"He's the one man of the crowd, Andrew," said Anthony Bathurst, "whose help should be invaluable. Look at his Secret Service record for one thing. He becomes an almost heaven-sent proposition."

"I have. And its particular relationship with Germany. Few men could serve our purpose better."

Anthony then discussed with the Inspector Playfair's story of the flat at Remington with its window of different-coloured dachshunds. "He's also told me," continued Anthony, "of when he was in Berlin, the night the Reichstag was fired. I've wondered since whether we ought to have looked further into that dachshund business. Suppose you have a look into things that way yourself, Andrew?"

MacMorran agreed, and on the following morning he took an early train to Remington, after 'phoning Legge that he was coming. A short walk from the police-station brought the two police officers to the block of flats which had figured in Playfair's story. An official of the company which controlled these flats was shown on a board as residing at Number 7.

"We'll knock there at once," said Legge, "and find out the time of day generally."

"The flat we are concerned with," remarked MacMorran, "is the basement one that's the farthest distance from the railway station. Suppose we scout round first and take a 'dekko' at it."

"All right," conceded Legge—"suits me. Come on then now—right away."

MacMorran piloted Legge to the particular flat which had attracted Playfair's attention. There was nothing in the window, which, as Playfair had said, was on the eye-level, remotely suggesting a dachshund, no matter what the colour might have been.

"Nothing much here," commented MacMorran. "I'm beginning to wonder—"

"No need for anything now," replied Legge, "this job, such as it was, may be all over and done with. Strikes me, Inspector Mac-Morran, that you and I are late on the scene. Still—we'll try a few inquiries. Judicious inquiries. We shan't lose anything by doing so. Let's come along over to Number 7 now."

MacMorran fell into step beside him. They came to Number 7. "I'll knock," said Legge. He stepped across the square grass plot and knocked on the door. MacMorran, true to police traditions, went to the side and looked through a window. Through the glass he saw dimly a man spring from a settee where evidently he had been lying. From what he was able to see of the man's face, MacMorran thought that he looked as though he were scared of something. An instant later the front door was opened and a stout, white-faced man was seen to be standing there, facing the two police officers.

"What is it?" he asked. "What is it you want?"

"We are police officers," replied Legge. "We want a few words with you. I don't think we shall take up any more than a few minutes of your time. May we come in?"

"Certainly. Come in and sit down." The stout man mopped his forehead with a large coloured handkerchief and gave a huge sigh of relief. "Come this way, gentlemen."

He led the way to the front room where he had been lying down. "Sit down—make yourselves comfortable."

MacMorran and Legge each found a chair and sat in it. "You have a number of residential flats here?"

"Yes, sir. I act as caretaker and also answer all inquiries. Employed by the firm of Barclay, Dines and Martin."

MacMorran looked across at the comparatively low windows. "I notice," he observed, "that each block has a common stair."

"Yes, sir. They're almost like private chambers."

Legge took up the interrogation. He described the position of the particular flat in which he and MacMorran were interested.

"I know the flat you mean, sir," replied the stout man.

"What is the name of the occupier?" demanded Legge.

The man smiled as though he had suddenly and very pleasantly come to the end of a long lane of troubles. "That's easy to answer. There isn't one. As a matter of fact that flat you're inquiring about is empty."

"Empty?" echoed Legge.

"That's what I said. Empty."

"How long's it been empty?" cut in MacMorran.

The stout man put in an effort of memory. "Let me see now. Some little time, I'm afraid. I can tell you. Since about the end of April. The people who had it went about the 29th of April."

Legge looked at MacMorran significantly. "Sure of your dates?" asked the former of the stout man.

"Yes. Pretty well certain."

"How do you fix it?" queried MacMorran.

The stout man wagged his head with a hint at superlative wisdom. "I'll tell you," he said with a glint of triumph in his eye. "I'm able to fix it by the murders at the 'Royal Sceptre'."

"How do you mean?" asked the local Inspector with a sharp glance in the direction of MacMorran.

"Why—the murders at the hotel took place about the middle of April. The people left the flat here very soon after. As a matter of fact I remarked on it. When they gave me notice. I said to the chap that does the electrical repair work here, I said: 'This place is getting a bad name already. Here's people on the "flit" at once as you might say.' I remember making that remark quite well."

The stout man paused for breath. But Legge was keen for further details. "These tenants that gave notice—who were they? We should like to know as much about them as possible. Tell us all you know."

The stout man nodded. "Very good, sir. I'll be pleased to. First of all—and I think it's important you should know—they were foreigners. German, I fancy. 'Uns and proper 'Uns at that! Went by the name of Wenzel. Otto Wenzel was the man's name. You notice I said 'the man' and not 'the husband.' Fact is, I was never certain as to who was who and what was what. There was a girl here, too. And a fair stunner to look at. You don't see many like 'er knocking about in a day's march—I can tell you. Took your breath away. He called her 'Elsa,' but whether she was his wife or his sister I could never rightly tell."

MacMorran began to wish that Mr. Bathurst had come with him on the inquiry. This seemed to be much more down his street than the Inspector's own.

"Could these people speak English?" he asked of the caretaker.

"Oh—yes. They could speak English all right."

"How far does that opinion actually go? Could they speak English *well*?"

The caretaker nodded. "As well as you and me. You need harbour no doubts on that score."

Legge had his note-book out. "How old were these people? Within a little."

The stout man pushed his hand through his hair and began to scratch his head. "The man—Otto Wenzel—was, I should say, somewhere round about thirty-five. Elsa, the girl, would be about ten years younger than that."

Legge made suitable notes. "Describe them, please. As closely as you can."

The caretaker's face fell a trifle. "H'm. Setting me a bit of a teaser, aren't you? I'm not much of a hand at that sort of game."

"Do your best," said Legge curtly. "It's a matter of necessity."

"All right. I'll have a go. I'll start with the man. On the tall side—not much under six feet. Slim. Thin, lean face. A hungry-looking face with deep-set blue eyes. Looked as though he'd gone through the mill a bit in his younger days and had never forgotten it. Kind of chap who was never still. Hands and fingers and eyes continually on the work. That's about all I can say. Oh—brown hair and a bit of a scar on one of his cheeks. The left cheek. How's that?"

"You're doing fine," replied Legge. "Now what about the girl?"

"That's easy. A blonde. Small features. Blue eyes that got yer directly she fastened 'em on to yours. A neat, trim way of moving and walking. Sort of pranced along! I'd 'ave left 'ome for her any day she'd ha' beckoned. Not too tall. Just right! Say about five feet six or seven. I can tell you, gents, I was downright sorry when they scrammed out of it. I've missed her."

The caretaker's countenance became doleful.

"What reason did they give for going?" inquired Inspector Legge. The man rubbed his chin between thumb and forefinger. "I've been trying to think. I've been reckoning you'd ask me that. They did give a reason, I remember. Now what the hell was it." Suddenly his face cleared. "I've got it. The man had got another job. A better job. That was it."

"What was this man Wenzel by occupation?' Any idea?" The question came from MacMorran. The caretaker shook his head.

"I couldn't tell you that, sir."

MacMorran persisted. "But when you have applications from people who wish to take up tenancies here, isn't it the usual procedure for them to fill up a form giving various particulars about themselves? How many in family? Where the breadwinner works and what his financial circumstances are, etc., etc.? Isn't that so? I've always been led to believe that."

"We don't trouble to have forms filled up here," replied the stout man. "As long as they seem all right and the colour of their money's good—well, I reckon they pass muster. In Wenzel's case, I can recollect that when he first came he paid a month's rent in advance. That suited my bosses all right. The question of the kids is a bit beside the point, naturally, because these particular flats ain't suitable for people with large families. We very seldom get applications from that kind. They know better than to apply, you see."

MacMorran shook his head at the information. He didn't seem altogether satisfied. Legge spoke again.

"You said just now that this German chap, Otto Wenzel, got another job somewhere. Have you any idea as to where that job was?"

The caretaker scratched his head again. "Not the exact locality, but from what he told me it was in the Midlands somewhere. That's vague, I know—but it's the best I can do for you, gentlemen."

Legge looked across at MacMorran. "The Midlands—eh? Not so good! Pretty big area when you come to work it out. The man might be anywhere between Northampton and Nottingham."

"I agree," commented MacMorran, "not to mention several other places." His tone was distinctly acid.

Legge looked through the notes he had made before closing his book. "I don't fancy we shall require this gentleman's services any more, shall we, Inspector MacMorran?"

MacMorran thought the question over before replying. "Yes, there's something else I'd like to ask him. These Wenzels—had they a car by any chance?"

"Yes. They had. I can say that without any hesitation. I often used to see them in it."

"What make was it? Can you tell us that?"

"Yes, I can tell you that as well without the slightest hesitation. A Rover."

"Good. Where did they garage it?"

"At the back of the flats here. There's a row of lock-up garages. As a matter of fact, Wenzel asked me about garage accommodation when I let the flat to him."

MacMorran came to closer quarters. "Remember the night of the hotel murders?"

"Rather. Very well. It was on a Saturday night. Saturday night-Sunday morning. What about it?"

"Were the Wenzels out in their car that night?"

"Have a heart, guvnor! Isn't likely that I could be sure about a question of that kind. Askin' me something, aren't you?"

MacMorran smiled at him and then transferred the smile to Inspector Legge. "I suppose I am—when you come to think of it."

He picked up his hat from the table where he had placed it. Legge followed suit.

"What do you make of it?" he asked MacMorran, when they got outside.

"Don't know—quite. Nothing emerges very clearly that I can see. All the same, I'm not sorry we came. The time hasn't been wasted. Because we've certainly learnt one or two things."

III

MacMorran discussed his visit to Remington with Anthony Bathurst. After he had told his story, he formed an impression that

Anthony's thoughts and attention were not wholly his, or had they been even during the telling of his story. He translated this impression into words. Anthony was quick to apologize.

"Sorry, Andrew, if I didn't seem to be paying a lot of attention. To tell the truth, my mind was on another matter. I'll give my best attention to Herr Wenzel and dame a little later on. In the meantime, have a glance at this with me, will you?"

MacMorran drew up a chair and sat down beside him. Anthony looked up from the cigarette he was smoking. "Have you had a close look into these stories that have floated your way, Andrew? Concerning the several warnings that have been received by various friends of ours who had attended Mrs. Clinton's party?"

"Well—close enough. Why—what's your point?" MacMorran sat up straight in his chair. Anthony began to tell him.

"Let's take 'em one by one. We're fond of taking 'em in alphabetical order, so we'll stick to that idea and do it that way once again. Take the story you had from Sir Edward Angus. Here it is."

He tapped the Ale which he had been examining when MacMorran had begun to tell of his Remington experiences.

"I see from these notes that you had questioned Angus a good deal as to his general movements after he received the first warning. That came to him, according to his story, when he was seated in the Lexicon Club. Talking to a man by the name of Adrian Anstey. Sir Edward says that he went straight back from the 'Lexicon' to his own flat. In answer to your inquiry he states that he travelled the journey in his own car, driven by his own chauffeur, Kingsford. The same Kingsford, you will observe, Andrew, who has already figured once or twice in this sordid history. Now when Sir Edward Angus was telephoned round about midnight, the message he received related to a humdrum box of 'Swan Vestas' that had somehow been placed in his breast pocket. I deduce, therefore, Andrew—and I think it's a fairly sound deduction—that Sir Edward made the necessary contact while he was still in the 'Lexicon.' Make a special note of that, will you, Andrew?" MacMorran nodded. "I agree with you."

"Good. We will pass on to Curte. His story runs as follows: The warning was delivered to him in his library by his manservant. Afterwards he went to a Ball. A Charity Ball—to be precise. In the Trent

Hall, Nottingham. Here he spoke to several people, and amongst others danced with a Miss Felicity Frayle. I suggest that it's again a sound deduction to assume that contact was made with him somewhere under the roof of Trent Hall. Observe in what circles these contacts have been made, Andrew. Now, who's next?"

"Garnett. The cricketer." MacMorran looked puzzled.

"He's an easier case to deal with. Access was obtained somewhere and somehow to his private bag. What did he do and where did he go? After the day's play at Lord's was over he dined at Murillo's and went to a cinema. According to what he told you he left his bag at each place in the cloakroom. So that contact, in his instance, occurred either at a cloakroom or in the dressing-room at Lord's. Again, please observe the surroundings, Andrew."

A second nod came from the Inspector. "I think I see what you're getting at, Mr. Bathurst."

"I thought that you would. Still we'll proceed. Who's next on the list? Miss Kingsley, our explorer friend. Now in her case we find ourselves confronted by a different set of circumstances. Contact was effected with her by means of either a subordinate member of what we will call the crime organization or by somebody employed specially for that one purpose and that one purpose only. In other words, the case of Rosamund Kingsley doesn't provide us with the proper soil on which to sow our theories. Now what happened in the case of Dean Langton? Think carefully, Andrew."

"His cigars were tampered with."

"Exactly. And in the Dean's own words: 'The substitution must have taken place when my coat was hanging in the vestry of St. Saviour's.' This is to say, while evensong Was actually going on. Cool work that, you know, Andrew. But notice *la galère* again, through which our criminal or criminals is or are still flitting. Which brings us to the last case with which we have to deal. The case of Capt. Ronald Playfair, V.C. Without whose help, if I may remind you, Andrew, you would never have got on to the track of Otto Wenzel and his charming sister, wife or mistress (you pay your money and you take your choice), Elsa."

MacMorran began to feel a little uncomfortable. It seemed to him, as he listened to Anthony, that most of the theories he had formed with regard to the case were going by the board. Indeed, were almost at vanishing point. Anthony continued.

"Now what does Playfair tell us? Not only that he was warned, but in his case certain direct and violent action was taken against him."

MacMorran appeared about to disagree. Anthony saw his point. "Well—if not actually against him, against his property and sufficiently intimate to him as to be undeniably unpleasant. Notice the difference in technique here, Andrew? With Playfair, the action antagonistic almost approximates that of the authentic gangster. But scarcely so in any of the other examples. The others are but hintings at the dreadful. With Angus—'it *might* have been a knife.' With Curte there was nothing beyond the insertion of a card in his pocket. With Garnett and Miss Kingsley there were harmless alarm clocks secreted in their belongings which '*might* have been bombs.' With Dean Langton, 'phoney' cigars were foisted on him, but he was advised 'not to smoke them but to put them on the fire.' But with Capt. Playfair, once of the British Intelligence Service, part of his garden is actually destroyed by fire."

Anthony sprang to his feet. "Frankly, Andrew, I'm worried to hell about it all. I've a strong idea that we're just running round in circles. That, as I've said before, we're missing and we keep on missing something essentially vital. Now tell me this, Andrew, is it possible that all those various contacts which we have just discussed could have been effected by the same person?"

"I think it is. I considered that point myself. There were days interval between them in several instances."

"So that all the jobs could have been done by one man?"

"I think so. Or woman. Indeed, I'm sure they could."

"That's worth noting, then."

MacMorran seemed to grow suddenly moody. "What's the trouble, Andrew?" asked Anthony.

"No trouble exactly, but I was thinking that none of this was getting us any nearer the Mrs. Clinton end of the business. Besides the deaths of Denver and Mrs. Ramage we've got to remember that Mrs. Clinton was murdered as well. Seems to me that we're apt to omit that part of it from most of our calculations."

Anthony shook his head. "I'm not forgetting it, Andrew—believe me. It's when I think of Mrs. Clinton that I'm much more inclined to the acceptance of Playfair's story. Which, if you like, co-ordinates the Wenzel incident. Do you get my meaning?"

Andrew MacMorran nodded. "Yes. I get that part of it." Anthony went back to his chair again. A silence of some minutes ensued. Then Anthony sat bolt upright in his chair. "Andrew," he cried, "check me up on something."

"What's that, Mr. Bathurst?"

"Didn't Mrs. Warren Clinton come over from the States on the *Myrobella*?"

"Ay! I believe she did."

"And didn't I read somewhere that a famous film star travelled on the *Myrobella* with her?"

"You did that. I've already had words with one of the journalists Mrs. Clinton gave an interview to, soon after she landed in this country. I made it my business to find out all I could about her. As a matter of fact and if you want to know, the famous Anne Assheton is the lass you're thinking of at this moment." MacMorran wagged his head with wise emphasis. "Yes, it was no less a person than Anne Assheton herself who travelled with her. But why do you ask me this? What is it that's worryin' you now?"

Anthony turned to him with a slow benign smile. "Bless your heart, Andrew. I'm not worrying, Andrew, far from it. All I've done is to make up my mind about something."

"What have you made up your mind about?"

"Why—this. That I'm going to call on the incomparable Anne Assheton. I've an idea that she may be able to pass on some very valuable information."

"In addition to being," supplemented the Inspector, "the widow of the late Wilfred Denver."

"Exactly," replied Mr. Bathurst.

IV

Anthony Bathurst found Miss Assheton at her cottage in the West Country. That is to say, when he called he first of all had conversation with her maid, who told him her mistress was out.

The maid added, and as a result of the addition his waning spirits soared, that if he cared to come in and wait, Miss Assheton would be back shortly. Anthony went in. The maid deposited him in a living-room which had all the outward and visible signs of grace and charm. Anthony waited. After a matter of ten minutes Miss Assheton came in to him. With an economy of movement she rid herself of her close-fitting hat and coat.

Anthony rose from his chair to greet her. He saw a slim, elegant figure with gloriously dark blue eyes set in a rather small face. Her skin was cold and clean and clear and in the face there showed unusual beauty, strength of character and the steadfast gaze of dynamic personality. Her body was straight and slender and slim as she advanced towards him with the hint of a welcoming smile. She said simply: "Mr. Bathurst, I understand? Now, do you know I'm much more than pleased to meet you."

And the moment that she had said that Anthony realized that her voice was as attractive as her appearance. At the same time he was conscious of receiving a definite impression that she seemed to be slightly on the defensive. On the whole he was not surprised at this. He had usually found women of her type like this. Anne Assheton looked at her watch.

"I'm so terribly sorry to have kept you waiting." She spoke again. All this before Anthony had said a word to her.

"There's no need to apologize, Miss Assheton," he replied quietly. "Any apologizing that is called for, strictly speaking, should come from me, not from you."

"Sit down again, please." She waved him airily to a chair.

He took advantage of the offer. Anne seated herself opposite to him.

"Now tell me, Mr. Bathurst, I'm simply dying of curiosity—what is it you've come to see me about? Wilfred?" Her voice faltered a little.

Anthony shook his head. "Not altogether. In a way—perhaps. But not directly."

She pushed a small gold cigarette-case over to him. "Please smoke, Mr. Bathurst. Then I can join you without a twinge of conscience."

Anthony's eyebrows questioned the last statement. "Yes," she continued with another of her deliciously provocative smiles, "smoking is harmful to my voice. That's the direction down which my semi-moribund conscience assails me. I'm sorry if you misunderstood." She lit a cigarette from the case which Anthony had handed back to her. "If not Wilfred—what then, Mr. Bathurst?"

"Mrs. Clinton," he answered laconically.

Anthony thought that his reply had disconcerted her. He proceeded immediately. "I understand," he said, "that you travelled with the lady when you returned from the States in the Spring, on the *Myrobella*."

Anne nodded brightly. "Yes. That's perfectly true. I did."

"Tell me, then, Miss Assheton, all that you can about the lady," said Anthony gently and persuasively.

Anne shrugged her shoulders and then went and sat in the window-seat. Anthony noticed that for a moment or so she looked away from him and out of the window. Suddenly she turned to him and he saw that once again her lips and eyes were smiling.

"In answer to your request, Mr. Bathurst, and I feel it must have been a request, I don't think that I'm in a position to tell you very much. I did see something of Mrs. Clinton on the voyage home and more than once I was profoundly grateful to her for her company. It is true also to say that she told me something of her plans. But only in a general way. To this extent. That she had inherited vast riches which she intended to devote to the cause of the Empire. That's all. She told me no more than that."

Anne became pensive. She lifted a slim foot in a beautifully fitting shoe. "I'm afraid that I rather let her in for it when we docked."

"What's the amount of the confession, Miss Assheton?" asked Anthony.

"Oh—quite meagre really. It amounts to very little. But when the Press fellows surged towards me, as they always do when I come off a boat, I stalled and put them on to Mrs. Clinton instead. Really, it was great fun. For me. But I do hope that she didn't get upset over it," Anne sighed.

"Did Mrs. Clinton ever hint to you when you were fellow-voyagers on the *Myrobella* that there were, to her knowledge, people strongly opposed to her plan?"

"No, Mr. Bathurst, I don't think so. I certainly can't remember her ever having done so."

"Did she mention any person to you by name?"

Anne looked a little bewildered. Anthony smiled. He had seen his error and could understand her difficulty. "I'm sorry, Miss Assheton," he said—"it's my fault. I didn't express myself clearly to you."

She swung her slim foot. Anthony went on. "What I should have said was this. Did Mrs. Clinton mention that she intended to get in touch with any special person when she landed on the shores of this country?"

Anne shook her head. "No. We never got as far as that point."

"Why do you think she invited your husband to the hotel at Remington?"

Anne's face was uplifted towards him like a flower. She was round-eyed. "If you knew the times that I've asked myself that question. All I can think is that she knew and had recognized his ability."

"Now it's my turn not to understand. His ability in which direction, Miss Assheton?"

"Wilfred was exceedingly well read and also had a perfectly marvellous memory," she replied. "I don't think I've ever known anyone with a better one. It's possible, I suppose, that news of this trait of his may have reached Mrs. Clinton. Somebody may have contacted her who knew of this particular flair of Wilfred's. At any rate, it's the only reason I'm able to think of."

Her voice seemed to have taken on a note of weariness.

Anthony cut in: "I infer from that, Miss Assheton, that you yourself were not responsible for the introduction? Personally, I had always considered that as the likeliest reason."

"I? Good lord—no, Mr. Bathurst. Wilfred and I weren't on such good terms that I splashed him about in my daily conversation."

Anne Assheton noticed Anthony's facial reaction to this statement. "Don't misunderstand me," she said, following it up quickly, "don't think that Wilfred and I were bad friends. Actually, we were nothing of the sort. We just agreed, as it were, to disagree. To live our own lives and carry on with our own careers. Occasionally we met each other and that was that."

She stopped and glanced at him keenly. "I hope that I've made myself clear."

"Quite clear, Miss Assheton," said Anthony in reply, "you have explained that position perfectly."

"I am so glad," murmured Anne. "I should hate you to misunderstand. Or anybody else, come to that."

"What was your impression of Mrs. Clinton—your general impression?"

"A remarkable woman," replied Anne promptly. "A woman of strong character with a fixed determination of purpose. In my opinion, Mrs. Clinton would have seen anything through which she had thought worth while to start."

"You rather surprise me," returned Anthony. "I had no idea that she appealed to you to that extent."

Anne's eyes regarded him with a rather disconcerting frigidity. "Really I don't know why you should say that, Mr. Bathurst. I can assure you that Mrs. Clinton was a woman in ten thousand. I formed a most tremendous admiration for her." She smiled at him provocatively. "Now mind, don't misunderstand me—I said 'admiration'—I didn't say 'affection'."

Anthony returned smile for smile. "I had already noted that, Miss Assheton. Now one last question of you before I retire. During the days you spent close to her, did Mrs. Clinton at any time give you the impression that she was afraid of anything? Or of anybody?"

Anne shook her head emphatically. "No. At no time. Even if she'd had cause to fear, she wouldn't have given way to it and *been* afraid. I'm absolutely positive of that."

Anthony rose to go. "Thank you, Miss Assheton, you have been most helpful. You have given me an eloquent picture of Mrs. Clinton—better, I'm convinced, than I should have obtained from anybody else, at least—in this country."

He took her outstretched hand. "Goodbye, Mr. Bathurst. I'm only too pleased to have been able to help."

V

Judiciously placed inquiries brought Anthony the information that when Mrs. Warren Clinton had gone ashore from the *Myrobella* she had given an interview to a journalist by the name of Redfern. Anthony found that this Redfern was attached to the staff of the *Morning Message* and he quickly arranged to meet Redfern at a time and place suitable to both of them. Actually—when they got down to things—Jerry Redfern agreed to come to a spot of dinner at Anthony's flat. When they came to the sweet course, Anthony, who had up to then kept off the important subject, opened out. Jerry Redfern smiled when he heard the opening.

"I guessed that was the reason you wanted to see me. Told the boys, too. Well, I'll make you an offer. When we've finished grub, I'll tell you all I can over a wine and a smoke—eh? On?"

"Certainly. Suits me down to the ground."

"That's O.K. then." Redfern grinned at his host.

Anthony kept to the bargain and waited until Emily had cleared away. He poured out a liqueur for Redfern, lit him a cigar and settled down to hear the journalist's story.

"Really," he said, "if I tell the truth, the whole truth and nothing but the truth, the boys and I were put on to Mrs. Clinton by Anne Assheton. And it was jolly sporting of her. As a matter of fact. I've met Anne several times on her various trips and we're quite good pals. Well—I followed up on it. Anne had spilt the beans that the lady was staying at Davidge's and I was lucky enough to get in there and scoop an interview out of her. True—it didn't last long— just a few minutes—but I was able to pad it well and make quite a decent news item out of it. Managed to get a 'snap' of her as well. Did myself a bit of good."

Redfern paused to knock the ash from the end of his cigar.

"Tell me your impressions, Redfern, will you? I don't quite know what I'm expecting to find—but I'm certain there's something tucked away somewhere if I can only get my fingers on it."

Redfern nodded understandingly. "I think I get you. I've had the same feeling myself when I've been after a good story. Well— Mrs. Clinton. What shall I say about her? A middle-aged woman of undeniable charm. Dressed in excellent taste, parried a devastating smile which she turned on most effectively whenever she felt like it. Which she often did. She was not a hundred per cent Yank. Born in England—so she told me. Claimed to be the fourth richest woman in the world, which cheery statement, of course, I wasn't in a position to contradict. She was distressed, she told me, at the sight of the war clouds gathering over Europe and was intending to devote her fortune to the task of dispelling them. You get the idea—the old country was the one hope left to a world in War-travail."

Anthony nodded. "Yes—so far your story tallies with other stories which have already come my way. But go on—you're doing excellently."

Redfern grinned at the compliment. "Thanks. Well now—where was I? Remember, I was only with the lady a few minutes, as I told you just now. Oh—I know. After talking about the Empire and the colonies, she mentioned Anne Assheton. I do remember that. It was an entirely natural thing to do, I suppose. Seeing that they had been companions on the voyage over. Said that Anne, although she hadn't been too fit, had been positively charming to her all the time. Gave Anne quite a testimonial—I can assure you. Anne was the bee's knees with the old girl all right, I can tell you. All the way and then some." Redfern paused again. He wrinkled his forehead as though he were endeavouring to remember something.

"She told me something else about Anne—now what was it?" He rubbed his top lip with his forefinger. "Give me a minute and it'll come to me." Suddenly his face cleared with a look of triumph. "I know. I've got it. Mrs. Clinton told me that she was dining with Anne and her husband, poor old Denver, some time in the near future. That's it."

Anthony looked surprised at the statement. "That's rather disturbing. I've always understood that Mrs. Clinton knew little about Denver. At least, I gathered as much from Miss Assheton." He thought for a minute. "How did Mrs. Clinton refer to Denver? I mean—in what exact terms?"

Redfern made no reply. His brow furrowed again.

"Can't you remember?"

"I was thinking. As far as I can remember she described him as the 'eminent Shakespearian actor.' Perhaps it was 'the famous Shakespearean actor.' It was one of the two, but I'm not quite sure which."

Anthony pondered over the answer. "I suppose you heard no more about this suggested dinner-party, did you?"

Redfern shook his head. "Well—it wouldn't have come under my notice, would it?"

Anthony smiled. "I'm sorry. I wasn't sure. I know how you fellows go after certain fragments and scraps of information, 'society gossip,' etc.—I didn't know whether you'd picked up anything more with regard to it. Still—never mind."

"You can easily check up on it," replied Redfern—"ask Anne herself."

"That's an idea. I will. Still—we'll leave it for now. It's not so important as all that. Have another Green Chartreuse?"

Redfern said he would. That it was one of his principles never to refuse a drink. Anthony supplied him. "Now what about the murders themselves? At Remington. Did you cover them for the *Message* in any way?"

"No. Sorry. Can't help you there. Not down my street—crime. You want Franklin for that. I can put you in touch—if you want me to."

"Doesn't matter. I was on it myself, as you probably know. With MacMorran and the local man, Legge."

"Didn't pick up much, did you?"

Anthony noticed that Redfern was eyeing him shrewdly. Before he could reply, Redfern had come in with a further question. "And if you have—you wouldn't pass it on, of course?"

Anthony grinned. "I don't know that I'm going to contradict you there. Although you've been extraordinarily decent to me. I can hardly—at this stage of the case—"

Redfern cut in on him. It appeared that the mood which had suddenly seized him had passed. "That's all right. Don't mind what I said. It's of no consequence at all. Forget it."

Anthony humoured him. "Have it your way, then. I understand. But there's one more question I want to ask you. You're about the only person who can give me anything like an answer. I'd rather trust your judgment in this particular direction than I would Miss Assheton's."

"Thanks for the compliment. Hope I shan't let you down—that's all."

"You weren't with Mrs. Clinton long, I know, but during the time you were with her did she strike you as a person of more than ordinary culture and erudition?"

Redfern hesitated. "In what particular direction were you—"

Anthony interrupted him. "Let me explain myself a trifle more fully. I think it will help you if I do. First of all, have you heard any of the more intimate details surrounding the actual murders at Remington?"

Redfern shook his head. "Scarcely any. That I feel can be regarded as authentic. Of course, I've heard sensational and garbled versions which are three parts wild rumour, but you don't want me to talk about them, do you?"

"No. Naturally. We have it beyond doubt that Mrs. Clinton put a sort of examination 'test' before her guests. This 'test,' as I called it, consisted of a number of distinctly unusual words. From what you saw of her and heard of her, particularly the latter, did she strike you as a woman equipped with the necessary knowledge to prepare a 'test' of that type?"

Redfern thought for a moment. "Your question isn't too easy to answer, is it? Seeing the short time I was with the lady. During which time, too, I was doing the best part of the talking. In effect, you're asking me to assess the strength and measure of Mrs. Clinton's vocabulary on an experience which lasted but a few minutes. Well—I'll try to answer it—but I'll hedge a bit on the answer. I'll say that it's possible for Mrs. Clinton to have had the required knowledge, but from my experience of her, gained in that interview, not very probable. There you are—that's the best I can do for you, Bathurst."

Anthony noted the terms of Redfern's reply. He had answered and yet not answered the question. Anthony decided to halt at this stage for the time being. He offered Redfern another cigar, which the journalist accepted with alacrity. He then let Redfern see clearly that his inquiries were over for that particular evening and diverted the conversation into many varied channels. He discovered that

Redfern was intensely interested in *hara-kiri* as practised by the Japanese. Redfern pointed out that it was also known as 'Happy Dispatch' and informed Anthony that the first recorded instance of the occurrence was that of Tametoms, the brother of Sutoku, an ex-Emperor of the twelfth century. Anthony listened to Redfern with the maximum of attention. So much so that the clock on the mantelpiece chimed the hour of midnight before either of them had realized how late it was.

"By Jove," said Anthony, "twelve o'clock."

"Yes," replied Redfern with a start—"midnight. Who'd have thought it?"

VI

Anthony Bathurst drove again to the cottage in the West Country which housed Anne Assheton. The same maid opened the same door with the same look on her face. Anthony smiled one of his best smiles and he was admitted almost instantly to the living-room in which he had sat but a few days previously.

Anne Assheton came to him eventually almost exactly as she had come before. Anthony rose from his chair to greet her. As he did so he registered the thought that Anne looked more adorable than ever, difficult though that task might well be. Her dark blue eyes opened to his and Anne exclaimed:

"Mr. Bathurst? Again? And so soon? Why am I thus honoured?"

She gave him her finger-tips. Anthony dealt with the gift. "You almost tempt me to the seas of compliment, Miss Assheton. I can think of at least a hundred reasons—and they are all to do with you."

"Much better to give me the real reason," returned Anne.

"I will. May I sit down again?"

"Of course." She motioned towards the chair which he had just vacated. "Now tell me truthfully," she said, "what brings you to see me again so soon after the previous visit? Because I am a consuming mass of violent curiosity."

"Since I saw you, Miss Assheton, I have stumbled across one rather interesting piece of news. It concerns you. That's why I have come back. To ask you about it."

Anne smiled sweetly. "And what is it, Mr. Bathurst?"

"I will tell you, Miss Assheton. When Mrs. Clinton landed from the *Myrobella* she went to an hotel where she stayed, I believe, for a few days."

Anne nodded. "That's quite right, Mr. Bathurst. I can tell you the name of the hotel. Because she herself told me on the boat that she intended to go there."

This statement of Anne's pleased Anthony. It tallied satisfactorily with the story as told by Jerry Redfern. Anne went on.

"It was Davidge's. Am I right?"

"You are, Miss Assheton. Davidge's was the hotel."

"I knew it. But go on, Mr. Bathurst—please."

"Well—Redfern, a journalist attached to the staff of the *Morning Message*, managed to interview her at this Davidge's Hotel."

Anne gurgled deliciously. "I knew that too. Because I gave him the low-down as to where Mrs. Clinton was staying."

Again, this coincided with Redfern's account. "Good. Now here's where you come in. I've seen Redfern—yesterday, as a matter of fact—and Redfern assures me that Mrs. Clinton informed him during that interview he had with her at Davidge's that she was dining with a certain two people 'in the near future.' I quote the phrase that Redfern used to me. And those two people were you and the late Mr. Denver. Now that's what I've come to ask you about, Miss Assheton. Because frankly I'm puzzled."

Anthony waited for her to reply. "But that's perfectly true, Mr. Bathurst," answered the lady. "There's nothing inaccurate about it." Anthony opened his eyes. "You and Denver did dine with Mrs. Clinton then?"

"Why—no," replied Miss Assheton, round-eyed. "The dinner didn't take place. We *were* to have dined together. At the hotel with Mrs. Clinton. Wilfred and she and I. It was all arranged. She extended the invitation to me when we were on the *Myrobella* together. But she cried it off. I was ever so disappointed. I don't know how Wilfred felt about it, but I know about my own disappointment. I was going to tell you about it when you called on me before, but you said something at a critical moment and I got side-tracked. It was on the tip of my tongue more than once, but you know what those things are—it just went."

Anthony nodded. "I understand perfectly, Miss Assheton. I'm guilty of the same thing, too often either for my liking or for my peace of mind." He paused before asking her another question. "How did Mrs. Clinton let you know with regard to her abandoned dinner party?"

Anne knitted her brows. "How do you mean, Mr. Bathurst?"

"Did she write or come to see you or 'phone you?"

"Oh—she 'phoned me."

"How long before the dinner was due to take place?"

"I shall have to think."

"Take your time, Miss Assheton."

"Let me see now. She rang me up on the morning before the evening the dinner was due. I'm almost sure of that."

"Did she give any reason for the change of plans?"

"No definite reason. As far as I remember she said that something unexpected had turned up to upset her arrangements and she just couldn't make the evening date for the dinner-party. She was full of apologies, naturally. I told her it didn't matter two hoots and that was that."

Anthony thought hard. "Did she mention your husband at all?"

Anne considered the question. "No-o—I don't think she did. But I think I said: 'You'll ring Wilfred, won't you?' and she replied that she would. I don't think that anything more was said actually."

"She wasn't apprehensive of anything?"

Anne was decisive. "As I told you before, Mrs. Clinton wasn't a woman of the apprehensive type. You can take that as an absolute certainty, Mr. Bathurst."

Anthony spoke as though he were thinking aloud. "So it's reasonable to assume that something happened to her between the Redfern interview and her 'phoning you about the dinner-party. Something 'unexpected.' That was the word used. That caused her to 'upset her arrangements.' Again, I employ the phrase she employed."

"It would appear so," commented Anne.

"It certainly would," echoed Anthony. "And I wonder what it was."

"I'd like to know," said Anne.

"You're not the only one," agreed Anthony.

Anne's eyes sparkled at him. "I don't believe I am," she countered. They were both laughing when Mr. Bathurst said his farewell.

VII

Once again Anthony discussed matters with Chief-Inspector MacMorran.

"Without a doubt, Andrew, the most baffling case I have ever encountered."

"I agree with you, Mr. Bathurst. I'm getting absolutely nowhere with it."

Anthony turned in his chair and looked at the Inspector. "My chief difficulty lies with Mrs. Warren Clinton. She had no English contacts, to speak of. Whom did she see between the time that Redfern interviewed her and the time she went to Remington?"

"I can help you there. I've followed that up. When she was at Davidge's she used to go out during the daytime, come back and dine quietly in the hotel at night. But the strange part about it all is that I can't trace a single person whom she visited or who visited her. Now you pick the bones out of that, Mr. Bathurst."

Anthony shrugged his shoulders. "I know. Take some doing, Andrew. What happened to her to break her dinner engagement with Denver and Anne Assheton? If we knew that, I've a hunch that we should have gone a long way towards solving the whole problem."

MacMorran replied with glum directness. "And how can we know? How shall we ever know? Who's going to tell us? Seeing that Mrs. C. is dead and there's nobody left who can give us a line."

"Exactly, Andrew. And that's just what I meant when I started this conversation."

He surveyed the Inspector with a look of unusual benevolence. "You have the whole business in a nutshell. Any suggestions?"

There was a considerable silence. MacMorran put his elbows on his knees and his head slumped into his hands. "Whichever way we look at the case, Mr. Bathurst, it seems to me we come up against that eternal blank wall. If we leave the Clinton murder out of it, and concentrate on the Remington murders, we don't seem to get anywhere."

"We *can't* leave the Clinton murder out of it, Andrew. That's the one thing we can't afford to do. It's the pivot of the crimes. I'm sure of it."

MacMorran nodded. "It's the important factor, I've no doubt."

"Important! I'll say it is, Andrew." Anthony rose from the corner of MacMorran's table. "Denver, Andrew! I keep on running up against Denver, the actor-fellow. Thespian of the Thespians. I could bear to know all about Wilfred Denver. Anne the incomparable tells me that he was a remarkable man."

"In what direction?" asked MacMorran dully.

"Personal ability. Much in advance of the ordinary. Well-read and marvellous memory. Thus—Anne."

"She ought to know."

"She should." Anthony waved a hand at the haze of smoke. "Interesting though, don't you think, Andrew?"

"How do you mean?"

"Well—I'm letting my thoughts stray a bit. Not a bad idea when you're stymied. Wandering sheep. Don't love the fold. Take Denver."

"We were on Denver."

"Mrs. Clinton wants certain people to do a job of work. Thus the story goes. She invites candidates. Picks 'em herself. Very carefully and slow. And lays 'em on an examination paper down below. Tennyson adjusted, Andrew! Denver's one of the candidates. We'll concede a reason. She wanted him tested because of those qualities I've just mentioned to you. Is that all in order? Does it suit your palate, Andrew?"

"Quite."

"Right then—what about Cedric Garnett with Denver, Angus, Ramage and Langton? How does Garnett fit *dans cette galère*? Sorry, Andrew. Don't get it."

MacMorran stirred uneasily. Then he smiled a wry smile. "Don't know that I do either. When it's put like that."

Anthony went back to his seat on the table. "That's the only way I can put it at the moment." He swung his legs.

MacMorran watched him. Then the Inspector had an idea. "There's one thing, you know, Mr. Bathurst. I think we're a bit inclined to forget it."

"What's that, Andrew?" Anthony gazed at him almost reprovingly. "That Mrs. C. came from the United States."

"What about it?"

"Gangsterdom," replied MacMorran curtly.

Anthony blinked. "Plus Playfair's 'Deutschland' vein?"

"Why not?"

Anthony shrugged his shoulders.

"Well—why not?" repeated the Inspector.

"You mean—"

The Inspector didn't give Anthony time to finish whatever it was he had been about to say. "That Mrs. Clinton wanted help of some kind because she had been put on the spot."

"Then she took a roundabout course and a hell of a long time to get it—that's all I can say."

MacMorran's brows drew themselves together in a heavy frown. Anthony looked at him, but did not speak for some time. MacMorran fixed his eyes on Anthony's face.

"Yes—I see what you mean."

Anthony shook his head with quick decision. "I can't take the Clinton 'tests' in the way you've just suggested, Andrew. Sorry and all that."

"Very likely. But look at it this way," MacMorran argued. "Isn't it far more probable that the reason for the murder of this woman from America, *went back* to America? Went back to the time that she spent there? What chance or opportunity did she have of making enemies over this side?"

Anthony rubbed the ridge of his jaw. "We don't know why she was killed, Andrew. Therefore, we don't know who might have been her enemies."

MacMorran waxed satirical. "Well—that's a sort of 'take away the number you first thought of' business. Instead of getting anywhere, you stay 'put'."

Anthony grinned at him. "I suppose it is in a way. Still—seriously—haven't you picked up anything from the American end?"

"Not a whisper, Mr. Bathurst. Not a breath of a whisper. Mrs. Clinton was just the widow of Warren Clinton as far as the American authorities are concerned. That—and nothing more."

"A primrose by the river's brim—eh, Andrew—and a yellow primrose at that. Well—that's too bad. Doesn't get us anywhere, does it?"

The Inspector shook his head. "It certainly does not," he replied.

Anthony became contemplative. "Strange, when you come to think of it, that not a single bird has sung a note from anywhere."

MacMorran looked at him with reproach in his eyes. "We shouldn't expect that to happen. If the 'Yard' can't get its claws in unless there's a 'squeak' coming from somewhere—well—it doesn't say much for the 'Yard'."

Anthony made a mock grimace. "It don't—do it?"

MacMorran cocked an eyebrow at him. "Seriously—though—I mean it."

"And equally seriously, Andrew—so do I."

At that moment the door of MacMorran's room opened and the Commissioner of Police entered. Anthony thought that Sir Austin looked tired and his face drawn.

"Ah, Bathurst," he said. "I heard you were here. So I came along to have a word with you. As a matter of fact, I'm rather perturbed at this lack of action in the Remington case." The Commissioner found the most comfortable seat in the room and appropriated it. "What's the real trouble, Bathurst?"

Anthony was glad of this second chance to unburden himself. He reiterated most of what he had just said to the Inspector. Sir Austin sat back in his chair. He shook his head at Anthony when the latter had finished.

"I can't accept that, Bathurst. You've had worse problems in your time than this Remington problem. By far. Candidly, I'm disappointed. You're missing something. Something that's probably staring you in the face."

"Well—you're sitting in line with me, sir. So what is it?"

The Commissioner brushed the remark on one side. "It's there all right and it's your task to see it and grasp it."

He saw the look on Anthony's face and repressed a movement of irritation. "Well," he went on as though finally closing the matter, "that's all there is to it. The clue's there and we must find it." He rose from his seat. "Well—goodbye for the present. Hope I've helped you. See you in a couple of days' time, Bathurst."

Sir Austin sailed from the room. Anthony looked at MacMorran and then at the uncompromisingly closed door. He smiled. But there was no smile on the face of the Inspector. On the contrary, there was something strongly akin to gloom.

"Not so good," remarked MacMorran, "when the old man's like that—verra definitely *not* so good."

VIII

Anthony passed quickly through the stage-door of the 'Marlowe' Theatre. It was about an hour before the time fixed for the rag to go up on the West-End production of 'A Heart in Exile.' He held his breath as he recognized the familiar signs which betokened that there was a show due to go on that evening. He walked up a dark passage which he had no doubt led directly to the stage and all the old smells came back to him from the years he had spent with the O.U.D.S. The odours of grease-paint, 'two-and-a-half,' 'three-and-a-half,' of cream, of spirit-gum, of liners, of powder and of painted scenery laid friendly siege to his nostrils and affected them as only they can. Here—close to him—they all were assembling for the evening's homage and honour. Flats, and men in shirt-sleeves, perspiring visibly, and firemen and carpenters and electricians—all of the integral parts of the painted pageant that was due to come.

From the O.P. side a man stared critically at the battens above him. "Try that amber, will you, Fred?" he cried in a thick, hoarse voice.

There came the inevitable click of the switch and the set was flooded with light. Anthony looked up to the electrician's platform and saw a man there peering fixedly in the direction of the stage. His face was pale and his eyes held a curiously strained expression. Anthony went on towards the dressing-room which was his goal for that particular evening. For the reason that he had an appointment with Lionel Rochfort and that Rochfort himself had fixed his dressing-room as the place where he could most conveniently see Mr. Bathurst. Anthony had been told that he would find the doors of the various dressing-rooms on the right of the passage and that Lionel Rochfort's room was the fifth to which he would come. He arrived outside the fifth door and knocked on it. His knock was answered immediately.

"Who's there?"

Anthony gave him the required information.

"Oh—come in, Bathurst," replied Rochfort, "come straight in. I was expecting you about this time, as a matter of fact."

Anthony responded to the invitation. Rochfort was seated in a chair at his dressing-table looking into a mirror that faced him. Anthony saw that Rochfort had already started to make-up. He was rubbing the grease into his cheeks with the tips of his fingers. All the smells that had come to Anthony when he had passed near the stage seemed to be essentially concentrated within Lionel Rochfort's dressing-room.

"Take a pew, Bathurst," said Rochfort, "and talk while I mess about with this ugly mug."

Seeing that Rochfort, in appearance at least, was very nearly the ideal *jeune premier*, he could afford to grin as he made the statement.

"Thanks," said Anthony. "I'll take you at your word. I gave you an inkling as to what I was coming about. I want to ask you a few questions concerning Wilfred Denver."

"I have a lousy little part in this show," answered Rochfort. "Cathcart's got all the fat. In fact, I don't know why I trouble to make up for it. Extraordinarily like waste of time. Despite what the critics say." He made play with his white 'liner.'

"And what do the critics say?" asked Anthony. He had accepted Rochfort's gesture. But for the time being only.

Rochfort uttered something like a snort of contempt. "That Lionel Rochfort makes an admirable foil to his brilliant colleague. My God! Can anybody tell me how anything like a foil can become admirable?" Steps came along the passage outside. A voice was heard calling. "Three-quarter hour, please. Three-quarter hour, please."

Rochfort grimaced. "All right, cock. I heard you the first time." Anthony grinned at him. Rochfort turned in his chair and smiled charmingly. "It's a great life, Bathurst—the 'profession.'"

Anthony's grin became a smile. "Once upon a time I was strongly attracted myself. Spare me the usual recriminations."

"Go on? Fact? Well, heartiest congratulations on having side-stepped it. What gave you the insistent inclination?"

"O.U.D.S."

"No! Well—I'm damned. Shouldn't have thought it of you. You don't look the type, somehow."

"Is that a compliment?"

Rochfort was inspecting his face at various mirror-angles. "If you like to take it as such. What I really meant was that you look more 'out-of-doors' than most of us do. Yes—it's a lousy life, Bathurst, but I expect if I had my time again I'd choose just the same way as I did." Rochfort picked up the 'bunny' and dabbed his face. Anthony saw that he was nearing the completion of his make-up. Mr. Bathurst coughed.

"*Re* Denver," he urged gently.

"Must I?" responded Rochfort.

Anthony made no reply.

"On what compulsion must I?" reiterated Rochfort.

"None. None at all. Merely a projection of personal goodwill towards me. I must concede that much in the preliminaries."

Rochfort was now powdering down. "You're frank—at any rate. I'll say that much for you."

"Needs must when all the circumstances drive."

Rochfort sat quietly in his seat and stared almost morosely at his reflection in the mirror. "I hate talking about Wilfred Denver," he said at length. "He's dead and gone—and he was sent to his death in a particularly foul way—which fact merely aggravates my reluctance to talk about him."

Anthony argued. "But that's also the reason why I want you to tell me certain things."

Rochfort fell to silence again. The steps sounded in the passage. "Half-hour, please. Half-hour."

"Hear that?" said Rochfort. "Time marches on."

"I know," said Anthony, "and he talks twice who talks quickly— *bis dat qui cito dat.*"

Rochfort grinned. "Persistent little fellow—aren't you?"

"I have to be. Especially with super-obstinate cusses like you."

Rochfort suddenly shrugged his shoulders. "All right. Have it your way. I'll talk. If you don't ask too much of me. What is it you're burning to know?"

"I'm afraid it's going to be a strange question. A curious question. Here it is: in what particular direction, apart from the stage itself, did Denver's ability lie?"

Rochfort looked puzzled. "You mean—"

"I mean just that and nothing more. If Denver *had* a special line of brilliance apart from any that he might have had or not, as the case may be, as an actor pure and simple, what was that line?"

Rochfort beamed at Anthony. "I get you, my lord. You've rung the bell. And I can answer the question *statim*. He was a 'whale' at 'crossword' puzzles. 'Crossword' puzzles of the most abstruse variety."

"Good. You've interested me tremendously. How good was he—at an actual assessment?"

Rochfort's answer was prompt and decisive. "In a class by himself. That is as far as the circle of *my* acquaintance goes. His background of unusual general knowledge, if I may employ the paradox, was profound. It was, really. Ask anybody who knew him and he'll tell you the same story."

"I see. That's most illuminating. Was this trait of Denver's well known?"

"That's not an easy question to answer. 'Well known,' you say. The term is relative. It must be. Now how can I answer it—and remain the perfect truth-teller?"

"Do your best," urged Anthony, "anything less will not be good enough."

"Well—within certain defined limits, I should say that it was. Certainly pretty well everybody who knew him knew about it. He'd toss off a couple of really 'sticky' 'crossword' puzzles in something like a quarter of an hour. At the same time, this knowledge of him may not have extended very far beyond his absolutely immediate circle. I feel that I should make that point clear."

The voice sounded outside again. "Quarter-hour, please. Quarter-hour, please."

Rochfort grinned with superb amiability. "Didn't know this place had an echo, did you?"

Anthony ignored the flippancy. "So that you would have backed Denver to knock-off a 'crossword' puzzle against anybody?"

"Against anybody and everybody, old son. With supreme confidence. And not only would I have backed him, I would have placed my dress-shirt on him. Than which no mortal man can say more. Have I satisfied you?"

"I think so."

"And is the information to your liking?"

"I don't find it unpalatable."

"Good." Rochfort stared into the mirror again. "I shall have to powder down again. It's on the hot side tonight, and an actor can't afford to take liberties with his grease-paint." He used the powder again. "Going in front?" he asked Anthony.

"I hadn't intended to. It's a crook play, isn't it?"

"Yes. You mean you don't want a busman's honeymoon? Still—it ain't so bad, though I ses it myself."

"I may go in front, then. A recommendation from you should be good enough."

"I'll get Cathcart to pass you out, then. He isn't on till the end of the first act. Doesn't start making-up till I've done half an hour's solid slog. Some people have all the luck. But I've told you that before. Well—cheer-o. I haven't over-long now."

The voice came again. "Beginners, please. Overture and beginners, please."

Rochfort went to his dressing-room door and opened it. "This way, Bathurst. Just along there, if you don't mind."

Anthony shook hands with him and wished him luck. "Many thanks, Rochfort."

"A pleasure, old man. Any time you want another basinful—let me know."

Anthony waited for a minute or two. He knew that in the space of a few seconds the curtain would rise on the evening performance of 'A Heart in Exile.' Should he try to find Cathcart or should he slip unobtrusively out, the way he had come, into the street? For a moment or so he pondered over the problem. He heard the opening bars from an orchestra, which seemed incredibly near at hand, as he stood there in the passage. Then he shrugged his shoulders and turned towards the exit door to the street. He would make his way home. After all, he had found out what he had come to find out.

IX

On his way back from Rochfort's dressing-room at the 'Marlowe' Theatre, Anthony formed another quick decision. Having investigated certain matters connected with Denver, he would make similar inquiries with regard to the late Angela Ramage. He therefore rang John Ramage on the 'phone and made an appointment with him for the late afternoon of the following day.

When he arrived he was at once shown into Ramage's library. Ramage himself, he thought, was looking a trifle better than on the occasion when he had interviewed him at Remington with Inspector Legge and MacMorran.

"Sit down, Bathurst," he said cordially, "and let me know what it is you want of me."

"I wanted to ask you one or two questions concerning the late Mrs. Ramage—if you can bear with me for a few moments."

John Ramage's fine face showed the incipient signs of a strong emotion, but he quickly threw them off.

"Ask me your questions and I'll do my best to answer them," he said simply.

"Thank you. Firstly—was Mrs. Ramage an expert, or anything like an expert, at crossword puzzles?"

Ramage stared at him. "Crossword puzzles?"

Anthony nodded. Ramage shook his head. "No. I can answer 'no' quite safely."

"Thank you again. That disposes of my first question, then. Here's the second. If Mrs. Ramage had a special point of distinction, or a special line of personal brilliance—in other words, an outstanding ability or quality—what was it?"

Ramage sat still and straight in his rather high-backed chair. Anthony waited patiently for his reply. When it came, Ramage spoke slowly, giving each of his words full weight.

"Didn't we discuss this before at Remington, just after my wife had been murdered?"

"Not altogether. In general terms—yes. In specific terms—no. You'll pardon me, I know, if I seem insistent on the difference."

Ramage's face suddenly cleared. "I agree. You're quite correct. I see your point. There is a difference—an undoubted difference."

"Well, then, having generously conceded me that, what would be your answer?"

"Well, my wife was an unusual woman. As I told you at Remington, she was capable and much above the average for a woman of her class even, and definitely well-informed. Er . . . exceedingly well-informed. But there's no denying the fact that her really outstanding ability was map-reading. I know only one person who can be justifiably compared with her in this direction. A major in the 'Sappers.'"

Anthony nodded. "I see. That's exactly what I wanted to know."

Ramage half-smiled. "That's good, then. I'm glad to have been able to help you. Now what else is there?"

"Before we leave that—one more question. With direct reference to Mrs. Ramage's ability for map-reading. Was this particular 'flair' of hers well known?"

Ramage knitted his brows. "Er—well known? I don't know that I quite—"

Anthony intervened brightly. "What I mean is this. Mrs. Ramage was a prominent figure. A Member of Parliament. Known to hundreds of people—beyond her own personal circle. Was this special ability of hers that you've nominated also known to the many?" Ramage nodded in understanding. "I follow you. I was a little in doubt at first as to what you meant. The answer to your question is 'yes.' I should say that it was very common knowledge. My wife was a doctor, you see, besides being a Member of Parliament."

Anthony shook his head. "I'm puzzled," he said almost with a note of despondency in his tone.

"How do you mean?"

"I'll tell you. This ability of Mrs. Ramage's you say—and certainly none should know better than you—is well known. You employed the term 'common knowledge.'"

Ramage nodded. "I have no hesitation in doing so."

"Well, then, look at it like this. Mrs. Warren Clinton, when she interrogates Mrs. Ramage, asks her the very question which on that showing was the very one she did not need to ask her. I don't get it. I don't get it at all."

Ramage looked startled. When he spoke, he spoke almost in a whisper. "Bathurst, I never thought of it like that. I believe you're on to something."

Anthony showed pleasure. "It's strange, isn't it? But I don't think that I have any clear conception as to what's behind it." He saw that he was taking Ramage with him. "Take your own experience at Remington as an example," Anthony continued; "in your case Mrs. Clinton asked you three questions. I think I can remember what they were. Correct me if I'm wrong. Had you ever grown chives? Were you interested in numismatics? And had you any acquaintance with the Black Forest?"

Ramage nodded his assent. "You are quite correct, Bathurst. They were the three questions the lady asked me."

"I thought so. And you were compelled to answer 'no' to two of them."

"Quite right."

"Well—there you are. Observe the astonishing difference in the lady's technique. She asks your wife something, not only that she can do, but at which almost all the world knows she's an expert. Again—I don't get it."

"I see your point clearly now. And neither do I."

"Crazy—isn't it, Ramage? The more closely one looks at it the more crazy it seems to be. And yet three people died. So that it must have meant something vital to somebody. There's no doubt about that. And all the time I spend on the case I seem to be running round in circles."

Suddenly he turned and asked Ramage another question. "I suppose *you* haven't been threatened in any way since the murders, have you?"

"No. Why should I be? Who would want to threaten me?"

Anthony shrugged his shoulders. "I thought it might have been that they were after you, too. Sort of 'continuation-vendetta.' But as you assure me it isn't so, I'm perfectly satisfied."

"No. Nobody seems to harbour designs on me. I don't think I should be unduly scared if they did. That is to say, now. Some months ago, perhaps, I should have thought otherwise." Ramage smiled sadly.

Then Anthony had something like a brain-wave. "It has been said," he remarked, "that everybody should know something about everything and everything about something. In other words, that every one of us should have a paramount interest in one particular matter. Would you agree?"

Ramage nodded. "Yes. I think that I can accept that. As a general proposition. But why? What's your point?"

Anthony smiled at him sympathetically. "Well—that conceded—what's yours?"

Ramage returned the smile. "I saw that coming almost immediately after I had spoken. And I suppose, bearing in mind what I have said, that I've let myself in for it and shall have to reply. Well— it won't take a lot of thinking over. My chief hobby-interest lies in the history and origin of the various livery companies. In case you shouldn't know, Bathurst, there are about ninety City companies of old standing, nearly all of which contribute freely from their own funds to charities. Chiefly in the direction of educational activities, and quite forty of them have their own 'Halls' in the City. To tell the truth, I have found a close study of them extremely interesting, and as the years have gone by my knowledge of them generally has increased considerably. I've answered you in the way you wanted, haven't I?"

"Absolutely. You've told me just what I wanted you to tell me. And is this interest of yours in the livery companies well known and generally appreciated?"

Ramage balanced a paper-knife on the tip of a finger. Then he moved his head. "Yes. I think I could truthfully say that it is. All my friends know of it and no doubt very many others."

"Yet Mrs. Warren Clinton was concerned about chives, coins and forests when she interviewed you at Remington?"

"Yes."

"Well," said Anthony, "I still don't get it."

Ramage stared at him. "Neither do I, Bathurst—and that's a fact. I'm beginning to see the line of your reasoning."

"It seems to me that I shall have to go home again and start afresh at scratch. Forget all the notions I've allowed myself to form about the case and commence again with a clear and absolutely unbiassed mind."

Ramage remained thoughtful. "I can see how you feel," he said at length. "And I can also see *why* you feel like it. As a matter of fact, you've made me think, too. Like yourself, I've been taking certain aspects of the case too much for granted. It's a mistake to do that. Like falling into a trap."

Anthony showed signs of making his departure. He held out his hand to the K.C. "Good-bye, sir, and many thanks for your kindness and patience with me."

Ramage took it and grasped it warmly. "It's a pleasure to help," he said simply. "I can only hope that I've helped you to the light and not towards a greater measure of darkness."

"No fear of that," declared Anthony, as he gathered up his hat and gloves.

"Then I am more than repaid for my trouble," responded Ramage.

X

But a few hours after his interview with John Ramage, Anthony Bathurst sat down to his self-imposed task of 'starting again.' He had determined to marshal on paper all the facts which he had so far been able to amass from the various individual interviews with the late Mrs. Warren Clinton and from the subsequent examinations by the two inspectors and himself. He listed the evidences in the same order as that in which the interviews had taken place. Which meant that he began with Sir Edward Angus.

Anthony wrote as follows: *Angus*—Did *not* produce Mrs. Clinton's letter of invitation to Remington. When questioned regarding this omission stated that he had destroyed it. The questions asked him by Mrs. Clinton all bordered on athleticism, (*a*) Was he a good shot? (*b*) An accomplished swimmer? (*c*) Able to ride a horse? (*d*) Did he understand the mechanical parts of motor-cars and tanks? Anthony considered carefully the direction of the questions. After a time he came to an inevitable conclusion. Which was this. That, taking into consideration Sir Edward's age, profession and obvious inclinations, the questions put to him were certainly not well chosen and, indeed, approximated foolishness. Anthony made suitable notes against Sir Edward's name and followed on with 'Curte.'

Curte *produced* the letter of invitation. The questions put to him were 'mixed' in type, (*a*) Could he row a boat? (*b*) Had he any knowledge of jiu-jitsu? and (*c*) was he a fluent speaker of German? Two of the questions on the athletic side and one academic. As with the case of Sir Edward Angus, Anthony considered the trend of the questions. On the whole, after due deliberation, he regarded them as reasonable and intelligent. Different, for example, from the technique distinguishing those put to Angus. Anthony thereupon started two categories. 'A'—'Proper,' and 'B'—'Irrelevant.' He placed Curte in the former and Sir Edward Angus in the latter.

Next on the list came 'Garnett.' Garnett *produced* Mrs. Clinton's letter to him. The questions she put to him were: (*a*) Could he pilot a plane? (*b*) Could he play a musical instrument? (*c*) Had he any knowledge of curling and ski-ing? and (*d*) Did he know anything about safe combinations? Here Anthony considered that he had found a difficulty. Like Curte's questions, they were a 'mixed bag.' Anthony analysed them with scrupulous care. Eventually he decided that, in the main, bearing in mind what he knew and had seen of Garnett in person, they might reasonably be classed as 'proper.' Garnett, therefore, he placed in Category 'A.'

This brought him to Rosamund Kingsley. Anthony remembered the interview with her. He recalled her physical appeal and the quality she carried about her. And of how he had associated her with Olaf, Eric and Thorvald. Miss Kingsley *had* produced the letter of invitation. The questions she had been asked were—Anthony searched his notes. After a few seconds' fruitless investigation he realized that he had been guilty of an almost unpardonable piece of carelessness. Neither he nor MacMorran had questioned Rosamund Kingsley with regard to them. And Legge had failed to remedy the omission. Anthony felt supremely annoyed with himself. He tried to remember how he could have slipped up on such a vital point. He endeavoured to recall the conversational run and sequence of the Kingsley interview. He remembered asking her about the various words of the test and her reference to 'etymological monstrosities,' and he remembered, too, that it had been right on his tongue to question her in relation to what had occurred between Mrs. Clinton and her at the personal interview. MacMorran or Legge—he fancied it had been the Scotland Yard inspector—had butted in then with a question about the bedroom she had occupied. And he, Anthony, had allowed himself to be side-tracked. Well—it was useless crying over spilt milk—he would have to remedy the omission as soon as conveniently possible.

After Rosamund Kingsley came Langton, Dean of Mannington. The Dean had *not* produced Mrs. Clinton's original letter of invitation. The reason given by him had been that he hadn't brought it with him to the interview with the police authorities. Hadn't realized probably that they would ask for it. Anthony noted these facts. The question Mrs. Clinton had put to him had been if he had ever played hockey and, as far as Anthony could remember, this was the only question which Dean Langton had mentioned. Again, as before, Anthony considered it as he had considered the others. With the utmost care. Finally, remembering the extraordinary physical prowess of the onetime Bishop of London, Doctor Winnington Ingram, Anthony decided that Mrs. Clinton's question was a reasonable one, and that therefore Dean Langton could well be placed in Category 'A.'

This brought Anthony to consideration of Playfair, the ex-British Secret Service Agent. Playfair *had* produced the letter from Mrs. Clinton. The questions she had asked him had been: (*a*) Had he any experience as a 'parachutist'? (*b*) Had he ever bred canaries? and (*c*) Had he ever studied the causes of sleeping-sickness? Anthony fell that a study of these was going to give him something of a headache. For one thing, they were once more of the 'mixed' or contradictory type. After most careful analysis and dissection, and bearing in mind Playfair's negative replies, Anthony decided that the questions, considering Playfair's antecedents, were more unreasonable than reasonable, and somewhat reluctantly he felt compelled to place Playfair in Category 'B.'

The only name that now remained for consideration was that of John Ramage. Anthony had seen Ramage but a few hours previously, and everything about him was entirely fresh in his mind. Ramage, therefore, was allotted to Category 'B.' Angela Ramage, as a victim, did not concern Anthony from the point of view of his present analysis and of Denver's questions he had no knowledge.

Anthony now decided to summarize his findings. First of all he dealt with the categories. Short of Rosamund Kingsley, there were six names to be allocated. In Class 'A' he had Lord Esmond Curte, Cedric Garnett and Dean Langton. In the 'B' category he found Sir Edward Angus, Ronald Playfair and John Ramage. There was one thing, he ruefully admitted to himself, the ultimate inclusion of Miss Kingsley would give a balance one way or the other. Langton and Angus, one in each list, had been the only two unable to produce the original Clinton letter. He was on the point of adding a note when his telephone bell rang. He picked up the receiver and found that MacMorran himself was at the other end.

"*Re* Otto Wenzel," said the Inspector, "and the beautiful Elsa. I can get no trace of them out of the most exhaustive inquiries throughout the Midlands. If they are up there anywhere it's a thousand to one that they're living under a different name. Not so good, is it, Mr. Bathurst?"

"It's on all-fours with everything else of this wretched case, Andrew. Whichever way I turn I seem to run up against an impassable barrier. Still—I think I can tell you one thing."

"What's that?" came back the Inspector like the crack of a whip.

Anthony grinned to himself at MacMorran's eagerness. "Just this, Andrew. That the guilty person's one of four people."

"How do you make that out?" demanded MacMorran.

"From much perspiration, Andrew, and I fear but little inspiration." MacMorran almost heard Anthony sigh. The Inspector resolved to come to closer grips.

"Who are the four people, Mr. Bathurst?"

This time MacMorran distinctly heard Anthony chuckle at the other end of the telephone. "I can't even tell you that, Andrew. All I can say is that the one name of which I'm certain is that of Rosamund Kingsley. In fact, I hope to have a few very vital words with her at the earliest opportunity. Cheero, Andrew. Keep smiling. We've groped in the dark before now and found the light eventually. Let's hope it will turn out like that this time. All the best."

Anthony replaced the receiver. He would call on Rosamund Kingsley in the morning.

XI

Anthony drove to Chislehurst, whenever and wherever he could, with a fierce speed. His annoyance with himself had, in all probability, contributed to this. When his car reached the house, the faithful Rhoda it was who took his card and carried it to her mistress. Rosamund Kingsley tip-tilted her nose and examined it critically.

"I've seen him before, Rhoda. At Remington. What on earth does he want with me again?"

"That he'll tell you. You may be sure that he won't tell me." Rhoda was gloomily severe.

"All right," said Rosamund, with a shrug of her shapely shoulders. "I suppose you'd better show the man in. Give me a couple of minutes to approximate my best."

Rhoda smiled her own slow, sapient smile. "Very well, Miss Rosamund. I'll give you the two minutes all right. With one or two over, I expect."

"I'll be in the lounge, Rhoda. So that you'll know where to bring him."

"Very good, Miss Rosamund."

Within the appointed time, Anthony Bathurst was ushered by Rhoda into Rosamund Kingsley's lounge. "Mr. Bathurst," announced the imperturbable Rhoda.

Anthony saw the Kingsley blue eyes again. He commenced with an apology.

"Miss Kingsley, please believe me when I tell you how sorry I am to trouble you again. You doubtless remember that we met at Remington."

Rosamund thought instantly of the letter she had received signed 'Heil Hitler!' and of what it had warned. For some strange reason which she couldn't have explained she felt that she must be on her guard. She must make sure that she answered no questions in a manner that would mean entrapping herself. She contented herself, therefore, with nodding to her visitor and saying: "Oh, yes—of course—I remember you perfectly."

Anthony Bathurst smiled at her engagingly. "That's very nice of you, I need hardly say how well I remember you."

"Thank you," she replied. Anthony was not slow to observe the curtness. He continued on his course of explanation.

"I have come to Chislehurst today, Miss Kingsley, to repair an omission. An important omission."

Miss Kingsley raised her eyebrows. "Indeed—and what is the omission—may I ask?"

"I shall be happy to tell you. You will remember that at Remington you were good enough to give me and the two police inspectors who were with me certain items of valuable information."

Rosamund Kingsley frowned. "I should prefer to be more exact. I don't know that I *gave* you any information. I should say rather that it was extracted from me."

"*Hardly,*" rejoined Anthony, still smiling.

"Well," replied the lady, "almost."

"Was it as bad as that?"

"Perhaps not—seeing that you're so persistent. But tell me about this alleged omission—please."

"That's what I want to do. On the night that Mrs. Clinton entertained you at Remington, and after the 'word-test' which she inflicted on you, I believe I'm right in saying that she interviewed you one by one." Anthony paused interrogatively.

Miss Kingsley nodded. "Yes. You are quite right. She did."

"Good. And judging by the accounts which have come to us of similar interviews, she asked you certain questions." Again Anthony paused—a question in his eyes.

Without the slightest hesitation Miss Kingsley gave him a second assent. "Yes. You are still right. She did."

"Good again. Now will you be good enough to tell me, Miss Kingsley, what forms these questions took?"

Rosamund Kingsley thought hard over the request. Her mind was still harking back to the 'Heil Hitler' letter. As far as she could remember it had contained no mention of these particular questions. She decided to hesitate no longer. «

"During the interview I had with her, Mrs. Clinton asked me three questions. I will tell you what they were. On the whole I thought they were rather amusing. The first was, 'Could I state the amount of the National Debt at the outbreak of the South African war?' The second, 'Could I give the names of the eight horses of Helios?' And the other, 'Was I able to play chess?'"

While she was speaking Anthony made suitable notes. "And what were your answers to those three questions, Miss Kingsley?"

"Does it matter very much?" She furrowed her brows.

"It would help me, I think, if I knew."

"Would help you in what—or to what? I don't think that I understand."

"To perhaps a clearer understanding of a most remarkable case—and after that, as a logical sequence, towards the administration of justice."

Rosamund Kingsley regarded him slightly contemptuously. "I wonder," she said aloud.

"Give me the benefit of any doubt you may harbour. That's all I ask of you." Again Anthony Bathurst smiled. This time his effort was successful. A companion smile played round the corners of Miss Kingsley's mouth.

"All right. You shall have the answers that you want. I did *not* know the amount of the National Debt. I did *not* know the name of a single one of the eight horses of Helios. But the third question did not find me wanting. I am able to play chess. Not terrifically cleverly—but quite a useful game. There—now you know all you want to know."

"Thank you very much, Miss Kingsley. I'm trebly your debtor. I suppose you've had no further trouble?"

She arched her brows questioningly. "In what particular direction?"

"Following the 'warning' you had a little time ago. When you consulted Inspector MacMorran." Anthony thought that her face cleared.

"Oh—you mean with regard to that wretched alarm-clock business. No—nothing more has happened. To tell the truth, I'm most annoyed with myself over that incident. I'm afraid I cut a rather inglorious figure. If Rhoda—that's my maid that let you in today—mentions it to me, I go for her up hill and down dale. In fact, she knows better now than to refer to it. Even in the most casual terms."

Anthony rose. "I expect we've all of us got something to reproach ourselves over, Miss Kingsley—if the truth be known. Well—I think I'll be off. There's no point in my staying any longer—and crowds of thanks, again."

Miss Kingsley extended an eminently business-like looking hand. Anthony grasped it. "Goodbye, Mr. Bathurst. I hope that you won't have to bother me again. I'm jealous of my time—if you only knew." On the way back to town Anthony considered the implications of the visit. In which category was he to place Rosamund Kingsley? He thought over Mrs. Warren Clinton's three questions and the three answers that had been forthcoming. It didn't take him long to place Miss Kingsley. He summed the questions up as definitely 'irrelevant' and cast the lady into Category 'B.' He now had companioned Playfair, Angus, Ramage and Miss Kingsley. His thoughts dwelt upon and played round these four names. Almost idly he noticed that the four initials made a word—'Park.' Having reached thus far, his thoughts revolved rapidly. Ideas crowded in upon him. His fingers itched for pencil and paper. He was keen to try an experiment. Directly he returned to his flat he would get right down to a job that he now saw right in front of him. He found himself wondering why he hadn't thought on these lines before. Anthony trod on the juice. The powerful car swept on towards London. Again Anthony drove swiftly and fiercely.

XII

Anthony Bathurst sat down for the second time within a space of thirty-six hours to perform another operation in analysis. For one thing he had altered his mind. Now that he had been enabled to 'separate' Mrs. Clinton's guests into 'groups' from the point of view of one particular angle, he felt that he must examine again with scrupulous care the aspect of what he described to himself as 'the veiled threats' before he tried the idea which had filled his mind on the journey back from Chislehurst. Firstly, he placed on record in front of him the names in the two groups of separation. In Category 'A' he had Curte, Garnett and Dean Langton. In the other, Playfair, Angus, Ramage and Miss Kingsley, as he had so recently determined. From that point Anthony now set out to adventure further.

He decided on this occasion to consider the various people in the order of the groupings which he himself had now given to them. The case of Lord Esmond Curte, therefore, came up first for this consideration. Anthony referred to the notes he had made in a consultation with MacMorran of the different threats which had been levelled against the Mrs. Clinton 'party personnel.' The notes with regard to Curte were more voluminous than most of the others. Anthony dissected them. There was the reference to the aeroplane before the incipient murmurings of the menace itself. Within the menace was the entanglement of Capt. Maitland, Curte's pilot. Maitland must not admit, if questioned by the authorities, that he had seen Sir Edward Angus's chauffeur. Anthony began to feel more puzzled than ever. There was no pattern in any of it, as he had complained before to Andrew MacMorran. The whole business was 'crazy' and seemingly opposed to all the natural functions and operations of intelligence. Anthony set his teeth and determined to make sense of it.

He went on with his task. To the *execution* of the veiled threat. A card had been placed in the breast-pocket of Curte's evening-dress. Ostensibly during the ball which Curte had attended in Nottingham that evening. Nothing tangible there, Anthony concluded. He began to assemble a second section of 'groupings' which he marked 'A' 'True,' and 'B' 'False.' Curte, after but a few seconds' consideration, was placed in the latter of these groups. When he compared his decision with his first scheme of separation Anthony shook his head. He felt another tinge of annoyance. Things were certainly not going as he would have wanted.

The subject of his next study was Cedric Garnett. Anthony went to his notes again. Garnett was threatened not to speak of what he had done at Remington before the arrival of Mrs. Warren Clinton. Anthony looked for MacMorran's examination of Garnett on this particular line of inquiry. Garnett's reply had been: 'I haven't the slightest remembrance of having done anything that wasn't absolutely normal and commonplace during the time between my arrival at the hotel and the arrival of the American woman.' Anthony pondered over the reply. He decided eventually that he could find no fault with it. As in the case of Curte, he now turned to the actual fulfilment of the threat. An alarm-clock placed in his cricket-bag. An alarm-clock that 'might have been a bomb.' Just as the card in Curte's pocket 'might have been a knife' in his back. But after all, and thus Anthony's judgment, an alarm-clock is not a bomb, and Cedric Garnett's menace went into Group No. 2 to take its place alongside Curte's. Again Anthony shook his head. Progress was still certainly slow.

He now had to deal with Dean Langton. The threat that had been levelled against the Dean had been that silence had been enjoined upon him with regard to his interpretation of the word 'Reldresal.' Anthony frowned. More craziness. No pattern at all. What had been the practical application of the threat? Anthony referred to his notes again. The Dean had stated that the word 'Reldresal' was unfamiliar to him and that he failed to answer the question. Subsequently he had found five cigars in his cigar-case which he felt certain were not his own. That is to say, the Dean is positive that his cigar-case had been tampered with. Having become in this way suspicious, the Dean states that he immediately decided that he wouldn't smoke the substituted cigars in any circumstances, so he went with them into the kitchen of his house and threw them into the boiler. Directly he had done this he was aware of a strong smell of bitter almonds. Anthony put down his fountain pen and thought hard. With regard to the execution of Dean Langton's threat there *might* have been something definitely lethal. Anthony came to the decision to place Langton's threat in Class 'A.' Which meant, summing up, that Langton's was the only case which fell consistently in the first grouping. He now had the first section of Category 'B' to investigate.

Firstly—Capt. Playfair. Playfair was to maintain a discreet silence and to take especial care to avoid all reference to the figure that hid behind the clock in the hotel on the evening of the murders. Anthony went carefully to MacMorran's notes and his own recorded account of Playfair's interview with him. 'I saw no figure conceal himself or herself behind the clock, and I haven't the foggiest idea what is meant by the allusion.' Still more craziness. And a further blurring of the pattern. Now for the tangible nature of the threat when put into execution. Part of the garden, reasonably close to his house, had been destroyed by fire. Anthony remembered Playfair's emotion when he had told him the story. With no further hesitation Anthony placed the Playfair threat very confidently in Group 'A.' Yet mother instance of a misfit.

Angus came next in order. Now the letter to Angus had been different from practically all the others. The terms of the threat had been general. Nothing had been mentioned of a specific nature. Neither Sir Edward Angus himself nor his chauffeur was to give any information if asked for it. The carrying out of the threat had been the placing of a box of 'Swan Vestas' in his pocket. Anthony wasted little time on Sir Edward Angus, and placed his threat without further consideration into the grouping of Category 'B.' Here was a second tribute to consistency. Anthony felt a slight sense of gratification as he turned to the next name, John Ramage.

Then he remembered that Ramage had not been threatened at all and that, therefore, he would have to be excluded from this second essay in grouping. Anthony thought again on this 'difference' with regard to Ramage. There was no doubt in his mind that if Ramage had been guilty he would have arranged to be the recipient of a 'greeting' just as all the others had been. Anthony now faced the last name of all to be considered. That of Rosamund Kingsley, whom he had so recently interviewed. Anthony made a further reference to his notes.

Miss Kingsley had been warned to be silent with regard to the 'incident which had occurred' on the journey down. Here at last, thought Anthony, was something moderately tangible. Anthony was inordinately curious as to what this incident had been. He went carefully through MacMorran's typed observations. Miss Kingsley *loquitur*: 'on the way down to Remington I stopped and pulled in so that I might smoke a cigarette. When I had finished this and was on the point of resuming my journey a car flashed by me, nearly grazing my off mud-guard. I noticed that it was a "Bentley," and to tell the truth it put the wind up me a little. In addition to making me uncomfortably hot under the collar. But nothing happened. No harm was done to either of us in any shape or form. The whole thing took only a second. Actually, Inspector, I shouldn't have given the incident a second thought, but for your question of a few minutes ago. When you asked me if anything had happened to me on the way down. I thought of it because, quite frankly, there was absolutely nothing else I *could* think of.' Anthony pulled at his top lip. Then, as his eyes went to the notes again, he caught sight of something else to interest him. The name of Cedric Garnett. MacMorran had evidently done an exercise in 'following up.' Anthony read on. MacMorran *loquitur*: 'I made inquiries with regard to Miss Kingsley's story, and I am pretty certain that the "Bentley" of which she complained to me had been driven down to Remington by another member of the Clinton party—namely, Cedric Garnett. Garnett most certainly journeyed to Remington in a "Bentley," and from a few feelers I put out, quite unbeknown to him, went the same road as Miss Kingsley took. Ultimately I decided that I could find nothing untoward with regard to the incident, and dismissed it as no more than yet another example of careless driving.' Anthony smiled to himself as he read MacMorran's comments. But the smile was short-lived. Anthony realized with strong misgiving and some despondency that his progress had been but trivial. He turned to the examination of the threat against Miss Kingsley as regards its execution. 'Another alarm-clock delivered to her home at Chislehurst by a man who seemed to be acting in the capacity of a messenger. Miss Kingsley was not alone when the affair occurred, and her story was corroborated in every detail by Rhoda Flowers, Miss Kingsley's maid.' Strange coincidence, thought Anthony. 'Alarm-clocks for both Garnett and Miss Kingsley. For nobody else.' Therefore, if Garnett's threat had gone into Category 'B,' Rosamund Kingsley's must be treated similarly. Which meant that from the entire exercise there emerged but one case which Anthony had been able to place from *each* of the two angles which he had considered, in Group 'A,' because it satisfied the demands of both intelligence and truth. This had been Dean Langton. The remaining 'consistencies' were Angus and Miss Kingsley, whose names appeared in the 'B' compartment on each occasion.

Anthony pushed back his chair. The case was ill-starred. Langton! Had the name been any one of three others he wouldn't have been surprised. But Langton's was a name he had not considered. Anthony sat silent for some minutes. Then, with a shrugged shoulder, he resolved that he would go straight on with the other task he had promised himself. The attack on the words of Mrs. Warren Clinton. Anthony found fresh sheets of paper and began again.

PART FIVE
THE WORDS

I

To BEGIN with he listed the words in the order that he remembered them. His memory, always excellent, was fully equal to the task. 1, Orpheus; 2, Iphicles; 3, Eagle (two-headed); 4, Edyrn; 5, Ulema; 6, Roup; 7, Reldresal; 8, Mazikeen; 9, Premonstatensian. Nine words, thought Anthony. Nine words for nine guests. One word per guest. Mrs. Warren Clinton had evidently a penchant for the figure 9. He noticed that by a fortuitous trick of memory he had listed first the words which began with vowels. He began to play with the initials, commencing with the O for Orpheus. Nothing appeared to him to fit until he tried 'Orpheus, Ulema and Roup.' Much to his satisfaction and delight he found that by using these initials he now had the word 'our.'

Anthony began to rub his hands. He thought that he might well be on the track of something, so he began to arrange the letters of the words which were left to him. These were Iphicles, Eagle (two-headed), Edyrn, Reldresal, Mazikeen and Premonstratensian. Which meant that he needed a word of six letters to prove that his idea was correct. His next step was to collect the initials, I.E.E.R.M.P., and the moment that he put them down in front of him his eyes caught and held the solution. The word contained here was obviously 'Empire,' and the whole arrangement—'Our Empire.' Anthony sat back satisfied. Pattern and fitness at last! Also—the phrase was entirely in keeping with what he had heard of the character of Mrs. Warren Clinton. She had written her various letters of invitation stressing the point in every instance that the salvation of the British Empire was the treasure of her heart and one of her main objects in life. Anthony felt a glow of gratification. He had proved to his own satisfaction that the nine 'test' words had been chosen simply to produce from their initials the words 'OUR EMPIRE.'

There now remained the other side of the Clinton word-picture. Each word, according to Mrs. Clinton's fertile brain, had a counterpart meaning which it had been the task of the competing candidates to find. Anthony, a grim smile playing round his lips, buckled to his work. He took it that the lady had meant by 'counterpart' an affinity of meaning. The first word to be tackled, obviously, was 'Orpheus.' Anthony furrowed his brow. A word of this kind might have a dozen counterpart meanings. His job would be to find the right one—according to the gospel of Mrs. Warren Clinton. Anthony began to see that the job was going to be the reverse of easy. After a few minutes' intensive thinking he came to the conclusion that the best thing he could do in the circumstances would be to list, say, three words, in each case, which more or less filled the picture, and then, having collected the words in this way, embark on a process of elimination afterwards. Anthony ran his fingers through his hair. He realized that he was going to need no small measure of good luck to construct the edifice of his intention. Unless, of course, some of the words to be considered later had but *one* counterpart which could be considered reasonable.

He concentrated on 'Orpheus.' If necessary, he was prepared to make the lock fit the key. Against 'Orpheus' he wrote unhesitatingly 'Eurydice.' The other two words which he wanted did not come to his brain anything like easily. He thought of Milton's lines from both 'L'Allegro' and 'Lycidas,' and then, discarding 'Pluto,' 'Hebrus' and 'Lesbos,' he decided on 'Thracian' and 'Music.' So that he now had opposite to 'Orpheus'—'Eurydice,' 'Thracian' and 'Music.'

'Ulema' was the next word. Not too sure of its exact meaning, Anthony turned it up. 'The learned classes in Mohammedan countries and interpreters of the Koran and the law.' He noted that it was not an ecclesiastical body and that the name really signified 'a number of wise men' under the presidency of the Sheikh-ul-Islam. Anthony chose his three words and wrote them down opposite to 'Ulema.' 'Wise,' 'Koran,' 'Interpreters.' 'Take care of the vowels,' he murmured to himself, 'and the consonants will take care of themselves.'

He next considered 'Roup.' At the back of his mind he had an idea that this was a word of Scandinavian origin which meant something like a 'shout.' As in the case of 'Ulema,' he looked it up in his dictionary. He was gratified to find that he was correct within limits, that the word's essential meaning was 'auction,' and that it was used in Scotland in this sense. Anthony wrote down carefully, therefore, 'Scandinavian,' 'Shout,' 'Auction.' 'And yet another vowel,' he whispered to himself; 'it's not going too badly after all—if you ask me.'

The next word to receive his attention was 'Eagle (two-headed).' Anthony carefully observed the brackets. The particular variety of bird was evidently relevant. Anthony racked his brain for what he could remember of the history of the 'two-headed eagle.' The German eagle had its head turned to the left hand, the Roman eagle to the right. When Charlemagne was made Kaiser of the Holy Roman Empire he joined the two heads together, one looking to the east, the other to the west. As a result of this, the late Austrian Empire, as the direct successor of the Holy Roman Empire, included the "Double-headed" Eagle in its coat of arms.' So far so good, thought Anthony. Now what else was there for him to remember? Something to do with Russia he felt moderately certain. Who was the man of whom he was thinking? Suddenly the correct answer came his way. Ivan Vasilievitch had assumed the two-headed eagle when he had married Sophia, daughter of Thomas Palaeologus and niece of one of the Constantines, an Emperor of Byzantium. The two heads thus symbolized the Eastern or Byzantine Empire and the Western or Roman Empire. After careful thought and some degree of head-shaking, Anthony selected 'Empires,' 'Charlemagne' and 'Vasilievitch.' But the selection in this instance was diffident and Anthony's spirits sagged a little.

'Mazikeen' came next for consideration. Anthony had an idea that the word had something to do with Jewish mythology, but he was far from certain. Research gave him the following facts. 'A species of beings in Jewish mythology, said to be the agents of magic and enchantment. According to the Talmud, when Adam fell he was excommunicated for 130 years, during which time he begat spectres and demons. There is also a Jewish tradition that a servant, whose duty it was to rouse the neighbourhood to midnight prayer, one night caught a straying ass and mounted it, thereby neglecting his duty. As he rode along, the ass grew bigger and bigger till at last it towered as high as the tallest edifice, where it left the man and where, next morning, he was found.' Anthony looked for appropriate words to select. After considerable thought he chose: 'Jewish,' 'Magician' and 'Ass.' The presence of the vowel in the gallery again, pleased him, for by this time Mr. Bathurst was more than toying with an extremely attractive idea.

He looked eagerly at the next word, after having written it down carefully. 'Premonstratensian.' Anthony shook his head. The word was unfamiliar to him. More research became necessary. This is what Anthony found. 'A Norbertine order, of Augustinians founded by St. Norbert in 1120 in the diocese of Laon in France. A spot was pointed out to him in a vision, and he called the spot "Pré Montré," or "Pratum Monstratum" (the meadow pointed out). The order possessed thirty-five monasteries in England—where they were known as the White Canons of the rule of St. Augustine—at the time of the Dissolution.' Anthony found the selection in this case considerably more difficult than in some instances previously. Eventually, after a close study, he decided on 'Order,' 'Norbert' and 'Augustinian.' And there again was the recurring 'vowel condition.'

'Iphicles' was the next to be tackled. Here was a province in which Anthony was much more at home. He remembered the famous 'tag,' *Quid hoc ad Iphicli boves?* Neleus had promised to give his daughter to Bias in marriage if he would bring him the oxen of Iphicles which were guarded by a very fierce dog. Melampus was caught in the act of stealing them and was cast into prison. He afterwards told Astyocha, the wife of Iphicles, how to become the mother of children—by steeping iron-rust in wine for ten days and then drinking it. Inasmuch as the treatment was highly effective—she became the mother of eight sons—Iphicles gave him the coveted herd and his brother married the daughter of Neleus. Anthony's three chosen words were: 'Neleus,' 'Herd' and 'Oxen.' Still the vowel. Anthony passed on—rather heartened than otherwise.

'Reldresal.' The word concerning which Dean Langton had been threatened. Of its meaning, Anthony confessed to himself, he was completely ignorant. Again he was compelled to research. When he found the meaning he smiled to himself and castigated himself for his forgetfulness. Of course—and he should have thought of it before. Dean Swift joined issue with Dean Langton! 'Reldresal,' so ran the commentary, 'was the Principal Secretary for private affairs in the court of Lilliput and became a great friend of Gulliver himself. When it was proposed that the Man-Mountain should be put to death for the crime of high treason, it was Reldresal who moved that "the traitor should have both eyes put out and be suffered to live so that he might serve the nation."' Again, thought Anthony, by no means an easy choice. Eventually, and after much weighing-up of the relevant words, he nominated for his three 'association' words: 'Gulliver,' 'Secretary' and 'Lilliput,' and wrote them down in the opposite corner to 'Reldresal.' But one word now remained for analysis. The word was 'Edyrn.'

All Anthony could recall about it was that its origin was in Tennyson's 'Idylls of the King.' Yet another case for research. Anthony turned up the word for more details and found the following information: 'Edyrn is found in Tennyson's "Marriage of Geraint," which was founded on the story of Geraint in Lady Charlotte Guest's translation of the Mabinogion. Edyrn was the son of Nudd and was known as the "Sparrowhawk." He ousted Yn'iol from his earldom and tried to win Enid, the Earl's daughter, but was overthrown by Geraint and sent to the court of King Arthur, where his whole nature was completely changed and "subdued to that gentleness which, when it weds with manhood, makes a man."' Anthony closed the book and surrendered himself to yet a further exercise in intensive thought.

At length he decided on his three words of association, and selected 'Geraint,' 'Sparrowhawk' and 'Idyll.' He was, of course, in the last instance, acutely tempted to the inclusion of the vowel. He had by this time considered all the words, and his next task was to assemble his various treble choices. He found that he had them listed thus:

1. Orpheus.	Eurydice	Thracian	Music
2. Ulema.	Wise	Koran	Interpreters
3. Roup.	Scandinavian	Shout	Auction
4. Eagle (Two-headed)	Empires	Charlemagne	Vasilievitch
5. Mazikeen.	Jewish	Magician	Ass
6. Premonstratensian.	Order	Norbert	Augustinian
7. Iphicles.	Neleus	Herd	Oxen
8. Reldresal.	Gulliver.	Secretary	Lilliput
9. Edyrn.	Geraint	Sparrowhawk	Idyll.

Anthony surveyed the list with some satisfaction. He intended now to seek a word that he termed the 'link' word. The word to fit the key. It must obviously be a word of nine letters, he thought, equalling in number those contained in the phrase, 'Our Empire.' Anthony attempted to put himself in the place of Mrs. Warren Clinton. What was her chief concern? The welfare of the Empire? No good—seven letters only. Preservation? Safety? Salvation? Ah—Anthony's nerves tingled—nine letters and a most likely word at that. In fact, considered Anthony, one of the most likely words of all. He determined to put its merits to the crucial test there and then.

Firstly he concentrated on the initial letters which were required, which appeared but once in the list he had prepared. The first was the letter 'L,' demonstrated once by 'Lilliput.' Anthony put his pen through 'Reldresal.' The second was 'V,' as given by 'Vasilievitch.' Anthony eliminated 'Eagle—Two-headed.' Then he rubbed his hands—he was beginning to get 'warm,' The third letter was 'T,' satisfied by 'Thracian,' so out went 'Orpheus.' These three letters exhausted his supplies of this kind, so he now considered what he had left. His requirements were S-A-A-I-O-N. He inspected his remnants. 'Sparrowhawk' he took from 'Edyrn,' 'Roup' and 'Mazikeen' gave him his two 'A's,' 'Ulema' yielded him his 'I,' and 'Premonstratensian' and 'Iphicles,' each containing an 'O' and an 'N,' gave him the last links for his 'key' word.

Anthony smiled to himself in satisfaction. Mrs. Clinton's test had become clear to him—'Our Empire' and 'Salvation.' But why? That problem still remained. Anthony thrust his hands into his pockets and began to pace the room. He was 'nearer' than he had been—and yet no nearer. As he had said so often before, the whole pattern of the affair seemed crazy and incoherent. And yet underlying it all there must be a reason of some kind operating, and it was his job to find it. He sat down again and thought hard. Chiefly on the death of Mrs. Warren Clinton and the failure of Dean Langton to make any answer concerning the meaning of the word 'Reldresal.'

II

Anthony went into conference again with Chief-Inspector Mac-Morran. The Inspector listened with admiration and approval to the account of Anthony's work in the research department. Anthony presented him with the full details of the lines he had worked on and what he had discovered. MacMorran produced several nods and gestures of appreciation.

"Now I call that most interesting," he said at length, "and it shows the value of a bit of book-learning. I'm not yieldin' to any-body in my admiration for education. Every man's the better for it. And every woman as well."

Anthony made no comment on this effusion. He had heard Andrew MacMorran in this strain before. He turned the conversa-tion, therefore, into another channel.

"Andrew," he said quickly, "tell me frankly. What *real* progress have we made in this case?"

"Verra little, I'm afraid," replied the Inspector, with an omin-ous shake of the head. "Certainly my people have picked up little or nothing."

"And I'm much in the same boat," returned Anthony—"that's really what I've come to talk about. There's a line, however, Andrew, that we haven't yet taken. I'm rather worried about it. I feel that we've been guilty of a certain amount of neglect. I want you to listen to me. It concerns Mrs. Warren Clinton. The lady herself."

"In what way do you mean?"

"I mean with direct reference to the last hours of that lady's life. The last days, if you prefer it." Anthony lit a cigarette.

"What about them?" MacMorran's question was both short and sharp.

"That's what I'm asking you," replied Anthony imperturbably.

MacMorran seemed to sense that he was under criticism. "Well, I've no doubt you've something in mind—but I don't know that I altogether get you."

Anthony noticed the line of the Inspector's jaw. He grinned. "Well—let's start at scratch. Tell me all you know."

"When the *Myrobella* berthed, Mrs. Clinton caught a train and went to 'Davidge's.' She stayed there for some time and then booked up at the 'Royal Sceptre,' Remington. You are well aware of what happened to her after that," concluded MacMorran with dry emphasis.

Anthony shook his head. "It hurts me more than it hurts you, Andrew," he said quietly, "but what does all that really amount to? See where I'm getting?" He pressed out the stub of his burning cigarette and lit another.

MacMorran puffed with contentment at his pipe. "Well—go on," he conceded, "I'm prepared to listen to you."

Anthony tossed away the burnt match he had been holding. "Well—what did Mrs. Clinton do while she stayed at 'Davidge's'?"

"Do?"

"Yes—do. How did she occupy her time? Where did she go? Whom did she meet? Who called on her? Can you give me any authentic information on any one of the questions?"

MacMorran paused a second before replying. "Inquiries have been made."

Anthony waited for him to amplify his statement. He made no intervention.

MacMorran continued. "But they didn't yield much. I have the details in the file here if you would care to hear them."

Anthony nodded assent to the suggestion. The Inspector took the green-coloured file and removed certain papers. Anthony gave him ample time.

"But few people called on Mrs. Clinton while she stayed at 'Davidge's.' This was understandable. She was an American visiting London for the first time for many years. She had no friends in London to speak of. And fewer, probably, acquaintances. Aren't they the likely explanations?"

Anthony shook his head again. "No, Andrew—I'm sorry. I'm not satisfied."

MacMorran showed signs of uneasiness. Anthony went on before he could reply.

"And what about her maid, Andrew? Or companion?"

MacMorran picked up this particular challenge with alacrity. "She didn't bring one. I considered that in the early stages of the case. I've examined the *Myrobella's* sailing list and it's been confirmed at the American end as well. Mrs. Clinton travelled alone."

"And she travelled farthest," commented Anthony whimsically.

MacMorran eyed him suspiciously, but made no remark.

"All right," said Anthony. "I'll accept your position with regard to Mrs. Clinton travelling solo. But let's proceed from there. With regard to one or two other points I put forward. How did Mrs. Clinton occupy her time? Where did she go? Whom did she meet? You still haven't answered those, Andrew."

MacMorran shrugged his shoulders. "I didn't have 'tabs' on her the whole time she stayed in the hotel. But all the inquiries I made were answered. I'll give you examples of what I mean. You ask how did she occupy her time? In the mornings she used to stay in the hotel and attend to her correspondence. Of an afternoon she would visit a cinema. She was heard in the hotel to say that she preferred the cinema to the theatre. In the evenings she dined alone quietly and invariably retired to bed comparatively early. There's one of your queries answered if not two of them—and answered, I venture to say, quite satisfactorily."

MacMorran was perturbed. He was beginning to roll his 'r's'—a sure sign in his case of mental disturbance.

"All right, Andrew. I'll give you that. What about the other question? Whom did she meet? What personal contacts did she make?"

MacMorran shook his head rather disconsolately. "That, I admit, I cant answer. I wasn't able to establish, that is to say enough to satisfy me, that she made any. For instance, I couldn't trace that anybody visited her at the hotel. Beyond Redfern the reporter. But as I said to you before, don't forget that she had no friends in London. She had none and she didn't appear particularly desirous of making any."

Anthony nodded. "Reversing the position, putting the boot on the other foot, can you trace that she visited anybody outside the hotel?"

Again MacMorran shook his head. "No. I wasn't able to do that. And I admit that there are too many loose ends sticking out at that side of the case to be at all pleasant. But there it is. I was unsuccessful all along the line, in that respect. They're the facts and we can't alter them."

"I agree, Andrew. But we might be able to investigate them again perhaps a trifle more fully. For instance, supposing I ask you a pertinent question?"

MacMorran smiled at the way Anthony had put it. "Well—supposing you do—what is it?"

"Quite a simple question, Andrew. Nothing elaborate. Who were her bankers?"

MacMorran looked disturbed. "Where?"

"Over here—in England. In London, if you like."

MacMorran named one of the better-known private banks. "Not one of the big five, you see," he said rather aggressively.

"Good," returned Anthony. "I'm pleased to hear it. You've taken a load off my mind telling me that. How much money did she draw during her stay at 'Davidge's'?"

A spot of colour showed in each of the Inspector's cheeks. "I couldn't answer that, Mr. Bathurst. To tell the truth I didn't attempt to find out. I don't see what bearing it has on the case. Nothing was stolen from her."

"As far as you know."

"Agreed with that. As far as I know."

"I think we'll inquire as to that, Andrew. Suppose we get on to—who are the people looking after her affairs?"

"Crabtree, Holt and Needham, Mr. Bathurst, Gray's Inn Road. I'll get them on the 'phone for you now."

The Inspector got the Exchange and dialled a number. Anthony waited. MacMorran obtained the desired connection in reasonable time.

"Ask them for information on what I just asked you. What were her drawings from current account while she stayed at 'Davidge's'?"

MacMorran nodded to signify that he understood the trend of Anthony's enquiry. He put the relevant question. "Placed to her credit, you say?"

Anthony heard the sequel question. MacMorran went on. "And exactly how much was drawn by her?" MacMorran waited for the reply. Anthony waited at MacMorran's side. "What?" came the Inspector's query. "Are you sure?"

A pause of some seconds' duration. Anthony saw MacMorran nod several times. Eventually the Inspector replaced the receiver. Anthony noticed that the blood had left his face and that he had become unnaturally pale. He sat heavily in his chair.

"I don't know what you'll think of this piece of news, Mr. Bathurst, but from the time Mrs. Clinton set foot on these shores until the day she died she drew no cash from her banking account. Not a penny. Five thousand pounds had been placed to her credit and it was untouched."

"What, then, did our lady friend use for money, Andrew?"

"According to Messrs. Crabtree, Holt and Needham, she had ample resources in cash when she landed from the *Myrobella*."

"Really! Which fact, of course, explains the point of the £5,000 credit at her bankers," remarked Anthony drily.

MacMorran looked discomfited at the thrust. "Not so good, is it?" he said rather lamely.

"On the contrary, my dear Andrew," said Anthony, "I rather like it. The idea that you have just projected suits me down to the ground. In fact, I should have been extremely disappointed to have heard anything else."

"Why? What help does it give us?"

Anthony's eyes twinkled. "It teaches us, for one thing, that Mrs. Clinton was determined to live frugally."

"What—at the 'Royal Sceptre.' Remington—where she invited no less than nine distinguished guests?" MacMorran was critical.

Anthony's eyes continued to twinkle. "Perhaps she was frugal and parsimonious at 'Davidge's,' Andrew, and extravagant at Remington."

"I don't see how you get that. Because she made no drawings whilst she was at Remington. The position, as far as she was concerned, was exactly the same in both places. No change took place in her." The Inspector seemed a trifle nettled.

"Perhaps she intended to mend her ways, Andrew, when Death took charge of things and dealt her a bad hand. In other words, if you prefer them, *La femme propose mais le Dieu dispose.*"

MacMorran shrugged his shoulders. "Well—whatever happened, I don't see where it's all getting us to," he declared impatiently.

"I do," returned Anthony crisply. "It's leading us to the discovery of the murderer of these three people. Angela Ramage, Denver and Mrs. Warren Clinton herself. Which at the present moment, my dear Andrew, is our primary job of work. Ours—yours and mine."

MacMorran relapsed into silence. Anthony's words and the point he had driven home had shaken him somewhat. The case of Mrs. Clinton had been a nuisance to him from the beginning—now it had become an intolerable nuisance. He came out of his brown study to hear Anthony's voice. MacMorran understood that Mr. Bathurst was making certain suggestions. He felt it incumbent on him to reply without hesitation.

"As to that, Mr. Bathurst," he said semi-defensively, "Mrs. Clinton's belongings at the 'Royal Sceptre' have all been carefully gone through and examined. Not an item was brought to light that caused us the slightest suspicion. She appeared to have made no acquaintances since she landed in England, and in all probability the only letters which she sent out were those of the now famous invitations. Nine in all."

"Which presumably were sent out by her from 'Davidge's' Hotel?"

"Presumably. At least—I have always supposed that they were."

"She had no secretary with her there—no stenographer. Don't forget she travelled alone."

"Quite right. I'm aware of it. She had to write all those letters herself."

Anthony seemed lost in thought. Suddenly he woke up and spoke again. "I suppose you haven't one of those invitations handy, have you, Andrew?"

MacMorran grinned with pardonable satisfaction. "I have. I made it my business to get hold of all I could—after we saw most of them at Remington. Which one do you want? Any one in particular?"

Anthony shook his head. "No. Doesn't matter." Then almost instantaneously he changed his mind. "Yes. For preference give me Dean Langton's. If my memory serves me correctly he didn't have it with him when he came to see me at Remington. Do you happen to have it, Andrew?"

MacMorran's grin broadened. "I have it all right, Mr. Bathurst. Give me half a second and I'll turn it out for you."

The Inspector went to the appropriate file. Eventually he produced the Langton invitation letter. Anthony read it quickly.

"I'd like to retain this for a day or so, Andrew, if I may. Also that copy of the *Morning Message* that I see you have there." Anthony had noticed the familiar letterpress in MacMorran's file. "I promise to let you have them both back unspoiled and unharmed by the end of the week. That a bet, Andrew?"

"That's all right as far as I'm concerned, Mr. Bathurst. I'm afraid you won't derive much information from either of those sources."

"You never know, Andrew. I'm going to put in a spot of visiting and I might run into a stroke of luck. Mind you—I only say 'might.'"

"Let's hope you do," returned MacMorran. "I don't mind confessing that the case has got me down—well and properly."

Anthony slapped him on the back. "Never mind, Andrew. Keep your chin up. We'll solve it—and more quickly than you imagine."

"I wish you meant it, Mr. Bathurst."

"Wish I meant it? My dear Andrew, I was never more serious in my life."

III

Anthony had conference with one Arthur Wellesley Sturt. Mr. Sturt, it may be mentioned, held the position of manager of 'Davidge's' Hotel. Mr. Bathurst's card had been sent up to him as he sat in his private room, and after a few minutes' frowning consideration of that card Mr. Sturt had directed that Mr. Bathurst himself should follow it. Mr. Sturt listened attentively to what Mr. Bathurst had to say.

"Mrs. Clinton's rooms here were booked by cable. Just before she left America in the *Myrobella.* When she came and all the time she stayed here she impressed me as a singularly charming lady."

Mr. Sturt closed his lips firmly and sat in his chair, rigidly determined, as it were, to keep his end up.

Anthony put another question to him. "Luggage? Oh, yes—pretty well what you might have anticipated. Neither too much nor too little. When Mrs. Clinton left here *en route* for Remington it all very naturally went with her."

Anthony was aware of this, more or less. The information coincided with what MacMorran had already indicated to him. "I see. Thank you, Mr. Sturt."

Sturt nodded his acceptance of Mr. Bathurst's gratitude. He was still an extremely dignified figure. More questions from Anthony.

"Friends? That called here?" Mr. Sturt shook his sapient head. "I can't recall a single one, Mr.—er—Bathurst. As far as I can remember, Mrs. Clinton while she remained here was unvisited." Mr. Sturt coughed portentously.

Anthony again thanked him suitably. At the next question asked him Mr. Sturt furrowed his brows.

"All accounts that were paid by Mrs. Clinton while she was here were settled promptly, and settled, too, by cash. Mrs. Clinton invariably discharged her bills in notes. To the best of my memory, she usually paid in high value notes on the Bank of England. I mean by that that she didn't use the ordinary currency notes. I trust I have made myself plain."

"Oh—perfectly. But there's another question that I feel I must ask you, Mr. Sturt. Didn't that cash arrangement strike you as peculiar?"

Mr. Sturt shrugged his shoulders. "No-o. Not so peculiar as you might imagine with no experience of running an hotel of this eminence. In many cases we refuse to accept cheques and insist on payment being made in cash."

"I quite agree. I was aware of that condition with what we may term ordinary guests. But my point was this. With a guest of the international standing of the late Mrs. Clinton, you would not have insisted on that procedure. I take it that I'm right in that idea?"

"Oh, yes. Mrs. Clinton's account was a formidable one. In amount. As a matter of fact, when she paid her account at the office she tendered something like an explanation. She pointed out to our cashier-receptionist that she had brought a considerable amount of English currency from the States and that she didn't desire to draw on her banking account until she had divested herself of most of it. I can recall our cashier mentioning the fact to me." Mr. Sturt coughed into his hand. Anthony mentally noted the terms of Mr. Sturt's answers. He put a final question to him.

"I'm afraid that this is rather a conventional question, Mr. Sturt, but I feel that I must put it to you. During Mrs. Clinton's stay here, did she ever seem at all worried or anxious about anything?"

Rather to Anthony's surprise Sturt answered readily. "I've been waiting for you to ask me that—in particular. And my answer is undoubtedly 'yes.' Especially, shall we say, during her first week here. After that first week I noticed a distinct change in her. Her anxiety seemed to be replaced by another condition. This second condition I should describe as one of unnatural excitement." Sturt paused.

"When did this second condition begin to arise? For instance—how long before she left for Remington?"

Sturt thought it over. "Well—not so very long before. Say three or four days. More than once, when I spoke to her she appeared to me to be all worked up, as you might say. Like somebody before an examination, or even before a serious operation—if you know what I mean. In fact, she reminded me of my mother just before she was carted off to the London Hospital to be carved up for something. Have I made myself clear?"

"Very clear, Mr. Sturt." Anthony rose to go. "I won't detain you any longer. Many thanks for your kindness and assistance. I am in your debt. Oh—one more question." Anthony produced the Langton invitation letter. "Is that Mrs. Clinton's signature?"

Sturt looked at the name. He smiled.

"Yes—or a marvellously good imitation."

"Thank you again, Mr. Sturt."

Sturt shook hands with him. Anthony drove home to his flat pondering over many things. When he arrived there he asked a question of Emily.

"When is a woman most excited, Emily? What's your answer to that question?"

Emily had her answer promptly on her tongue. "Why—just before she's going to be married, of course, sir. Ask any girl—and she'll tell you that."

Anthony smiled. "But supposing she's not a girl—but an elderly woman? How about it then?"

"Oh—then," said Emily, keenly and obviously disappointed, "when she's going to buy a new hat."

Anthony watched her as she walked back to her own room. "I shouldn't be surprised, Emily," he said to himself, "if you aren't right."

IV

Two days after Anthony's interview with Mr. Sturt, manager of 'Davidge's' Hotel, a stroke of good fortune came his way. As he, himself has said more than once, 'the first break that the case gave us right from the start.' He had risen at a comparatively late hour for him—the day had dragged by and he was standing looking out of the window of his flat when he saw a car drive up, stop directly outside and two people get out. As they made a straight path for his front entrance he saw, to his surprise, that one of them was none other than Rosamund Kingsley. With her was a man. A man whom he couldn't remember having seen before. Shortly afterwards he heard Emily admitting the two visitors. Anthony began to wonder what it was all about, but his mind had but a few seconds to exercise, and before his thoughts could take intelligent shape Emily was announcing "Miss Rosamund Kingsley to see you, Mr. Bathurst."

The tall, fair goddess advanced towards him with outstretched hand. At her side came an odd-looking man. He was small and spare. His face was lean and twisted-looking.

"Mr. Bathurst," cried Miss Kingsley as she crossed the floor, "I've brought you a previous acquaintance of mine. If you'll allow me to refresh your memory, he used to travel in alarm-clocks. Half an hour ago I ran into him on the Embankment and was able to persuade him to come along to see you."

Miss Kingsley looked flushed but triumphant. Anthony glanced sharply at the man she had brought with her. He looked sullen but defiant.

"Perhaps," continued the famous explorer, "he will be more communicative with you than he has been with me. Maybe your methods for making him talk will be more successful than mine."

Before Anthony could reply, the man himself took a hand.

"I haven't done anything wrong and you've got nothing on me. I'd like you to know that."

Rosamund spoke with a dangerous sweetness. "Look here, my man, you came along with me of your own free will. In other words, you fell in with a suggestion I made to you. You entered my house the other night, and after talking a lot of nonsense you dumped an alarm-clock on me and bolted for your life. I think it's up to you to give me an explanation. And as Mr. Bathurst here is a friend of mine, I'd like him to hear it."

Anthony listened carefully. The situation was an extraordinary one—to say the least of it. The thin man altered his tactics and assumed a truculent expression.

"It's no crime to do what I did. I was only acting as a messenger for somebody else—nothing more. You can't hold me for that. I know the law as well as you do, perhaps better."

"We aren't holding you," said Anthony grimly, "you're simply our guest for the evening, just as Miss Kingsley explained a moment ago. The best thing you can do is to make yourself thoroughly at home. Like you did at Miss Kingsley's house the other day."

The man made no reply. Anthony's retort appeared to have nonplussed him. Anthony himself realized that Rosamund Kingsley's quick initiative had presented him with an opportunity far too good and promising to throw away. After a moment or two's consideration he resolved to ask Inspector MacMorran to come along as soon as possible. He went to his telephone and asked for MacMorran's number. When the Inspector came, Anthony gave him the full story of Miss Kingsley's recent action.

"Good work," said MacMorran into the telephone. "I'll come right over at once; I shall have to be careful, but I'll get something out of him. Even if I only make it a nice, friendly little chat."

Anthony hung up. He was glad he had telephoned to the 'Yard. Handling this man was much more MacMorran's line of country than his own. The result was that he waited rather impatiently for

MacMorran's arrival. The latter came to the flat within twenty minutes. In the meantime Miss Kingsley's companion had maintained a sulky silence.

MacMorran was ushered in by Emily, and Anthony took him straight to the point. The Inspector listened with hard lines playing round the corners of his mouth. "I see," he said at length, "Miss Kingsley brought him along as the life and death of the party—eh?"

He turned to the thin man. "Good evening," he said curtly. "What's your name?"

"That's my business," replied the man.

"Really," returned the Inspector. "Now you listen to me and take careful note of what I say—because I shan't weary you by saying it again. I'm Chief-Inspector MacMorran of New Scotland Yard. Got that? Good. We shall now understand one another better. What's your name?"

There was still no answer.

"So you won't talk?" remarked MacMorran. "I see. Well, then—get this. I happen to be investigating a case of murder—not the theft of a box of kippers. I must ask you to come along to the 'Yard' to make a statement."

"What am I charged with? Tell me that," said the thin man querulously.

"Charged with? Nothing at all. All I want from you is a voluntary statement."

The man stared sullenly at MacMorran. "Wait a minute," he said eventually. "If I talk—I'll talk here."

"That's a lot better," declared MacMorran—"quite the little gentleman—eh?"

The man glared at him venomously.

"What's your name?" demanded the Inspector.

"Joseph Carter."

"Where do you live?"

"Oban Street—Poplar."

MacMorran made suitable notes. "Who sent you to Miss Kingsley's house at Chislehurst the other day?"

There was a silence. "Come," said the Inspector, "it will pay you to make a clean breast of things."

The man made a curious lifting movement of his shoulders, almost as though he had decided to rid himself of an unpleasant burden. "I don't know who sent me to Chislehurst, so it's no use my pretending that I do."

"Give me the full facts," ordered the Inspector. Anthony watched Carter's face with keen interest.

"All right," conceded Carter, surrendering his position, "I'll give you the dope. I can see there'll be no satisfying you until you get it. Mind if I smoke?"

He took a partly-smoked cigarette from his pocket and struck a match. He lit the cigarette and looked towards Rosamund Kingsley. "I know the lady smokes because I've seen her, so I hope that there's no offence. I'll tell you how I got dragged into this business. I use a house, very often, in Aldgate, 'The Walrus and the Carpenter.' Not a hundred yards from the big underground station. I used to use it more regular than what I do now. I've fallen on bad times, if you want to know, and cash is by no means as plentiful as I should like it to be. Not by a long chalk. Well, I was in the old 'Walrus' one evening—about the end of May it must have been—when a young lady came in,, ordered a glass of port and sat down near me. She was a fair 'stunner' to look at—I don't mean her clothes—I mean in herself—her face and everything. I didn't speak to her and she didn't speak to me, and I'd have thought no more about it, but the next evening, the very same thing happens. I dropped in for a pint of brown ale and lo and behold, almost on my heels in comes the same Jane, orders the same drink and sits herself down in almost exactly the same spot as she'd sat in the previous evening.

"Well—to cut a long story short, this goes on for six or seven nights running. The same identical performance. At last, on a Monday night it was—I can remember that because the bar was quiet—she changes her seat and comes and planks herself down next to me. Before I could collect myself so. as to know what was what, so to speak, she tells me that she's been looking for a likely man to do a certain job and that I'm the man for her money. Which was a cool tenner, almost for the asking. I 'boxed clever' for a time, but we soon got down to brass tacks and she told me what she wanted me to do. Well—you know what that was. I was to go to your place, lady, down at Chislehurst and take a parcel which she would bring me. She gave me the fullest instructions and coached me up as to what I'd got to say if you, lady, asked me any questions. As I felt certain that you would question me, I got her to give me the replies she wanted given in full. I told her I must know where I stood in the matter and that I couldn't be put off with meagre details."

He then spoke directly to Rosamund Kingsley. "As far as I could gather from what she said to me, you had been a member of some society or association, and you had sort of thrown a spanner into the works by leaving it all of a sudden. The lady said it was all quite harmless, but that a warning must be sent to you to give you a chance to come back to the society before it was too late. She said that in her own country—"

Anthony broke in sharply: "What do you mean? What country was that?"

Joseph Carter showed signs of surprise. "Oh—I should say she was German without a doubt. She spoke English well, but the accent was there all the time. In every word she spoke. You couldn't mistake it. But she was a smart Jane, I can tell you. A proper drop of 'omework and no mistake. Oh—and something I've just remembered. The last time I clapped eyes on her, when she dropped me the parcel for this lady here, when the time came for her to clear off, she lowered her voice and gave me the old 'Heil Hitler' joke."

MacMorran interrogated him. "What name did she give you?"

"None at all."

"Any address?"

"No. No address."

"Did you give her your name?"

"Not 'arf, Guvnor. I had to get my fingers round that tenner I mentioned."

"How do you mean. Explain yourself."

"Why—after I'd delivered the parcel to this lady at Chislehurst I had go back to the 'Walrus' to draw my dough. The young lady had it left for me, when I got there, in an envelope. Left it in charge of Len, the barman, who was to give it to me when I called in. The envelope was addressed 'Joseph Carter, Esquire'—blimey, what a thrill."

The man looked round the room as though daring any one of the others to challenge either him or any of the statements he had made. Anthony felt that it was time he took a hand in the game.

"I have been privileged to read Miss Kingsley's account of your call upon her at her residence in Chislehurst. And I have been particularly struck by the answers you gave her when she questioned you. I'll be candid and say that I consider them extremely 'pat.'"

Carter shifted uneasily in his chair. "I told you about that. The German girl coached me in the answers. For two or three nights in the 'Walrus' we talked of nothing else. She wouldn't give me the parcel till she was satisfied I was 'word perfect,' as you might say."

"I see. What guarantee did you have to give her that you had delivered the parcel to Miss Kingsley?"

Carter shook his head. "None at all. The girl had to take my word for it. What guarantee could I possibly give? You couldn't very well expect Miss Kingsley to sign a receipt for it, could you?" Carter's tone was becoming aggressive again. Rosamund Kingsley was quick to notice it and intervened sharply.

"You certainly could *not*. Or put down the red carpet to mark your arrival at my house."

Anthony put another question. "As far as you can tell from memory, what was the date of your first meeting with this girl?" Carter rubbed his nose with the edge of his finger. "That's askin' me something. I really couldn't say as to the exact day. But it would have been about the end of May. That's as near as I can get to it." Anthony looked significantly at MacMorran. Their thoughts had reverted to the interview with the caretaker of the flats at Remington. Otto Wenzel and Elsa, his companion, had left Remington, according to his story, somewhere about the end of April. There were certainly possibilities here! As Anthony had heard the story in the way that Carter had told it, he was inclined to the opinion that the man was telling the truth. MacMorran addressed himself to Carter again. "What work do you do?"

"When I'm at work I'm a bookmaker's clerk. I used to work for Hoppy Dick Isaacson round Aldgate. But things didn't go too well with him. The 'busies' kept pinchin' him and he stood me off."

MacMorran scrutinized him carefully. "Where were you before that?"

"In the same line. With 'Bluey' Oldfield. But 'Bluey' got pinched by a couple of interferin' 'busies' down at Lewes during the Sussex fortnight; He'd had a bad time at Goodwood, and stood up for the first race at Lewes with about fourteen bob in his 'sky.' Somebody must have put the 'dicks' wise, because they came and pinched him a few minutes after he put his boards up."

MacMorran nodded his assent. "I used to get on the racecourses a good deal a few years ago, and I fancy I must have seen you. Your face is certainly familiar." He patted his pocket. "Well, Mr. Carter, we have your name and address, and we're very much obliged for the statement you've given us. You shall come back to the 'Yard' with me now. I'll get it typed out and read over to you, and then you can put your signature to it. How does that appeal to you, Carter?"

Carter licked his lips. "Well—I hadn't bargained for that, Inspector Couldn't it wait for a day or so?"

"I'm afraid it can't, Carter. Sorry if I'm inconveniencing you."

Carter shrugged his shoulders. "All right. I'll come along with you, Inspector. I've nothing to fear, as I told you when this job started. Is the 'Rolls' outside?"

He walked out and down the stairs with the Inspector. Anthony and Rosamund Kingsley watched them go.

"What do you think of him?" asked the lady. Anthony smiled at her.

"Of him or of his story?"

Miss Kingsley smiled back. "Either—or both. Just as you choose."

"Well—I think he's a wrong 'un, if that's what you mean—but I'm inclined to think that his story this time is true. That is to say in the main. But as regards that, I should be interested to have your opinion."

Rosamund Kingsley knitted her brows. "His answers were very 'pat'—to use your word—when he came to Chislehurst that night. So 'pat,' indeed, that I think he must have rehearsed them many times."

Anthony nodded, "Exactly, Miss Kingsley. Which confirms my own opinion."

Rosamund Kingsley rose to make her departure. "Goodnight, Mr. Bathurst. And thanks for your help."

She held out her hand. "Surely," replied Anthony Bathurst, "the boot should be on the other foot."

V

Anthony moved to answer the telephone. He found MacMorran at the other end.

"Hallo, Andrew. What is it this time?"

MacMorran chuckled at the question. "I've got Playfair here. In accordance with your request. Will you come along now—or after lunch?"

"Now, my dear Andrew As near now as ever was. Expect me within half an hour. In fact I'm on my way already. Cheero."

Anthony shoved the receiver back, called out to Emily regarding his intentions, and clattered down the stairs. He was with MacMorran in his private room within twenty-two minutes. Capt. Ronald Playfair was sitting at the side of the Inspector's desk. He nodded cordially as Anthony entered.

"Morning, Bathurst. How are things?"

"Not so bad," returned Anthony—"but they're going to be better."

"Confident?" smiled back Playfair.

"Very," returned Anthony—"almost, in fact, at the end of the road."

MacMorran came in. "When we've done with you this morning we shall be more confident than ever. Now this is what Bathurst and I want to talk to you about. Sit down here, Mr. Bathurst, will you?"

Anthony took his place on the other side of the Inspector's desk. "It is only appropriate," commenced MacMorran, "that we should confer with you with regard to this particular point because we owe the 'contact' to you in the first place. If it hadn't been for your help we should never have been in touch with the matter at all." MacMorran paused—to go on again almost immediately. "I refer to the flat at Remington where the dachshund was shown in the window." Playfair moved eagerly towards the Inspector. His face was alight with interest. "Really—and what have you discovered?"

MacMorran held up his hand. "Just a moment, Capt. Playfair. Don't let us travel too fast, if you please. Mr. Bathurst and I made certain inquiries at the Remington flats. Some time ago. We weren't able to pick up very much. In fact, when we arrived there, such animals as dachshunds were conspicuous by their absence. But we were fortunate enough to run across one other rather important detail."

"What was that, Inspector?" Playfair cut in without ceremony. He obviously believed in the theory he had put before Anthony some time previously.

"The flat to which you called Mr. Bathurst's attention some time ago was empty. Note that, sir. It had become empty, according to the caretaker, somewhere about the end of the month of April. The caretaker was able to fix the date from the date of the Remington hotel murders."

MacMorran paused again—to see the effect of his words on Playfair. But the latter was still keenly interested and nodded eagerly.

"Yes, yes," he said, "that's significant—say what you like—go on!"

"The caretaker told us about the people who had been in the flat. A man and a girl. He wasn't sure of their actual relationship. But he told us their names. The man's name was Otto Wenzel."

Playfair started in his seat. "German," he exclaimed.

"Yes," said Anthony quickly. "We thought you'd be interested."

"What was the name of the girl?" demanded Playfair. "Unfortunately we're not sure of that. Our friend of the flats wasn't able to tell us. Beyond the Christian name. Which was Elsa."

"Elsa," muttered Playfair. "Otto Wenzel and Elsa."

"Well," inquired Anthony, "can you tell us anything? Do the names rake anything off the memory-heap?"

Playfair sat back, deep in thought. He saw again the crowds running down the Konigsgratzer Strasse while the Reichstag was burning. He saw the red dachshunds when the moron, Van der Lubbe, stood his trial.

"What were these people like to look at? Any idea?"

MacMorran glanced towards Anthony Bathurst. Anthony nodded. "I'll have a go," he said, "entirely from memory. These are the words of the caretaker. Otto Wenzel. Tall, nearly a six-footer. Thin. Lean, hungry face. Yon Cassius himself. Blue eyes. Deep set. Nervous. What else was there about him?" Anthony thought hard. He closed his eyes and put his head in his hands. Suddenly he looked up. "I know. I've got it. Hair brown and a scar on the left cheek. Now for the girl. Elsa Query. A blonde. Neat and trim. Blue eyes. Middle height. Five-sixish. But according to our caretaking friend, definitely 'easy on the eye.' He was prepared, he told us, to dare all for love."

"Anything else?" questioned Playfair.

"Don't think so."

"The descriptions might well fit thousands. That's the worst of them."

There was a silence as Playfair thought things over. After a time he glanced across and asked another question. "Just a minute; something you haven't told me. Ages. What were the ages of these people?"

Anthony responded readily. "Again, according to the taker of care, Otto in the middle thirties, Elsa about ten years his junior."

Playfair repeated the ages. "Otto Wenzel, say thirty-five, Elsa, twenty-five." Then he swung round on the Inspector. "Where did these people go when they left Remington?"

MacMorran shook a disappointed head. "We've run up against a blank wall. In fact, we haven't been able to trace either the man or the woman. The only information we've been able to get is that they went 'somewhere in the Midlands.' All our inquiries in the likely towns and places have drawn blank."

Playfair frowned. "Why did they leave Remington like they did? Do you know if any reason was given?"

"The ostensible reason was that the man left to go to a better job."

"What was Wenzel by trade? I presume you have made inquiries about it?"

"Naturally. I've been in touch with the firm that employed him. His trade was rather unusual. He was a scientific instrument maker. He worked for Fry and Davis, the Exeter people, who have a small factory on the outskirts of Remington."

Playfair frowned a second time. It was evident that he was feeling far from pleased. "Well—surely that fact would help. Help materially. It would have made the man much more easily traced. How many firms are there in the Midlands where Wenzel could have got a job? Find that out—and get into touch with them."

MacMorran held up his hand. "Exactly," he commented drily. "Nothing easier. Nothing more simple. That's what I thought when I first started the Wenzel line. But unfortunately it hasn't turned out like that. We've made inquiries of *all* the likely firms up there and not one of them has ever heard of Otto Wenzel, and what's more—not one of them has engaged a man anything like him. So you see, Capt. Playfair, there's a wide gulf between theory and practice." Having delivered himself of this homily, MacMorran sat back in his chair and looked at Playfair. The latter looked more annoyed than ever.

"I should have thought—" he began.

"I know," said the Inspector, "so should I. But it didn't and it wasn't. I'll tell you this. We can't trace Wenzel. We've tried everywhere. Not only in the Midlands. We haven't confined our efforts to that one district. Not on your life. It's my belief he went back to the Fatherland. Straight from his job at Remington."

Playfair seemed lost in thought. "Tell me," he said after a time, "did this firm you mentioned—Fry and Davis, wasn't it—know what relation of Otto Wenzel's the girl was?"

"No. She wasn't employed by them and they knew nothing about her." MacMorran half-smiled. "No, Captain Playfair, I'm very much afraid that I can't help you at all. I apologize for my—" He paused, seemingly at a loss for a word.

Anthony supplied the necessity. "Negligences and ignorances."

MacMorran grinned. "All right. Have it that way if you like. It's all the same to me."

Playfair sat there, his left leg raised and his two hands clasped across the knee-cap. "I'm wondering if I can do anything in the way of identifying them. It's a pretty difficult job, believe me—on the evidence you've put in front of me. The description might suit at least a hundred couples of whom I could think without the slightest difficulty. That's the trouble."

His eyes took on a far-away look. After a time he broke his reverie and came down to earth again.

"Look here, you chaps," he said, "leave this to me. When I get back home I'll have a look at one or two things I've got there, and I may be lucky enough to run across something. I've got several records that I can look into, and I may strike a clue as to the identity of your two Remington suspects. It would be useless for me to take a shot in the dark when by waiting a few hours I have access to so much important data in my house. See what I mean?"

MacMorran concurred immediately. "All right," he declared. "That suits me. Mr. Bathurst and I will wait to hear what you may have to tell us."

He looked towards Anthony as though requesting his support. Mr. Bathurst rose and stretched his arms to the ceiling.

"Very well, then," he said quietly, "we'll wait for Captain Playfair to communicate with us. Let's hope he won't be too long over it."

Playfair laughed gaily, shook hands with the two men and made his way out. When he had gone, Chief-Inspector MacMorran sat back in his chair and delivered himself of a profound judgment.

"The most difficult problem that I've ever been called upon to solve. What do you say to that, Mr. Bathurst?"

"On the contrary, Andrew—as I see it, matters are becoming more simple every day. By the end of the week—"

MacMorran interrupted him. "You'll be as far away from a solution as ever."

Anthony shook his head in denial of the statement. "By the end of the week, Andrew, I hope to be in a position to say: 'Andrew—your handcuffs—here's your guilty person'—and it's something more than a hope—believe me."

PART SIX
THE NET

I

ANNE Assheton was due to return to America again at the weekend. The two or three days prior to her departure she decided to spend quietly in her cottage in the West. She loved her country cottage and every hour she passed in it. She had just finished her dinner, her maid had repaired to the kitchen to do the washing-up, and

Anne was prepared to settle down to an evening's entertainment as provided by her radiogram.

At about ten minutes to nine, just as she was anticipating hearing the news bulletin, she was somewhat startled to hear a knock on her front door. She heard the footsteps of her maid as she left the sink in the kitchen and made her way up the old-fashioned passage to open the door. A few seconds later she heard her name being called. Anne jumped up from her chair and went towards the door.

"What is it?" she asked.

A tall, fair-haired young giant was standing there in the porch. Anne saw that he was hatless and agitated.

"What do you want?" she called out.

"I'm frightfully sorry to trouble you at this time of the evening," said the giant in a cultured voice, "but there's been rather a nasty accident at the top of the lane. A car smash. There's a young lady very badly hurt, I'm afraid. I'm wondering—"

"Oh, I'm so sorry. Can I do anything? Do tell me." Anne was definitely on offer.

"Well—if you could come along—"

"How far away is it?" Anne asked, simulating an eagerness which she was far from feeling.

"About two hundred and fifty yards, I should say. The car's turned right over. I'm afraid it's bent pretty badly. I simply must get Lydia to a hospital or to a doctor's somewhere. Do you know anywhere reasonably near? Do try to help me—please." The young man's agitation was increasing.

Anne heard herself answering his pleas almost mechanically. "There's a cottage hospital about five miles from here. Are you alone?"

"No. My brother's with me. He's looking after Lydia now. She's unconscious. It's her head, I think. If we could get hold of another car—"

"I have my car in the garage," returned Anne. She felt that she was compelled to give him the information. His spoken gratitude gushed forth and nearly engulfed her.

"Oh—if you could. If you would be so good—whatever's done for Lydia should be done at once. Every second's delay is so dangerous.

on." Anne skipped backwards and the tall young man came across the threshold and stood in the passage. Not far away he could hear sounds of Anne making her arrangements. He heard her call to the maid not to worry if she were late back. He heard the maid's voice in reply. Soon she rejoined him and was impressed by the intense look of anxiety showing in her visitor's face.

"How far's the garage?"

"Just round the corner here. Follow me, will you, and I'll have the car ready in a brace of shakes;"

Anne called a second message to her maid and ran towards the garage with the tall young man on her heels. Within a few minutes Anne was in the driving-seat and the car was gathering speed.

"Direct me," ordered Anne curtly. She was annoyed by the incident.

"Straight up to the top of the lane—please. I'll tell you when we get near the place of the accident. You'll see my brother there."

Anne put her foot down and the car leaped forward. It was a darkish night and the moon was obscured by heavy cloud-wrack. Anne drove the car up the lane at a fast pace. She peered forward to look through the glass of the wind-screen. Suddenly she felt her companion's clutch on her arm.

"There they are. Look! Richard's kneeling on the grass beside Lydia. God help me if she's dead."

Anne saw him put his head in his hands. "I'll stop the car here," said Anne quietly. This was an evening she had intended to spend seated by her radio. Anne stopped the car and her companion got out on the side where the kneeling figure was. Anne followed him and tried to make out the condition of the recumbent figure on the grass. She bent forward in an effort to discover the age of the girl lying there. She found to her annoyance that she could see nothing. She bent forward again, and at that moment received a violent blow on the back of the head. Anne Assheton went quickly into unconsciousness. The man who had been kneeling down picked a long fawn-coloured mackintosh from the grass, threw it into Anne Assheton's car and then picked that lady up by her trim shoulders.

"Give me a hand, old man," he muttered to his companion—"we'll hop out of this as soon as possible."

The fair giant helped to put the body of Anne Assheton in her own car. The other man quickly made a pad of a handkerchief and deftly forced it between Miss Assheton's teeth, into Miss Assheton's mouth. The two men arranged her body comfortably on the seat at the back.

"Right away," said the older man, "and put as many miles between this place and us as you possibly can in the next hour or so."

The fair man nodded. His companion slammed the door and the car started off. They drove fiercely for some hours with no sign of life emanating from Anne Assheton.

"She's well out," said the elder man, with a jerk of his head towards the prostrate figure on the seat.

The other man nodded. "I didn't hit her very hard either. She'll be all right before long." He gestured comfortably.

The elder man grinned in appreciation of the remark. "Timing, my boy—perfect timing—that's the secret. Garnetts don't hang from every bough."

"Some people would tell you what a damned lucky thing that is. There's no accounting for taste." As the man spoke he heard a slight movement from the figure on the seat. He turned his head and looked back at the girl. She was stirring slightly.

"Good job she's gagged," murmured his companion; "if she hadn't been she'd have been giving tongue by now."

"How far have we come?"

"Over a hundred and forty miles. We'll make for the Shropshire border. Somewhere round Shrewsbury or Church Stretton."

"Or Ludlow. There are plenty of quiet places round there where we can leave the car. Agree with me?"

"Oh, quite." He turned to look at Anne Assheton again. But she was lying quite quiet again. He could see her eyes, however, bright and watchful in the darkness. "I think she can hear what we're saying, Garnett."

"Expect she can. Hope she enjoys it. Listeners never hear any good of themselves." Then a further idea occurred to him. "Good evening, Miss Assheton," he said in a louder voice. "Heil Hitler!"

There was no audible response, but the keen senses of Miss Assheton, now entering their kingdom again, took in the significance of the remark. Although thoroughly frightened and even more in fear of what the immediate future held in store for her, Anne had an abundance of courage, so in order to give some semblance of consciousness she moved her head from side to side slowly and, to tell the truth, rather painfully. The gag in her mouth proved extremely effective, and coherent speech was impossible. She could see now that she was in the company of two men. One was the man who had lured her from her cottage and the other, doubtless, was the man who had knelt on the grass administering to an injured person who had never known an existence outside the flights of the conspirators' imagination.

It was rapidly coming home to her as she sat there in the car that she was in a distinctly tight place. But Anne, who had never yet quailed before an issue, was determined that she wasn't going under without a struggle. She sat very still, therefore, and awaited events. It was getting light now and with every promise of a glorious morning. Anne watched every trivial movement made by either of her companions. Even if she were gagged, her hands were free. Suddenly she heard one of them say:

"We're getting pretty close to the place now, Garnett. If you take my advice we shouldn't delay a minute longer than's absolutely necessary."

Garnett nodded acquiescence, and for the first time in her life Anne's blood ran cold. She dug her nails into the palms of her hands, resolute to sell her life as dearly as possible. She heard whispering tones from the front of the car and realized that it was slackening in pace. From what she could see of the country by looking through the windows it was wooded and pastoral. The car came to a standstill. Anne wondered in what form the blow would come. She hadn't long to wait before she knew. One of the car doors was opened and the voice of the man who had been addressed as Garnett told her to get out. Fearful of the next step, Anne obeyed. She saw the second man coming towards her. He held something in his hand. Anne looked wildly round the landscape for help, but the hope was vain. There wasn't a soul in sight. The man who approached her caught her by the shoulders, and almost before she knew what was happening she felt a bandage being tightened and tied across her eyes.

"Walk straight ahead," said a voice, "and keep on walking until you are ordered to stop."

With her heart in her mouth Anne obeyed. Suddenly the same voice commanded her to stop. Again Anne Assheton obeyed. She heard the sound of footsteps—close at hand. She was seized and held high in the air. From the position in which she was carried she felt certain that two men had hold of her. The pressure of four hands on various parts of her body was too plain to be misunderstood.

"On the way to the hot seat," she heard one of the men say, "and less than a hundred yards to go."

Anne realized the sinister significance of the remark and shuddered. What on earth were they going to do to her? She felt herself being lowered from the height at which she had been carried.

"Mind the juice," said the same voice that had spoken before; "don't start it working before the dame's ready."

"Don't worry," came the reply. "Lower her gently, will you?" Lower and lower went Anne Assheton until she was actually sitting on a seat of a kind. Her wrists were seized and the next moment they were tied together. Anne felt that the end, no matter in what way it was destined to come, was now perilously near to her. She leant back against something hard and then merciful oblivion came to her, for Miss Assheton lurched forward suddenly and toppled over.

"And that's that," said the man addressed as Garnett, "or even more appropriately perhaps, 'Heil Hitler!'"

The other man laughed. "A quick walk to the station and we can get the first train back to London. First stop Wolverhampton."

"Suits me," responded Garnett, "if there's breakfast on the train."

"There's bound to be," came the reply.

II

The ringing of the telephone bell disturbed Inspector Andrew MacMorran. He was working late in his room and the noise annoyed him extremely. He picked up the receiver, and the operator's voice came through to him almost immediately.

"Trunk call waiting for you, sir."

MacMorran frowned. "Right. Put it through. I'll take it." To his surprise it was Playfair's voice at the other end.

"Inspector MacMorran? Captain Playfair this end. I wanted a word with you over those two people in the flat at Remington. You remember, I promised I'd let you know if anything occurred to me with regard to them."

"You did. Well—what of it? Any luck?"

"I've been thinking things over and I've turned up one or two cuttings I have in a book down here, and I'm very much afraid those two people at Remington were none other than Ernst Zimmerman and his wife Helga. It's not certain, of course, but from the description given me of the lady I don't think I'm far off the mark."

"Well—and who may they be when they're at home?" growled the Inspector.

"Two of the most daring agents in Hitler's allegiance, my dear Inspector. Been chosen by the party for some of the most dangerous jobs that have been tackled in recent years, Helga particularly. A noteworthy illustration of the axiom that 'the female of the species is more deadly than the male.'"

MacMorran pulled a piece of paper towards him and made certain notes. "Zimmerman—eh? I'll see what I can do with that. That's something much more tangible than we've had before." Then an idea seemed to occur to him. "Captain Playfair," he said down the telephone, "tell me this, will you? If either of these Zimmermans ran across you, would he—or she—know you?"

Some few seconds passed before the reply came. "I don't know. I shouldn't like to say, exactly. Either of them might. They must have contacted me once or twice when I was over in Germany. But why do you ask, Inspector?"

MacMorran gave him the first answer which came to his mind. "Well—it might be good strategy on my part to use you. But I'm not going to do that if you can't hide your identity from either or both of the Zimmermans."

"Yes. I see what you mean," replied Playfair.

MacMorran judged from his tone that he seemed unconvinced. "Anyhow," continued the Inspector, "I'll see how the inquiries go before I definitely decide on anything. In the meantime many thanks for your information."

MacMorran finished the conversation and replaced the receiver. Then he stood up and walked to the window. He looked across the river. A slight rain was falling. The summer was failing to live up to its early promise. The Inspector looked at his watch. He wondered how Bathurst was faring and when he himself would get a request from him to move. The men and the telephones had all been covered, but the longer the delay the less confident he felt he must become. With a shrug of his shoulders MacMorran turned away from the window, the drabness of the river and the drizzling rain. After all, Anthony Bathurst had never let him down before—there was no reason why he should do so on this occasion. And if he himself had insisted on a show of proof, who in his senses could blame him?

III

Jennifer, maid in the cottage inhabited by Anne Assheton, went to bed soon after ten o'clock on the evening that her mistress had been called out to help in the 'motor-car' accident. Her mistress had told her not to worry if she didn't return to the cottage until very late, so the dutiful Jennifer went to bed early, untroubled by Anne's non-return, and in a very short time had slipped into that variety of sleep known to most as the 'sleep of the just.'

When Jennifer woke to find the sun streaming through her window and discovered soon afterwards that her mistress was still away, she remained calm and complacent. Miss Assheton could take care of herself all right and had, no doubt, driven to a hospital miles away. Miss Assheton would come back, of course, some time during the morning. If not then—some time in the afternoon. So Jennifer busied herself with her daily tasks and generally bustled round the Assheton country cottage. In addition, Jennifer sang 'little old West Country airs that her mother had taught her.' Such was Jennifer's description of them. Midday came and Jennifer had her lunch. Miss Assheton would come back soon now, and Miss Assheton would want an early tea, so Jennifer began to prepare early. Miss Assheton would be tired and hungry.

Shortly after Jennifer had finished her lunch the telephone bell rang in what Jennifer always called Miss Assheton's 'boodooer.' Jennifer had been waiting for this all the morning. She knew that she would have a telephone message before Miss Assheton arrived in person. So Jennifer dashed to answer it. To her surprise a man's voice spoke to her.

"Thus is the secretary," he said, "of the Wessex County Hospital. Is that Miss Assheton's maid? Yes? I've a message for you from Miss Assheton." There Jennifer interpolated. "No. She is quite well and there is nothing for you to worry about. Will you please catch the 2.17 from Croxton and meet Miss Assheton on Dorch station platform? No—she won't be using her car. She wants you to accompany her home. Now—is that all understood—or shall I repeat the message? All right? Good. That's all for now."

Jennifer looked at the time by the big ticking clock in the hall of the cottage. She was pleased to see that she had ample time for her journey. Croxton station was about half an hour's walking distance. She would have time to wash and then lay the tea-things for Miss Assheton's return. She wondered once or twice why her mistress was not using the car for her homeward journey, but eventually she came to the conclusion that she had lent it to the poor lady whose husband had come to the cottage for help on the previous evening. The lady was probably better by now and was using Miss Assheton's car to get to her own home, which might well be miles away. It was Jennifer's habit to find quick and moderately satisfactory solutions to problems which puzzled or occasioned her more than ordinary thought.

So Jennifer attired herself for her unexpected journey and set out blithely for Croxton station. It was a glorious afternoon and she was quite pleased to be able to spend an afternoon of such a nature in so pleasing a manner. Jennifer did not get too many afternoons off, and this one, as she put it to herself, had fallen off the tree into her lap. Jennifer strode along, pleased with the world and pleased with herself. We will leave her in that condition.

IV

Dean Theodore Langton, Dean of Mannington, handled the missive which had descended upon him through the channels of the post with a delicacy and a care far beyond the ordinary. He had read the message it contained three times already. It was evident, or it would have been had anybody been in the room with him, that the Dean was sorely troubled. The palms of his hands were wet with the sweat of fear. There was a hunted look in his eyes as though he couldn't be at all sure which was the best way for him to turn.' The letter he had just received was couched in the following terms. It bore neither address nor date.

'My dear. The game is up! We must get away at once. 'Phone me directly you receive this with regard to arrangements. I won't sign this typed note for obvious reasons.'

Dean Langton picked up the letter again and read it for the fourth time. His eyes were haunted by anxiety. He paced the floor of his study—to and fro—several times. This wretched letter he had just received was to do, of course, with that unfortunate business at Remington. There was that other abominable piece of impertinence which had been delivered to him in the vestry at St. Saviour's that night he had preached there. No doubt they were part and parcel the one with the other. Dean Langton was excessively annoyed. But only, he persuaded himself, because he hated and loathed everything which hid cravenly behind the thickets of anonymity. He abruptly stopped his pacing of the floor and almost fell into the comfortable recesses of his own big armchair. It was appalling—the whole business—and he regarded it as most unfortunate that he should have been 'mixed up' in it as he had. He picked up the letter from the floor to which it had fluttered from his nervy fingers. "Phone me directly you receive this with regard to arrangements.'

He bitterly regretted the day when Mrs. Warren Clinton had written to him. At the time it occurred he had accepted it as a compliment. A well-merited compliment. Now he was very far from feeling like this. Dean Langton rose from his chair and took the telephone directory from the bookstand which invariably was placed at the side of his chair. He fluttered the pages with his fingers. The Dean was evidently seeking a number. At last he found what he wanted. He replaced the directory on the bookstand and dialled a number. The curious look which his eyes held deepened. An answer came to him from his telephoning.

"Is that you, Greenaway? This is Dean Langton speaking . . . from Mannington. . . ."

V

John Maxwell Ramage, K.C., sat in his breakfast-room and moodily surveyed the letter, which, *inter alia*, formed his morning's post. Some minutes passed before he brought himself to open it. When he had read it the lines on his face were clear evidences of his perturbation and his sensitive features were sorely troubled. The letter to John Ramage ran thus:

'My dear. The game is up. We must get away at once. 'Phone me directly you receive this with regard to arrangements. I am not signing this typed note for obvious reasons.'

Although Ramage was annoyed, to put the matter somewhat mildly, a thin smile began to play round the corners of his mouth. He carefully examined the envelope which had enclosed the letter for any indications of interest, but he met with scant reward. He then propped the envelope up against his teapot and subjected it to yet another close scrutiny. All that he found were the typed address and the prosaic stamp. The postmark was a little blurred, but he fancied that the three final letters were TON. When he spotted this he frowned heavily. There might be more significance in this letter than he had previously considered. He wished he had never become entangled with Mrs. Warren Clinton. If he hadn't met her on the voyage home from the States he would never have been invited to that grotesque gathering of hers at Remington, which had culminated in the death of his wife. In the murder of his wife—for that his wife had been murdered John Ramage was absolutely certain.

He moved the letter from its stand against the teapot and poured himself out another cup of tea. As a rule he ignored anonymous letters, but there was something different about this one from most of the others which had come his way. He knew that it undoubtedly had some connection with the Remington murders and that it was incumbent upon him to do something about it. The whole business was getting on his nerves, and if he weren't careful would soon begin to take further toll of him. That would never do. He lit a cigarette and he noticed that the hand which held the match was far from steady. All this 'nerviness' was unlike him, and the realization of it chafed and worried him. He went to his telephone and picked up the receiver. He began to dial. He wondered where MacMorran and Anthony Bathurst were. Then the operator's voice, cutting in on his thoughts, brought him back from his reverie.

VI

Rosamund Kingsley was in her morning-room at Chislehurst when the telegram came. The telegraph boy touched his cap, clicked, his heels and pulled the garden-gate to with a snap which betokened (as he himself considered) his own smartness and efficiency. Rhoda looked out from the kitchen as Miss Kingsley opened the familiar buff envelope and read the message it contained.

To Rosamund Kingsley, Zerzura, Chislehurst. My dear Rosamund. The game's up. We must get away at once. 'Phone me directly you receive this with regard to arrangements. Your opposite number.'

Rosamund half-turned to see if Rhoda were watching her as she read. Rhoda came out of the kitchen.

"I hope you haven't had bad news, Miss Kingsley?" Rhoda couldn't help being struck by the strange look on Rosamund's face. Miss Kingsley didn't reply to her question. Rhoda repeated it. "Not bad news, I hope, Miss Kingsley?"

This time Rosamund Kingsley shook her head. "No, Rhoda— well, that is to say, I don't know."

"Is there anything I can do? Anything I can get you?"

"No, Rhoda—thank you all the same. There's nothing at the moment. I've had a rather sensational telegram—that's all. I think I'll go into the library and think things over. If I want you I'll call you."

Rhoda nodded and withdrew to her kitchen again. Rosamund went into the library. In her chair there she sat and studied the telegram that had just come to her. It had been handed in at 'London.' The actual office she was unable to discover from the telegram itself. She sat for some moments with her chin cupped in her hands. Her thoughts went back to the first letter she had received from the late Mrs. Warren Clinton and to the night at Remington when two people had died. The events which had followed all seemed incoherent parts of a disordered dream in which unpleasant incidents had occurred thick and close upon each other, and so quickly that each one seemed to delete instantaneously the memory of its immediate predecessor. Rosamund shuddered as she recalled some of them—particularly the night when the man Carter had come to Chislehurst and delivered to her the mysterious parcel. And now this telegram had come—out of the blue, as it were. Rosamund Kingsley sat in her chair and swung her foot.

She had had no further news of Carter since Inspector MacMorran had taken him to Scotland Yard to sign his statement, which fact, as far as she was concerned, had not been devoid of anxiety for her. She had been responsible for taking Carter to the police, and she had desired to be left in no doubt as to the wisdom of her action. Rosamund Kingsley sat in her library, the prey of her thoughts, for over a quarter of an hour. Then she rose and went to the kitchen to speak to Rhoda.

"Make me a cup of tea, Rhoda, please, and bring it into the library. I may be going out in a few minutes' time."

"Yes, miss. I'll do it at once for you." Rhoda beamed on her mistress as she put the kettle on the electric stove.

Rosamund returned to her chair in the library and waited for her maid to bring in the tea. Leanings forward to her desk, she picked up the telephone directory and began to search the pages for a certain number. She soon found it, removed the receiver from the telephone and dialled a number. As Rhoda entered with the tea she heard the voice of her mistress speaking. Rosamund motioned to her maid to place the tea-tray on the table. Rhoda obeyed. As she made her way out of the room she heard Miss Kingsley say: "This is Rosamund Kingsley speaking . . . may I speak to Mr. Cedric Garnett, please?"

VII

When Lord Esmond Curte received his telegram the sky was grey with the promise of rain. He had been annoyed at this from the first moment of his morning awakening. For the reason that Kent were due at Trent Bridge that morning, and there was no clash on the cricket field that appealed to Lord Esmond Curte so much as the annual struggle at Trent Bridge between the counties of Kent and Nottinghamshire. Not even the hardy Whitsun tit-bit, Nottinghamshire versus Surrey. Kent invariably brought a dash and an élan to their cricket which attracted his lordship tremendously. And on this particular occasion, when each county had advertised a most attractive side on paper—the weather chose to be grey, sullen and forbidding. So thoroughly, indeed, that Lord Esmond Curte could already see in the headlines of the evening papers the dreaded phrase: 'Trent Bridge—no play today—Rain!'

At the very moment that this thought was beginning to take shape in Lord Esmond's brain there came a tap on his door which heralded the arrival of his manservant, the ubiquitous Pollard. Pollard entered, and on the salver he carried reposed a buff-coloured envelope.

"What's this, Pollard? A wire for me? So early? This is unusual, surely?"

Pollard bowed and muttered something which sounded suspiciously like the opinion 'that it was and it wasn't.'

Curte split the envelope and took out the thin paper of the telegram itself. He read it with a furrowed brow. For Lord Esmond Curte was in a state of even greater annoyance now than he had been. Which is no mean statement. The telegram he had just read ran thus:

"My dear Esmond. The game is up. We must get away at once. 'Phone me directly you receive this with regard to arrangements. Your other half."

Curte read the telegram for a second time and pulled impatiently at his upper lip. Then he looked up and saw that Pollard was still standing there, almost at his elbow. "You may go, Pollard," he said brusquely; "if I want you for anything I'll ring for you."

Pollard bowed again and withdrew. Lord Esmond Curte followed the example of many of his fellows. He solemnly execrated the day that had brought him that fateful letter from the late Mrs. Warren Clinton. He strode to the window and looked savagely across to the roofs of Nottingham. It had begun to rain. More than that—it was going to be a wet day. Lord Esmond Curte cursed aloud. His cup was becoming full. What had MacMorran done? Nothing! What had the great Bathurst done? Nothing! And now this wretched telegram had been delivered to him. What should he do about it? What should he do with it? Then he remembered something. The night at Mona Shacklock's Charity Ball when he had encountered Felicity Frayle. The girl who had been stopping with the Ratherdons. That was the night on which he had been given that absurd warning!

If he had only—His eyes went to his telephone. This action caused him to make up his mind. He lifted the receiver and dialled a number. When the time came for him to speak he spoke very quietly.

"I want to speak to Captain Maitland, please . . . is that you, Maitland? . . . Esmond Curte this end. . . ."

VIII

For many years it had been the habit of Sir Edward Angus to have his correspondence addressed to the 'Lexicon' Club. If one speak the truth, it must be admitted that the hours which Sir Edward spent at his club were the only hours which could be counted by him as serene. When he was on his way to his club his pace, as he walked through Manners Street, was astounding for a man of his years. When the time came for him to leave his club his gait was as relatively slow as it had previously been fast. The fact, therefore, that John, the waiter, brought a telegram to him as he sat in his favourite corner with his old friend and colleague, Adrian Anstey, occasioned him no surprise.

"Telegram for you, Sir Edward," said John, "and if I'm not mistaken, sir, I think that it might contain birthday congratulations. Am I right, sir?"

Sir Edward Angus smiled and shook his head. "No, John. You are wrong. My birthday is on Wednesday next. I hardly think that congratulations would arrive *so* early."

"I'm sorry, sir. I was aware that your birthday fell during this month some time, but the exact date eluded me. I trust that you will overlook the inaccuracy." The waiter handed over the telegram and retired.

Adrian Anstey grinned cynically. "Birthdays"—he almost spat—"faugh! Never worry about 'em."

"Nevertheless, my dear Adrian," said Sir Edward, "you cannot escape them. They're like time and tide and death—they wait for none of us."

Anstey made an impatient movement with his head and watched Sir Edward as he opened the envelope of the telegram. The words of the telegram were these:

'My dear Sir Edward. The game is up. We must get away at once. 'Phone me directly you receive this with regard to arrangements. Your next in command.'

When he had read the message, Sir Edward sat quietly in his chair. He made no comment whatever. "Well," barked Adrian Anstey, "what have you got there? An affiliation order or a notice to quit?"

Sir Edward ignored the sally. His mind had already left the 'Lexicon' Club and was occupying the magic carpet. The letter from Mrs. Warren Clinton . . . the dinner in the 'Royal Sceptre' at Remington . . . the test of the words . . . and then the murders . . . followed by the menaces of word and deed. Evidently the wretched business was not finished yet. Sir Edward came out of his brown study to find Adrian Anstey's odd-coloured eyes watching him closely. Anstey coughed.

"You're an interesting companion today—I must say. About as interesting as a Bazaar Committee. What the hell's the matter with you, you miserable old sinner?"

"I've often wondered," replied Sir Edward, "whether the Litany is right when it instructs us to describe ourselves in that way."

Adrian Anstey glared at him. "You need have no doubts," he replied pointedly.

"Leave me out of it," returned Sir Edward, "the crimes I've committed in my time I'm perfectly prepared to expiate. For anything I've done that might seem to be atrocious, believe me I've had excellent reasons. No—what I meant was rather more like this. Why should we be content with describing ourselves as 'miserable sinners'? Shouldn't our misery, our wretchedness, our—er . . . moral squalor be wiped out by our knowledge of the atonement, and because of that shouldn't we describe ourselves as jubilant and thrice-blessed?

Why shouldn't our souls be more often magnifying the Lord instead of existing in this regrettable state of perpetual abasement?"

Anstey frowned. The frown turned into an uncompromising scowl. "Oh—you think that, do you? Well, let me tell you—I don't agree with you. By a long way. If you ask me, seventy-five per cent of the population *are* miserable sinners, and the act of magnifying the Lord, on their part, would be an example of barefaced and audacious hypocrisy. Faugh! The Lord might do worse than destroy them. Just as he did the Ammonites and the Jebusites and all those other 'ites that persistently flouted the moral law."

Sir Edward Angus smiled a cold smile at Anstey's utterance. "I am gratified that the Lord Himself is not of your opinion, my dear Anstey."

He rose from his chair. But Anstey was determined not to let the matter rest where it did. He stood up and held Sir Edward by the lapel of his coat.

"Do you mean to tell me seriously," he said, "that you wouldn't be prepared to destroy evil when you encountered it? Destroy it as ruthlessly as you would slash with a stick the head of a venomous snake?"

"It mightn't be in my power to destroy it."

"You're hedging. If it were in your power?"

"Well, in those circumstances—yes. I might be prepared to agree with you on those lines."

"There you are, then. That's what I've been saying all along."

"No, you've not. You've travelled quite an appreciable distance since you started."

Anstey's face broke into a huge grin. "Trust you to have the last word. I never knew an occasion when you didn't." Then he guffawed loudly and boisterously and slapped Sir Edward on the shoulder.

The latter turned and regarded his companion quizzically. "Tell me, Anstey," he said, "I suppose that I ought to know—but I seldom use the things—where is the nearest club telephone from here?"

Anstey stubbed his finger in the direction of the door. "Just at the side of the staircase," he answered.

"Thank you, Anstey," acknowledged Sir Edward, "then will you excuse me for a few moments?"

Adrian Anstey rubbed his cheek with his forefinger as he watched the retreating figure of Sir Edward Angus.

IX

Capt. Ronald Playfair was feeling by no means displeased. He had just arranged an 'eighteen holes' with a bosom companion on the Sid Valley course, and as the weather was wholly delightful Capt. Playfair's personal barometer was undoubtedly advertising a condition of 'set fair.' As he stood looking out of his morning-room window he hummed to himself the air of a favourite musical-comedy number and felt that life wasn't so bad after all.

As he watched from the window of the morning-room he saw to his surprise the figure of a telegraph-boy coming towards his front door.

Playfair walked to the door in anticipation. The boy put the envelope into his waiting hands. As he opened it Playfair's dominant emotion was that of disappointment. Somebody was evidently going to let him down over something. He read the words of the message, therefore, with some excitement. They ran as follows:

'My dear. The game is up. We must get away at once. 'Phone me directly you receive this with regard to arrangements. You know who.'

Playfair crumpled the telegram into a ball, tossed it savagely on to the table in the hall and went back to look out of the morning-room window. All thoughts of his anticipated game of golf vanished from his mind. By a stroke of a wand, as it were, he had been transported to the days of the murders at the Royal Sceptre Hotel, even though the hand that had wielded the wand had been the hand of a humble telegraph messenger. He was forced to admit to himself that this business was getting on his nerves. Not exactly worrying him, but definitely causing him annoyance. Playfair looked at his watch. In less than two hours from now he was due on the Sid Valley golf course. If he ignored the telegram he would be able to . . . he began to walk up and down the room. Bathurst and Inspector MacMorran had been working on the case for some time now . . . it was quite on the cards that they had run up against something vitally important. Ernst and Helga Zimmerman had been run to earth, possibly. There are times when Scotland Yard acts swiftly and strikes hard. Ronald Playfair considered many things as he paced the floor of his room.

Suddenly he walked from the room and made his way to the table in the hall on which he had thrown the crumpled telegram. He picked up the ball of paper and unfolded it so that he might read it again carefully. It had been handed in, he saw, at Exeter. Playfair took a notebook from his pocket. He flicked its pages as though searching for certain information. Apparently he quickly found what he desired. He studied the page for some time. When he seemed satisfied he replaced the book in his pocket and walked to his telephone. He was forced to wait some little time for the number he wanted. When he was connected he said in a lowered voice, "Playfair speaking. Is that you? Good! Now listen. . . ."

X

The two plain clothes men on the pavement who were watching the premises knew that the matter of the various telegrams was in the hands of Inspector MacMorran and Anthony Bathurst himself. When they received their final orders they were by no means sure as to whether they would click for anything in the nature of action. One pair of MacMorran's squad most certainly would, and they might have the luck to be that pair. They arranged themselves near the house they had been ordered to watch according to their usual plan and disposition for jobs of this kind. Chatterton said a few admonitory words to Evershed before they parted company and made silently for their respective positions.

"Don't make a mistake, Sid, on this particular job for the love of Mike. Because if you do you'll never hear the last of it and your career will be blasted for all time."

"Why pick on me?" replied Evershed. "Same goes for you, only more so. So long—see you later. And don't forget—when we move, we move together. If I get the 'how d'ye do' first I'll let you have the usual signal."

"Right," returned Chatterton. The two men took up their positions.

It was early evening now, but the sky was overcast and a thunderstorm seemed a good bet before midnight. As he took up his watching-post, Chatterton could hear the distant rumbles of the approaching storm and could see the vicious white flashes of lightning as it streaked and slashed across the summer sky.

At a quarter-past seven a car came quickly out of the garage attached to the house he was watching and made rapid pace almost immediately. Chatterton communicated' with Evershed according to the arrangement; Evershed made use of the police-box, gave certain vital information, asked for orders, obtained orders, gave orders. The hunt was up. And Anthony, with MacMorran in the big 'Yard' car, was once more on the track of a ruthless murderer.

XI

Anthony had smiled at the Inspector when the news came through.

"Well, Andrew," he said almost teasingly, "was I right?"

MacMorran, who had gone to the telephone immediately, smiled back at him, but the smile was grim. "Seems like it, Mr. Bathurst. But I'll tell you for certain when it's in the bag."

He turned his head to speak into the telephone. "In two minutes. Good. And you know what to do. Right. Mr. Bathurst will be with me." He jerked his head towards Anthony. "Fit? That's O.K. then. Car in two minutes. Less—very likely. Got a revolver?"

Anthony grinned. "You bet I have, Andrew. What about yourself?"

MacMorran patted his pocket with a significant gesture. "I'm breeched all right."

At twenty-four minutes past seven the big 'Yard' car rolled out on its way. MacMorran had asked for a special driver by the famous name of Owen Kettle. The Inspector had sublime faith in Kettle's driving and had made eloquent expression of his faith more than once. Anthony looked at his watch. Twenty-five minutes past seven now. The car screamed along the Embankment; Kettle had taken his orders from the Inspector and knew that MacMorran meant what he said rather more than most people. MacMorran actually felt safer with Kettle at the wheel than he did with Anthony there. Which was strange—seeing that Mr. Bathurst was incomparably the better driver. The car's speed, considering the amount of traffic that was still holding the road, was astounding.

"Making eastward," remarked Anthony.

The Inspector nodded. The car sped by the Mansion House, down Lombard Street, past Aldgate Pump, past the Three Nuns Hotel and held on down the Mile End Road. Through Bow, through Stratford, Forest Gate, Manor Park and Ilford. As they passed the Town Hall, Ilford, a police car, startled from its normal nonchalance, began to follow it at breakneck speed. But one of the occupants leant forward to the driver and spoke seasoned words. He had noticed something on the car in front which told him all that he needed to know. He knew that the car in front of them was on urgent work and not engaged on mere flippant flighting. Kettle's horn sounded incessantly as they turned the corner by Seven Kings Station.

Anthony looked at his watch again. Forty-two minutes past seven. Suddenly he realized that Kettle was slowing down. A motor-cyclist was approaching them travelling at a fast pace. The car came almost to a standstill. Anthony looked out of the window, and it struck him that the motor-cyclist was also slackening pace. His idea was right. The motor-cyclist stopped by the car and, holding on to the window, asked for Inspector MacMorran. MacMorran stuck out his head so that he could reply.

"Through Romford? And making for the coast, you think? Right-o. Many thanks."

He gestured to Kettle, who had the car in its stride again and roaring on the road towards Romford. MacMorran leant over towards Anthony.

"Probably making for the Chelmsford by-pass," he said curtly.

This time it was Anthony's turn to nod.

"We may get some further information later on," he added.

The car flashed through Chadwell Heath, Romford, Gidea Park and began the ascent of Brook Street Hill for the old Essex town of Brentwood. By the Martyr's Memorial the car stopped again and MacMorran took another message from a uniformed cyclist. Anthony failed to hear what was being said. MacMorran, however, as soon as the man had departed, passed the news on to him.

"This is a bit of a surprise," he stated. "The car's hung up at a place near Margaretting. They tell me it's a sort of super-roadhouse. I understand it's called The Glade.'"

"I know it well. So should you, Andrew."

MacMorran knitted his brows. "Should I? Why? Tell me."

Anthony regarded him quizzically. "Don't you remember the case of the three Somersets and the visit we paid to that ancient ruin who called himself Simon Gildey?"

The Inspector's face broke into understanding. "I remember."

"Good. Well—we passed The Glade' that day when we drove down to see him. I should describe it as a good-class roadhouse. With the usual attachments—swimming pool, dance hall—you know."

"Where are we now?" enquired MacMorran.

"This is Shenfield," replied Anthony, "in a few minutes we shall be at The Glade.' The car's pulled in there, I suppose."

MacMorran gestured his assent. He leant over to Anthony. "Which side of the road is it?"

"The left. You'll see the advertised notice-board in a minute or so. Keep your two eyes skinned for it. Have you made up your mind yet?"

MacMorran smiled at the question. "I'm more or less in your hands. I shall have to be convinced. And especially seeing it's a lady concerned."

Anthony grinned. "Same sound old ruffian as ever. Still—I can't find it in my heart to blame you." He looked up to see where they were. "Here we are, Andrew. Tell Kettle to turn in, will you? Let the car park over there on the left."

MacMorran gave Owen Kettle his instructions and the car ran in and parked as Anthony had suggested.

"Together?" he inquired of the Inspector. MacMorran shook his head.

"No. I think not. If we're seen when we go in and we're together we're almost bound to be spotted. Whereas if we enter separately, cock an eye round for the time of day, we *may* be able to join up at a table, say, in one of the corners. There's a much better chance that way."

"There's just this, Andrew," said Anthony, "we don't know exactly where we shall run our quarry to earth. If we have no luck in the restaurant—and I doubt whether we shall—we'll drift round on our own and then join up if either of us has any luck."

"I agree," answered MacMorran; "that's settled, then. Enter the pair of us."

As he broke away from the Inspector and walked towards the entrance to the roadhouse, Anthony looked at his watch. The time was twenty-two minutes past eight. He went into the restaurant portion of the establishment, saw an unoccupied table at his elbow, sat down immediately and picked up the menu that lay on the table. From its cover he inspected the surprisingly few occupants of the apartment. Then he remembered that it was a glorious summer night—the threat of the storm had passed—and that the swimming pool, doubtless, was one of the main centres of attraction. There were seven people in the restaurant besides himself. There were three couples at three different tables, and the remaining man's back seemed familiar to him, but he was too far away from Anthony and his general posture so cramped and huddled that Anthony was unable to judge his height with anything like accuracy. He seemed to be wearing some sort of clerical attire. Anthony decided to watch him closely to see if he were joined by a companion. By this time a waiter in evening dress had appeared and Anthony had given him an order. When the drink came Anthony found time to look round at the three couples who were the other occupants of the room.

He noticed that, with the exception of one couple, sitting at his extreme left, a girl in her late 'teens and a boy in Air Force uniform, the other two pairs all had their backs to him. At one table sat a prosperous-looking, middle-aged couple, and at the other there were a nurse and a man of whom Anthony caught an occasional glimpse, side-face. This man, Anthony thought, looked French from his neatly-trimmed beard and moustache and his pale cheek.

Suddenly, as he sat there watching, Anthony heard footsteps behind him and saw Inspector MacMorran come in. MacMorran gave him no sign. As he turned his head Anthony saw that the Inspector had pulled some of his hair over his forehead and put on a pair of horn-rimmed spectacles. The same waiter who had attended on Anthony went to MacMorran. MacMorran picked up the menu, studied it for a few moments and then gave an order. Anthony's eyes met his across the tables, but still the Inspector gave no sign of recognition. A few seconds later, after the waiter had brought MacMorran's order, Anthony noticed that the Inspector had a pencil in his hand and was scribbling something on the back of the menu. Anthony sensed that a message of some sort was coming to him. He waited, therefore, ready and watchful, for its reception. He saw MacMorran replace his pencil in his pocket and push the card towards the edge of the table on his, Anthony's, side. He realized. that by a quick movement he and MacMorran would be able to effect an exchange of menus. He prepared himself for the precise moment when MacMorran would move. This came even sooner than he had expected. Suddenly the menu from Mac-Morran's table came unsteadily to the brink and fluttered to the floor. Anthony bent with alacrity to pick it up, and when the two men sat back in their seats again the necessary transfer had been accomplished. Avoiding all semblance of haste, Anthony looked to see the message which MacMorran had written for him. What he read made his heart beat a trifle more quickly and his pulses throb a little more rapidly.

MacMorran had written very lightly round the edge of the menu: "Your trick! Congratulations! You've spotted the quarry, of course. Don't stir an inch or move in any way until I do."

Having read the communication, Anthony gave MacMorran an almost imperceptible nod of assent, but at the same time took himself to task. He had certainly *not* spotted the quarry and was forced to admit to himself that the Inspector had beaten him to it. MacMorran had seen something which so far he himself had not seen and which was still eluding him. He deliberately unfolded a newspaper which he had brought with him to the roadhouse and, half-turning, watched MacMorran's movements from under its cover. He soon saw that the latter had his eyes fixed on the man in clerical attire. Then, impulsively, MacMorran pulled the menu card towards him again and began to write in a similar place to where he had written before. The Inspector waited his chance. When the coast seemed to him to be clear he passed the card to Anthony with a quick movement.

Anthony read the second message. 'I don't want you to be recognized. But I'm afraid of it happening. I'm confident that I shan't be. Go out of here the way you came as soon as you've read this and work round towards the other entrance which leads to the swimming pool. You and I will then be on each side of them, and you will be in a position to cover any retreat which may be attempted. Get within earshot, and then when I move it will be up to you—if necessary. You must be the judge of that.'

Again Anthony nodded. He folded his newspaper, turned quickly and made his exit as MacMorran had indicated. From there he quietly made his way round the back of the restaurant portion and took up his position between the door and the swimming pool. He reasoned that directly he heard MacMorran's voice he would move towards the restaurant again. Unobtrusively he waited here for the critical moment. It was not long in coming.

A hush seemed to come over the restaurant apartment. Even from his post outside Anthony sensed this. He heard what he felt sure were MacMorran's footsteps as the Inspector crossed the floor. Anthony moved up closer, in case of a precipitate retreat. The next thing he heard was MacMorran's voice.

"Excuse me, but I'd like a word with you outside." There came a dead silence after the Inspector had spoken.

Anthony heard a man's voice in reply, but was unable to detect what was being said. MacMorran spoke again.

"My request was made in your own interests, but, of course, if you prefer to—"

Anthony saw three figures appear and approach him. MacMorran had a man and a woman with him. He was between the two of them. The woman turned and saw Anthony Bathurst. She uttered a shrill cry. But there was little fight in her companion. He stumbled rather than walked, and the beard that he wore merely accentuated the pallor of his face. Once or twice he shook his head as though endeavouring to convince himself that what was taking place was unreal and bore no relation to real life. Anthony heard MacMorran speaking again.

"John Maxwell Ramage and Anne Denver . . . you are arrested for the murders of Wilfred Denver and Angela Ramage . . . at the Royal Sceptre Hotel, Remington . . . of April last, and of Miriam Clinton . . . warned . . . used in evidence against you."

MacMorran's words trailed off into thin air. Anthony stepped up to his side to be ready if wanted. But the man who had been arrested was as a pricked balloon, a man in whom no virility or power of effort existed, and his companion was petulant and sullen now that devastating crisis had come to her. The four people moved silently towards Owen Kettle and the big car.

Chapter Seven
THE SOLUTION

I

It had been the whim of Sir Austin Kemble, the Commissioner of Police, that Anthony and MacMorran should drive him to 'The Glade.' The Commissioner had, indeed, insisted that he be conducted to the roadhouse where the arrests had been made in the matter of the Warren Clinton case. As they walked past the swimming pool MacMorran pointed out to the Commissioner the restaurant portion of the premises where he and Anthony had sat a few minutes prior to the arrests being made.

"I was amazed," admitted Sir Austin, "when MacMorran telephoned the news to me. For once I had formed no clear opinion of the case. As a matter of fact, I haven't been able to devote much time to it. Take me into the restaurant, Bathurst, and we'll drown our sorrows." Sir Austin smiled benevolently. He felt in high feather on this particular morning because the Warren Clinton case had been a source of worry to him for some time, and he had been facing the possibility of answering awkward questions with regard to its investigation. Questions, too, that he would have found grave difficulty in answering. Indeed, Sir Austin was now so overjoyed that he became unlike his normal self. When the waiter appeared he ordered drinks. Anthony and MacMorran exchanged quick glances. The drinks came.

"Now, Bathurst," said the Commissioner, beaming, "let's hear how you arrived at your successful conclusions."

Anthony smiled. "I took too long, sir. Things—many things—should have been plain to me long before they were."

MacMorran shook his head at Anthony's remark. "I don't know that I agree. In many respects we had to face the most baffling case I have ever known." He continued to shake his head.

Anthony went on. "I think I know what the Inspector's referring to, Sir Austin, but I would describe the case differently. It was a combination of 'awkwardnesses.' For quite a long time nothing fitted. Whereas it *should* have done. Or rather we should have *made* matters fit. I think that expresses the Inspector's attitude, sir, in a nutshell." Sir Austin Kemble drank up his whisky and soda and nodded. Anthony motioned to the waiter and ordered another round.

"In my opinion, Sir Austin, the lady in the case was the *fons et origo* of the entire plot. Everywhere I look I see evidences of her love of sensation and of her overwhelming desire to dramatize everything. Ramage, I feel convinced, was the subordinate partner in this malevolent and unholy alliance. When she and John Ramage fell in love on the voyage home in the *Myrobella* it was her fertile brain which manufactured the plot as we know it and have known it now for some weeks. In fact, I think it's a considerably odds-on proposition that her hand fired the shot in the cabin on the *Myrobella* which ended the life of the late Mrs. Warren Clinton. Not long before the time came for disembarking."

Anthony paused. MacMorran pushed back his chair. Sir Austin Kemble put down on the table the glass that had been on its way to his lips.

"What was that, Bathurst? I did not quite catch that."

Anthony repeated his previous statements.

"But how on earth," expostulated the Commissioner, "did Mrs. Clinton get to 'Davidge's' Hotel and after that to the other hotel at Remington when she—"

"After Mrs. Clinton died," said Anthony, "the part was admirably played by Anne Denver, the accomplished screen actress. But don't be disturbed. It took me a long time to realize the truth of that and to understand how the whole thing had been worked out." Anthony lit a cigarette which Sir Austin Kemble offered him. "Remember, sir," continued Anthony, "how Mrs. Clinton, when she arrived at 'Davidge's' Hotel and during all the time she stayed there, avoided every possible contact with people—even the most simple and elementary ones. She let Redfern interview her and she took a risk over it. This fact puzzled me rather when I first found myself toying with the idea of an impersonation. But I think that can be explained in this way. She wanted the personality of Mrs. Warren Clinton established in the minds of the British public. Firmly established. The only satisfactory way in which this could be done was through the medium of the Press. So she tipped Jerry Redfern off for the essential interview."

Sir Austin Kemble nodded. "And while that was going on the body of Mrs. Clinton—"

"Was in one of her own cabin trunks. That same trunk that afterwards finished up at Waterloo Station. When Anne Assheton left the *Myrobella* I suggest that she disembarked as herself with her own luggage, disposed of it for the time being, got back to the ship on a plausible excuse, effected the necessary changes in appearance and went off a second time in her character of Mrs. Clinton. With that lady's luggage including a trunk with a body in it. She was an accomplished actress and a perfect mistress of make-up, remember."

MacMorran intervened. "She certainly weaved a most ingenious web. I can't quite see that all of it was strictly necessary. But Mr. Bathurst here has given me his opinions with regard to that. Tell Sir Austin, will you, Mr. Bathurst?"

Anthony lit another cigarette. "I think that when the truth eventually comes to be revealed—if that ever does happen—you will find something like this. Ramage and Anne fell hopelessly in love with each other. But Ramage was afraid of any shadow of scandal in bus life which would blight his career. Scarcely anything in the nature of glittering prizes, remember, considering his political position, was out of his reach. So they decided on murder. This decision has been made many times before in criminal history. I could cite quite a number of cases. Then came the perfecting of the plan. Born in the brain of the ubiquitous Anne. A gathering was wanted—which would include Ramage and his wife and Denver, her husband.

She herself would be present in the capacity of *dea ex machina*. The Mrs. Clinton, whose love for and whose plans on behalf of the Empire she had already broadcast to the general public through the agency of Jerry Redfern. Thus was born the idea of the Remington invitations. Which, I submit, had at least two features of extreme cleverness. They are worth considering. A reason had to be obvious as to why Mrs. Ramage and Denver, of all people, were murdered. And it was necessary for that reason to be other than the naturally obvious one."

"Just a minute," intervened Sir Austin, "let me have that again." Anthony repeated his two previous sentences.

"The naturally obvious one?" queried the Commissioner.

"Yes. I suggest that finding the bodies of Denver and Mrs. Ramage under the conditions in which we know they were found, the natural inference would be for suspicion to be directed against either Ramage or against Denver's wife. Complications of the 'triangle,' etc. Ramage and Anne were acutely conscious of this, so that the whole machinery of the murders was set up in order to turn the affair from a private matter to what was made to look like an 'international' one. You see where all this is leading to?"

Anthony waited for a reply to his question. MacMorran made no reply, but Sir Austin broke into a denial.

"I don't know that I do. Yet awhile."

"Well—it all comes back to what I said just now. Another reason had to be furnished for the deaths of a certain two people. That's where the plot was fiendishly clever. Denver and Mrs. Ramage had to be *paired* in some manner before the murders took place. Hence the fantastic words 'test' and the equally inconsequent questions put to the various candidates by 'Mrs. Warren Clinton' afterwards. There was no set plan or order, I discovered, about any of these. But remember this. Denver, *as Anne well knew*, was an expert on words and etymological meanings. He qualified for selection with supreme ease. It was a simple matter to pretend that Mrs. Ramage had also triumphed. There was your 'pair.' Chosen for special work on behalf of the British Empire, and therefore natural victims of the deep-laid schemes of the Empire's enemies."

Anthony paused. MacMorran nodded. "Denver, of course, took his selection as a matter of course?"

"I think so. He expected to do well. The questions in the words were right down his street."

"What about Angela Ramage? Wouldn't her selection have surprised her and caused her to wonder?"

"It didn't matter much if she did. She could still argue to herself that she had scored high marks, as it were, in the questions she answered at the personal interview." MacMorran nodded.

"Yes—that's so. I see that point."

"How were they killed?" demanded Sir Austin Kemble.

Anthony shrugged his shoulders. "Shall we suggest that Mrs. Clinton, the benevolent hostess for the evening, made an appointment with each of them to meet her in one of her rooms at the hotel at a late hour? Concerning secret plans that were to be discussed regarding the jobs they had just been selected to fill? I think we may—with reasonable confidence and certainty. They were shot through the eye, in each instance. By Ramage, I fancy, standing behind the door. He couldn't miss. Anne lured them in. Ramage finished them off."

"I agree with you there," put in the Inspector. "I'd figured it out much in that way myself. The bodies were stripped, the clothes packed into suitcases, and Mrs. Denver, as I'll call her for once, skipped away from the hotel in her own car, which she had lying handy somewhere, to her West Country cottage, less than fifty miles away from Remington. Am I right, Mr. Bathurst?"

Anthony smiled. "Entirely, Andrew. From there she drove to London, parked the trunk containing Mrs. Clinton's body at Waterloo and caught the boat train to Southampton *en route* for Hollywood."

"Just a minute," said Sir Austin. "Where had Mrs. Clinton's body been all this time?"

"In her trunk at the cottage. Ramage took it down there while Anne was at 'Davidge's.' Jennifer Rapson, the maid, will give evidence for the prosecution on that score. I've already had a word with MacMorran here in respect of that."

Sir Austin looked reproachfully at his glass, which was empty. Anthony noticed the expression on the Commissioner's face. He gave further orders to the waiter. Sir Austin beamed eternal gratitude.

II

Having refreshed himself again, Sir Austin Kemble was ready for more revelations.

"Tell me," he said, almost on the point of entreaty, "what happened after the murders in the hotel and the woman was on her way to America?"

Anthony rubbed the ridge of his jaw before he replied. "The 'international conspiracy' atmosphere had to be sustained and fostered for all it was worth. So the warnings came into being. With the appropriate and topical attachment of Herr Hitler. The warnings, like the 'word test,' had no rhyme or reason about them—they were simply a means to a certain end, and I frankly admit they were couched in such terms that they had me running the wrong way for a long time. And in this connection our two criminals showed cleverness of an extremely high order. I refer to the omission of Ramage himself from the list of people who received the mysterious threatenings."

Anthony stopped for a moment to see the effect of his last statement.

"We discussed that," remarked MacMorran.

"I know we did. But Ramage reasoned that we should reason exactly as we did. The fact that he alone of the invitation people was omitted from the warnings meant that the finger of suspicion must point towards him. Therefore, so we agreed, had he been the instigator he would never have left himself out. It would have been too glaringly obvious. Which is just what he did do. In other words be double-bluffed—and it very nearly came off."

"Did he send them?" queried Sir Austin.

"I think so. Although in one or two cases they employed a 'down and out' named Joseph Carter to carry out certain work. Anne, now back from the States—she returned almost immediately—dealt with him, I fancy. By the way, MacMorran, did Carter give anything more away when you got him to the 'Yard'?"

MacMorran shook his head. "Not a thing. He was as dumb as an oyster."

Anthony went on. "Round about this time we were distinctly unfortunate. We ran up against the remarkably zealous Captain Playfair."

MacMorran nodded vigorous corroboration. "And I rather fancy," continued Anthony, "that Playfair was deliberately chosen for the 'invitation' party for that very reason. For he certainly assisted in no small degree to help the 'German menace' idea to be very closely associated with our investigation! Ramage, I imagine, must have been aware of Playfair's close antecedents with Berlin. And in this connection I would call your attention, gentlemen, to the fact that Playfair alone, of the threatened people, suffered any real damage when the threats were actually translated into action. There was quite a serious fire in part of his garden."

Anthony nodded—almost to himself. "Yes—we were undeniably unlucky as far as Playfair was concerned. His zeal and his general intelligence gave us information and genuine approaches to follow up—but they all turned out to be complete and utter red herrings. So much so that, greatly as we appreciated Playfair, we could very well have done without him."

"You think, then," said Sir Austin, "that Ramage carried out most of the threats besides being responsible for their deliveries?"

"Yes, Sir Austin. I should say so—undoubtedly. He dodged about here and there, from place to place, in his car and pulled off most of the jobs. But as in the case of the actual deliveries, Carter must have given him some assistance—and even Anne herself may have done so—particularly in the later instances—when she had returned from Hollywood."

"What eventually put you on the right track, Bathurst?" inquired the Commissioner.

"Well, sir. I learned, I think, by experience. I explored all the unlikelinesses, all the glaring absurdities, and all the things that didn't fit into the pattern and got nowhere! I was *intended* to, of course. Then one day the truth flashed on me. That there was *no* sensational side to it, as we were all being directed to think and believe, but there was a solution sticking out a mile that was based on sheer simplicity. An adulterous intrigue between a man and a woman whose respective and no longer desired partners had been murdered. I had little doubt now as to who were the murderers. Then I ran into trouble."

Anthony smiled and looked towards Inspector MacMorran.

"Why?" queried Sir Austin—"what was that?"

Anthony gestured towards the Scotland Yard Inspector. "Ask Chief-Inspector Andrew MacMorran," he replied.

The Commissioner took the cue and turned towards MacMorran. "What does Mr. Bathurst mean by that remark, Inspector?"

MacMorran grinned a little ruefully. "I'm afraid I took rather more convincing than usual. But—"

"But what?"

"Well, sir, I was worried, and am still worried—though not quite so much now—by lack of evidence. Eventually I conceded Mr. Bathurst his point and proceeded on the lines that he desired. Things went his way, or rather they went as he predicted they would—so I came to you for the final authority to act."

Anthony smiled his acknowledgment of MacMorran's semi-confession and began to amplify the explanation.

"You see, sir, it was like this. I had to convince the Inspector that I knew the guilty parties. He agreed with me and had agreed for some time that the murderer had been present at the Remington 'invitation' party. I agreed with him that if the guilty party received an 'all is lost S.O.S.' from his fellow-criminal that he would immediately attempt to get in touch with her, and in that manner give himself completely away. But to do that we had to remove Miss Assheton from possible contact with this man we were endeavouring to make betray himself. We took a big chance, of course, but I felt convinced that Cedric Garnett would help us in the matter. So I approached him, told him what I wanted, and within a few minutes he grinned, said O.K. and told me he knew another fellow who would lend him a hand. In this way Miss Assheton was removed for a matter of about twenty-four hours. Ramage fell into the trap. I had to make *him* make *her* move. He could only do that by moving first."

"I don't quite follow you there," said the Commissioner, wrinkling his brows.

"Think it out, sir," continued Anthony. "If Ramage had 'phoned through to Anne's cottage and had been able to find her there, she would have denied all knowledge of the letter which we had arranged he should receive and he would have at once known it had not emanated from her and suspected a trap. But we had removed her! He was forced, therefore, in her absence, to take the initiative. In other words, he was compelled to be active. He did exactly what the Inspector and I felt certain he would do. Left a message at the cottage for Anne to pick up when she returned, advising her of a rendezvous. To which rendezvous he would eventually lead us when the time came for him to answer the summons she sent him."

The Inspector and the Commissioner nodded their approbation. "You see what I mean, don't you?" added Anthony. "I made *him* make *her* go to him without any real communication passing between them beyond the bare order from him that she was to do so. I felt positive that he would do nothing beyond instructing her to keep an appointment, possibly in disguise. That appointment, gentlemen, was made and kept—and MacMorran and I kept it with them."

MacMorran nodded agreement. "I'll say we did."

"What first made you suspect Ramage, Bathurst?"

"When I realized that he had travelled on the *Myrobella* with both Mrs. Warren Clinton and Anne, I felt that it wasn't a factor I should neglect. It fitted, too, with the personnel of the two people murdered. But there were snags attached to it that I simply had to consider. It wasn't until I understood the significance of the impersonation that I began to see my way clear again."

"Would they have married? In time?" demanded the Commissioner.

It was a moment or two before Anthony replied to these two questions. "They're questions which are not too easy to answer. He and Anne obviously weren't ready to jeopardize his career on the rocks of divorce. And to have married quickly after the murders might well have courted suspicion. Still—I'll have a shot at an answer. I think they would have married eventually. After a reasonable time. But quietly and with little fuss."

"You really think that?"

"I do, sir. And I think we shall know before long."

Sir Austin Kemble and the Inspector looked surprised. The former translated his surprise into words.

"Why? What do you mean exactly by that statement?"

"If I read Ramage's psychology aright there will be a confession. I shall be extremely surprised if there isn't. Another whisky, Sir Austin?"

He signalled to the attendant without waiting for the Commissioner's assent. Then he turned again to his two companions. "But in the end I think it all came back to the 'words.' And the questions put to the candidates at the interviews. They were obviously 'hooey'—they were neither intelligently placed nor logically ordered. Entirely irrelevant questions were put to some and obviously relevant questions were omitted when it came to questioning certain of the others. When the truth of that position came home to me I was able to establish the position that the 'selection' of Denver and Angela Ramage had been deliberately arranged for a specific purpose *before* the party sat down to dinner. And that purpose, gentlemen, was murder!"

Anthony rose from his chair. "And now I'm going to extend an invitation to you two gentlemen. An invitation that I trust will *not* be attended by disaster. Sir Matthew Fullgarney has a highly promising two-year-old running at Sandown Park this afternoon. I'm informed by him that, with luck, we may be able to get 'sevens.'"

"Is the colt really good?" asked the Commissioner with a doubt in his voice.

"She's a filly, sir, and rumour has it that she can catch pigeons." Anthony smiled.

"I'm notoriously unlucky," grumbled the Commissioner.

"But surely not with the sex, Sir Austin?" Anthony smiled again. Sir Austin Kemble coughed. "I admit that—er—does make a difference."

THE END

www.ingramcontent.com/pod-product-compliance
Lightning Source LLC
Chambersburg PA
CBHW030752190726
48285CB00003B/815